IN THE MISLEADING ABSENCE OF

LIGHT

IN THE MISLEADING ABSENCE OF

LIGHT

JOANNE GERBER

COTEAU BOOKS

Edited by Edna Alford.

Front cover detail and back cover painting: "Wounded Angel"
1905, Hugo Simberg . Owned by The Museum of Finnish Art
Ateneum, Helsinki, Finland. Photo courtesy The Central Art
Archives, Helsinki, Finland. Photographed by Hannu Aaltonen.
Reproduced by kind permission.

Excerpt from "Choruses from 'The Rock,' IX" , from *Collected
Poems 1909-1962*, by T. S. Eliot, © Faber and Faber, Essex.
Used by permission.

Cover and book design by Duncan Campbell.
Printed and bound in Canada.

The publisher gratefully acknowledges the financial assistance of
the Saskatchewan Arts Board, the Canada Council for the Arts,
the Department of Canadian Heritage, and the City of Regina
Arts Commission, for its publishing program.

Canadian Cataloguing in Publication Data

Gerber, Joanne, 1953-
In the misleading absence of light
ISBN 1-55050-115-1
1. Title.
PS853.E64157 1997   C813' .54   C97-920095-4
PR9199.3.C472157 1997

COTEAU BOOKS
401-2206 Dewdney Avenue
Regina, Saskatchewan
S4R 1H3

AVAILABLE IN THE U.S. FROM:
General Distribution Services
85 Rock River Drive, suite 202
Buffalo, New York, USA   14207

Light
Light
The visible reminder of Invisible Light

—T.S. ELIOT

This book is dedicated
to Don Coles and
to the memory of
Brenda Macdonald Riches,
wonderful teachers and writers,
and to my mother, the most
courageous woman I know.

CONTENTS

I.

II.

I

THE BLACK MAGIC NIGHTS

She would keep him up long after the windows of the attic flat had gone dark, twice a week, while she ironed. Julio hated this. But he hated even more the terrible sound of his mother's weeping, which might follow him to bed if he left her. So late into the night he sat up, half in dream and half waking. He listened until his throat and chest burned from the smell of hot metal and fabric, from his mother's words, and from the secret he carried about his father.

Full of rage in those days, she spared nothing as she worked. It frightened Julio to see how the tablecloths, the crested pillowcases and sheets were thrown onto the board, then yanked, sprayed, pressed hotly into shape by his mother's broad hands. The clothing came later, when her face and hair had grown even darker and glossier with heat, her smell strong as that of the Greeks who ran the bakery.

With their stubborn collars and sleeve cuffs, Julio's shirts seemed to provoke her especially. Yet she refused to buy him coloured T-shirts, which the other boys wore with their blue jeans. For Julio, only the grey or blue-almost-black woolen shorts worn by Peruvian boys of good fam-

1

ily, with dress shirts of bleached cotton. And a tie, which he hid in the leather book bag which had also come with his mother from long-ago Lima.

The white shirts. When she had exhausted herself pressing everything else, his mother would unwrap and separate the first of them from the damp-sheeted bundle in the wicker basket. "Tssst. This one! Grass on the elbow. Do you not *think*, Julio, when you are ruining a fine shirt?"

Sometimes, maybe. But there was the soccer ball in front of him. And the other boys in their blue jeans.

"You will be just like your father. Just like a man. Caring for nothing but your own pleasure." She would flail and fling out the shirt as though she were beating a rug crusted with mud, making him wince. Flattening it on the board, she'd reach for the starch. She would shake the can as if it had scorched or stung her. "*Julio.* You think I don't know what men are?" Men again. Julio would sit very still, hardly breathing. With her arm swinging fiercely, she sprayed and resprayed, sprayed and resprayed until he began to cough and blink from the choking cloud which hung in the air.

"*Listen.* A man will hand over his friend that he loves like a brother, his own family and all that is holy—" finally, she picked up the iron. This moment, he liked to watch—on the can was a picture of Niagara Falls, and the glistening cloth hissed mightily when the smoking iron first rode over it, as he imagined the great river might hiss. The ironing board itself shuddered. But in another moment—less than a moment—the shirt would shrink, stiffen, become simply papery and hateful. The material burnt his neck and under his arms even after cooling on the hangers for days.

"—to follow his eyes."

It was such work to stay awake listening, breathing the starch, shirt after shirt. It was such work to pretend that he was only a boy and these things about men had nothing to do with him. Leaning exhausted against the wooden arm of the sofa which was also his mother's bed, Julio would follow with his eyes the yellow cone of light from the lamp shade to the ceiling. The pattern caught in the plaster leapt up sweeping and mysterious above him, like waves of the sea or clouds passing quickly, heightened and deepened by the single lamp and the evening. This amazed him. In the morning the ceiling looked rough and ordinary as a crumpled towel, nothing more.

He would study what was left of their belongings—the heavy chairs, the trunks, the tasselled curtains—whatever lay beyond reach of the lamp. How was it that all the colour went dead for the night? Squinting, he tried to decide whether he could still make out wine-dark red in the matching chairs, or, across the room in the kitchenette, scrambled-egg yellow on the shadowed doors of the cupboards. Could he? Or could he not? The night spread a weird blanket of grey and he was never sure whether he detected the daytime colours through it, or just remembered them.

His mother would bend to seize another shirt from the pile. "You think I am just a woman, who knows nothing? So, tell me. Where is your fine papa?" Snapping the limp flag angrily by its sleeves towards the corners, "You see him around here someplace?"

If Julio pressed his ear hard enough against the upholstery then and closed his eyes tightly, his memory might open like a miracle. Letting him look far back, to when he was very young—letting him see Papa.

IN THE MISLEADING ABSENCE OF LIGHT

THEY WERE LIVING STILL IN THE OTHER PLACE. In a fine old apartment, with many rooms and much furniture. His hair tufted luxuriously as his white cockatoo's, Julio sat on a polished wooden floor and played with tops—on one, a parade of circus horses chased each other's tails musically; another whistled in a white motion that slowed into whining, then hiccupping colours. He batted at it with his hands.

There was his papa! Darting across the room with a handkerchief and hat. "Goodnight, Julio," he was saying, making the bit of silk disappear, then reappear in the pocket of his jacket, making the hat sit not quite straight on his head. Clever Papa. He paused to touch Julio's top with his shoe, "Your ponies—they are fast? I could tell you such stories about horses—" He was winking, waving, all the time moving towards the door as Julio watched him. Smiling and touching his finger to his moustache, "But, my little man, we will save our stories for later. Don't make trouble for Mama, now, while I am gone."

Next, Julio sat in a tub full of bubbles, sailing a wooden boat from South America, a gift from his grandparents. He tugged a string to set the rudder, then upset the direction by moving his wave-making legs. He splashed and smiled into the shiny taps at the end of the tub. There had been four candles on his cake, his boat had real portholes and sails, his mama would scrub his back with the scratchy brush and sing; if he threw the bubbles at her so that the soap made her sneeze she'd laugh and pretend to pinch him. Although he wished to be going out with Papa, it was nothing. He had Mama and his fine boat.

Later, her laughter went flat. In that room which was used only for eating, she sat at the table between Julio and Papa, and silence sat with her; they had eaten their dinner again without speaking. She pushed back her chair and took the dishes on a tray to the kitchen. There she dropped the knives and forks into the sink with a clatter which frightened Julio. If he had done such a thing, he would have been sent to his bed at once. He, a boy of six years old.

"So, Eduardo, you are going out somewhere tonight?" She placed a pair of steaming custard cups in front of Papa. And Julio held his breath.

"Consuela, you know I would stay with you tonight— every night! It is only that my business takes me away. I must go to see people at the hour that is convenient." Papa winked at Julio then, pushing his dessert across the table toward him. Custard under a burnt-sugar crust.

"Business!! Oh yes, always it is business—" Her face very red, his mother backed toward the kitchen doorway. "Tell me, who are these strange people who work only at night? Who?"

She did not want his answer. "Eduardo! Hear me! Do you tell me one single night where you have been? Do you think I am a child? Still a schoolgirl in Lima? Do you think you are back in Buenos Aires with your foolish friends?" Then she threw a plate at him and rushed down the hall. Papa leapt up and rushed after her, shouting. (Many dishes must have been broken in this way, because later, when she and Julio moved, few of their beautiful plates and bowls would come out of the boxes.)

Julio ran down the hall too, not waiting to finish his custard. He wanted his pillow more than the sweet. Because once it had started, this fighting, there was no telling when it would stop. From behind the bedroom wall came his parents' voices—now louder, louder, every minute louder—until it seemed to him that surely the world was ending and the three of them with it. He stuffed his pillow into his mouth to hold his crying. Against his ears to block theirs. He wanted to scream at them to stop, to stop, that he was so scared of their shouting that he could not listen to another word of it.

When the apartment grew quiet at last, he had to finish with his tears quickly and rub his face. He had to quit shivering. Because very soon, he knew, his father was coming to him, dressed in a cloud-white shirt and fine leather coat, smelling sweetly for evening.

Papa would lift the damp pillow and toss it aside. If Julio had not been fast enough about his wet cheeks, he would cry, "What is this I find?"

Making him look up, holding his face, Papa would click his tongue and say, "Julio, Julio." Shaking his head as though he had seen something which disgusted him in the newspaper, "Julio, be a man!" he would say. "You listen too much to your mama. She weeps because she is only a woman and cannot help herself! But–*hear me*– nothing in all the world can be so bad that a man makes such tears."

Papa's words filled Julio with shame so great that he had to cover his face one more time with the pillow.

"Julio! How would it be for a boy in my country, if they found him weeping?"

He had no answer. He had never been to his father's country.

"The shouting means nothing. You must stop acting like a woman."

And Julio did stop. He lay shivering but quiet.

"There." Smiling, Papa would punch the air beside Julio's face then, or rub his scalp playfully with his knuckles, to end his shame. "Now, look after *Mamacita*. Who knows, maybe when I am finished working tonight I will find something sweet in my pocket. Promise me?" He would wink and be gone.

How could Julio do that, take care of his own mother—she of the weeping and shouting? Papa asked an impossible thing. No, he must try not to get up from his bed, even for the toilet. If he was very quiet, Mama might forget him. She might forget to make him sit at the table to finish his custard; then he would not have to look at the redness in her eyes or the way she soothed the back of her hand as though it were a sparrow fallen from its nest in the courtyard. It was better to lose himself in his dreams until morning. Then he could not be troubled by his mother's sadness or by the summer storms which lit up his window to frighten him. So, rewrapping his head so tightly that the feathers in the pillow crackled against his ears, he would try to sleep.

It often happened, though, that later in the night his bed would sag.

"*Julio.*" Someone touched and startled him.

"Wake up, sleepy one. I brought something." Julio woke to the smell of his papa's leather coat and of far-off flowers. His pillow was gone. Cool hands, sweet with cigar, tapped his cheek. And tapped him again, patting his head, twisting his damp curls until he opened his eyes at last and managed to sit.

His father held a finger to Julio's lips, and spoke as though they shared a great secret. "Shh. Quiet, little man, we do not want to wake your mama yet, do we? Your surprise, now—" rattling something under his coat, "you have not guessed?

"No? Good! Are you ready?"

Julio would grin and open his eyes wide then, trying to be surprised. He was so tired. And what Papa took from inside his coat was a box of Crackerjacks, every single time.

"See!" His father liked to announce, "I did not lie to you!"

"You did not lie." Julio would take the foil-wrapped box, which felt waxy as crayons. He'd shake it to loosen the contents before his father tore the top off. Digging out the favour, he'd exclaim over it as though he had been hoping for just such a prize. It might be a silver elephant or a tiny pink whistle. It might be a minnow-sized car. Then, his throat dry from sleeping, Julio would try to eat the sticky popcorn to please Papa.

He did not like the burnt sweet taste of it. He did not like the way it stuck in his teeth. Also, the peanuts tasted dark and rotten to him, like the single peanut in the song the kids sang while swinging. *Found a peanut... Went to heaven...* He prayed that he would not get a stomach ache and die. Just one bad peanut had killed the child in the song—and how many was he eating, night after night?

He could never say these things to Papa, though, who had remembered to buy him a treat. Who woke him to eat it when the window was black as the smokestack on his battered little boat, as though he were big. The prizes, at least, could be traded for glass marbles. He had started to fill a bottle.

While Julio ate, his father would whisper to him. "Now, what can you tell me of Mama? Did she come out of her bedroom tonight, after the trouble about my going out?

"No? She is a barracuda, that woman!

"Yes? When?"

Time meant nothing to a boy of six. "I don't remember." Julio looked at the floor, "I was sleeping."

"So. *Sleeping.* Well—" Papa would smile and push him playfully, or pretend that he was going to snatch some popcorn, until Julio ducked. Then Papa would frown, look over his shoulder at the wall which separated the two bedrooms and ask, "But tell me this one thing: was there more crying or banging of dishes?"

If Julio had no answer, Papa would uncover his watch and stare as though it knew and could tell him. "Almost two!" he would exclaim. Or, clapping his hand to his forehead, "Can it really be three o'clock?"

In a few moments, he would brighten, "Maybe she has been dreaming all this time and has forgotten to be angry. A man can hope."

Julio nodded, hoping too.

Papa did have one trick. A good one.

Some nights, he would tiptoe out of the room, then come back carrying something behind his back. He would say, "*Guess!* Guess—" but then he would bow and present his secret before Julio could say "Black Magic." A box of Black Magic chocolates, every single time.

"There! She will be pleased, will she not? It is not every man who empties his pockets to bring chocolates to his wife!"

Setting the box down where the edge of the blanket hid it, he'd urge Julio to hurry and finish his treat so that Mama could have hers. He would sit on the bed for a minute, jump up, sit, then jump up again, until Julio felt sweatier and sicker. Tapping the floor with his stockinged toe, Papa would push back the sleeves of his coat to touch his cufflinks, straighten then restraighten his shirt front and tie. He'd slip out to the hall to comb his hair, already as shiny and perfectly smooth against his head as the black feathers of a bird, and come back again. Until at last Julio managed to choke down the last mouthful.

Then his father would ask him triumphantly whether he needed a drink. He must never say no. Getting the glass of water was part of the trick.

Papa always put his shoes back on first. And Julio cringed as the half-moons on the heels scraped and clicked across the kitchen tiles. Papa made the taps squeal and the water blast loudly into the sink, rattling the dishes. He found it necessary to open the cupboard door and slam it shut two or three times, then the refrigerator door. To loosen the ice cubes, he had no choice but to bang the metal ice tray against the stove top or counter. All this noise, because Julio wanted water. From Papa, who was so quick, so light, in daytime. It made Julio want to reach for his pillow again.

Still, the water, when it came, was cold and delicious. He gulped it gratefully.

While he did, Papa would begin to tell him stories. Stories about anything. About horses which could break a man's heart, about Argentina—a country with history—about bears he had seen once in a circus, about gorillas fighting each other with guns in Chile, about swans in great gardens.

"Julio, I think someday you must see fighting cocks. You will have to go to Mexico, maybe."

"Mexico?"

"Yes, to see with your own eyes these proud roosters which will rather die than let another humiliate them. It is not a game for women.

"And in Patagonia, birds so strange they are not interested in flying. Penguins." Papa would poke him, "Almost as big as you."

Julio would make his drooping eyes round, "Pigeons as big as me?"

"Penguins. Shaped like the pins men knock down in the bowling lanes. Black and white as the keys of a piano."

Sickened by the lateness, the sweet popcorn, and the thought of peanuts rotting inside him, Julio hardly followed the stories. They were not for him, anyway. Papa always began quietly, but his voice grew louder and louder every minute and he would keep turning his head to check for Mama. Julio listened for her, too. Thinking about the chocolates under his bed and hoping that this night would end well.

If his mother did wake up and come in to them, Papa, playing with Julio's hair, would click his tongue and look up with surprise. "Consuela! Did we disturb you? I'm sorry—I found this little mosquito awake in his bed." *My little mosquito* was Mama's name for Julio. "For hours I've been sitting here with him, telling him things to make him sleep. Stories, stories, always another story. But in one more moment, I think he will be dreaming."

And he'd push Julio's head softly into the pillow and kiss his cheek, making his face burn. At no other time did his father kiss him, because Julio was going to be a man someday. But to get the chocolates without being seen, Papa needed to press his face and leather coat against Julio, while he reached under the edge of the bedspread.

"Look, what is this? Magic!" As he sprang up with the dark box behind his back, he would say in a voice like chocolate, "See, Consuela *linda,* even when I cannot be here with you, even when I am working, I think only of you."

The chocolates were magic, truly. On the Black Magic nights, there might be murmuring from his parents' bedroom, but Julio could go back to sleep without burying his head under the pillow. He planned to buy them himself when he had a wife.

"FOR HOW MANY YEARS HAVE I SEEN THIS, JULIO? All the time closing your eyes when I speak of your father?" Mama. The starch again. Shirts with stains in new places. A new iron, surge of steam in a room full of shadows.

The cut velvet sofa like mossed bark against his cheek; the wooden arm a wedge against both temple and ankle, he was getting so tall.

"Hear me, Julio: it would be better to put a sword into my heart with your own hands, than to grow up to be a man of secrets like your Papa."

But he would grow—he *was* growing—to be a man. His face was no longer smooth. When he changed his shirts, there were yellow stains under the arms. He had hair, now, where there had never been hair. His dreams had changed. He had always been a boy—would surely be a man—of secrets.

ONE WARM SATURDAY when the fine rooms were still theirs, his mother had promised to go to the christening of a baby. Julio was happy. Although there had been shouting in the night, had he not heard Mama tell Papa at breakfast that for one day out of his life he would have to keep Julio? And had Papa not taken her hand, kissed each finger slowly and agreed? She could stay at the celebration as long as she wanted.

As soon as they were alone, Papa told Julio that they would be going out themselves. "A man can take his son out, after all, on a fine summer day. There is a park I know, with a lake. The lake has more ducks and swans than a boy can count. How would it be if we went to see them?" How would it *be*?

He made Julio change into clothes which were worn only for Sunday Mass with his mother. To make Julio's hair as sweet-smelling and shiny as his own, he squeezed something white from a tube and combed it through his curls. Then he dressed as though it were evening and business, making the bit of silk reappear in the pocket of his snowy shirt, sitting his hat not quite straight on his head. Julio still thought him clever. But thinking also of the lake and ducks, of maybe buying ginger ale or a bag of marbles, he could hardly wait for him to finish.

He had trouble sitting still as they crossed the city. The streetcar lurched and rattled, throwing him now against Papa, now against the window. The doors swooshed and hissed every time they jerked open. People had to get on and off quickly, before the doors folded in and trapped them. When it was his turn, he was hit by fear. The rubber step gasped and gave as he stepped down. He felt Papa's hand on his back. The door wavered, about to swoop shut.

"Julio, jump!"

He let go the handrail, squeezed his eyes shut and jumped to the cobblestones. He whirled—Papa had followed!

But the streetcar shrieked at once and started, making lightning overhead and underneath, terrifying sparks on the metal tracks. Julio whirled again. On either side cars flashed diamonds off their windshields. Panicked, he grabbed Papa's hand.

And it was all nothing. They made the sidewalk in a few steps.

Papa took him right away for ice cream at a red and white wagon steaming with frost. Across the street Julio could see the entrance to the park, where other wagons were selling roasted chestnuts, candied apples, popcorn and balloons. He could kiss Papa for taking him to such a place! His ice cream was pink strawberry, rolled in paper. Snapping the paper off, the man offered it to Julio for licking.

Papa stopped him, almost slapping his hand. "No, my son is not a dog! Keep the wrapper." His nostrils quivered. But he smiled at Julio and told him, "You chose well, truly. No ice cream is better than strawberry—I would have some myself but for my moustache."

Crossing the road beside his father while all the cars waited, Julio felt hot with pleasure. The sun was even hotter. The ice cream began to run down stickily onto his hand and shirt front. Papa shook his head and laughed at this, so it didn't matter.

The park was wonderful, full of trees, and along the sidewalks, flowers. Papa took him to see swans, as he'd promised. They walked a long way first, to where there were not so many people. The swans were birds that came along the water without movement, white as clouds in a green sky. Julio loved them, with their rippling reflection beside and behind them. He tossed bits of the slippery cone, but the ducks and geese were faster, driving him back. Papa looked around to be sure no one was near, then got down and made wings of his arms. He chased the startled ducks, making their own funny sound. Julio laughed and laughed.

He chased the geese himself, making Papa laugh too. He ran around the screen of bushes and back again. He stood on the roots of a huge oak and watched a pair of black squirrels leap and disappear among the branches. He launched twigs and willow leaves like a fleet of ships into the moss-green water. Afterwards, he lay on the hill, smelling grass, strawberry and the smoke of his father's sweet tobacco. The sunshine felt so warm on his face that he gave up and slept.

"Wake up now." There was a shadow over him. Hands. Papa, crouched, wiping Julio's shirt and then his face with a tissue.

"Julio, listen to me. We must have a little visit now with a lady Papa knows. Can you believe it, she has come to see the swans too!

"But to play a trick on her, we'll pretend we are nephew and uncle."

Julio squinted.

"Yes. You must call me *Uncle* Eduardo. For a trick. If you forget, you will ruin it. So in front of the lady, call me Uncle Eduardo. Not Papa."

Julio stared at his father, not understanding.

"Also we won't speak to her of Mama. Why should we? She doesn't know Mama, so there's no need." Papa smiled and winked. "Now promise me, I am your Uncle Eduardo!! Not one word of Papa—*or Mama*—to the lady!!"

He helped Julio to his feet and led him through the trees to a bench where the lady waited. Julio stared. The lady was dressed like and smelled like a garden of flowers. Her hair wasn't black, like theirs, but as shiny and bright as new pennies. Her eyes were green as the moss or the water where it passed under willows. How had anyone so beautiful come to know his father? Confused by his sleep, the lady's dress and hair, and the trick they were playing, he couldn't speak.

She asked him questions—about how old he was and whether he went to school, about what he thought of the swans, about where he got such curly hair—but still he said nothing. She smiled and told him, "You have lovely eyes and eyelashes, so dark! With those eyes, you're sure to be a heartbreaker—just like your uncle!"

His father looked at him with anger then and clicked his tongue, reminding him of his promise. Julio wanted to answer something, something nice, but wanting did no good.

"The monkey pretends to be a mute!" Papa turned away from him and went to sit by the lady.

He sat very close to her. Then with his arm around her. Then with one hand tossing her hair into the sunlight like a stream of pennies. He whispered to her and played with her ear, making her laugh in a way Julio's mother didn't laugh. When a breeze lifted her dress from her legs, he caught at her skirt and teased her. Julio stood nearby, watching. He wanted suddenly to pee and also to cry for no reason. Ignoring him—he was only a nephew—his father visited with the lady until Julio was afraid of wetting himself. Finally he had to ask, had to, and his father pointed and sent him alone along the path to find a washroom.

"Uncle Eduardo," he practised in the echoing Men's Room, "*Uncle* Eduardo." He used his hands to drink from the rusty water. He stared at his lovely eyes in the tin mirror. They were two prunes, he thought.

Back at the bench he managed the trick at last. He stood next to his father. Quickly, not daring to look at her face, he told the beautiful friend, "We fed the swans, my Uncle Eduardo and I. Before you came. I ate strawberry ice cream—without the paper."

Papa laughed then, and rubbed Julio's head. Pointing to the pink stiffness on his shirt, he told the lady, "You see, there will be trouble for me when I take the boy home to his mother's house! My sister is a tyrant. A real barracuda! There will be trouble for the two of us, I am afraid, over that ice cream." But his voice was not afraid, it was full of laughter. He tapped his watch and told Julio to go and say goodbye to the swans.

Julio went, looking over his shoulder once to see his father rubbing the lady's arm and neck, slowly, as he whispered something. Her neck was very white above the bright dress and against Papa's hair. She had closed her eyes. He turned away toward the spot where he'd fed the geese.

Afterwards, Papa came and took his hand to lead him away. Papa's hand was hot, hot and damp, and he whistled as they followed the path back around the end of the lake. Whispering, "Eduardo, Eduardo, my Uncle Eduardo," Julio had to trot to keep up. The trees and the water trembled with a small wind, warm as the summer afternoon. And for some reason, he trembled, too.

A white and black soccer ball rolled across their path all at once. Papa darted aside and stopped it with his quick feet just at the edge of the water. Then with a great kick he sent it back up the slope to the players. They cheered him and he gave a little wave. Flushed with pleasure, he told Julio that on his team at school in Buenos Aires, he had once made a little name for himself with his footwork.

A little name—*Eduardo.* Julio felt sticky and exhausted.

While they waited for the streetcar to come, Papa took him into a crowded cigar shop. He collected Crackerjacks, chocolates, and two bottles of ginger ale, then stood in line. Julio stood with him, afraid to ask for potato chips instead of the sweet popcorn. He felt as shy with his father as he had with the lady. There were no marbles here, he could see that for himself.

"Hey, Eddie!" the man behind the counter said when it was their turn, handing over cigars without asking.

"Mac. The sunshine has been good for business today?"

"Can't complain."

Eddie.

The ginger ale was cold and sweet. Julio had never tasted anything so good. And the Crackerjacks, Papa agreed, could be saved for later.

On the streetcar, Julio wondered how it would be at dinner. Could he tell Mama about the swans and squirrels, about having ice cream? The funny way Papa honked and flapped his arms to make the ducks run? Maybe not.

He saw his father's legs flying after the soccer ball, his hands tossing the lady's coppery hair. *Uncle Eduardo.* Maybe not.

This time, Julio jumped down without being pushed. Papa stopped him on the sidewalk in front of their building. He squeezed his shoulder and said, "Now we have a secret, for always." He winked. "We can never tell Mama about the lady, because we didn't tell her about Mama. You see?"

Julio saw.

"Good! This day will be our own." Papa touched Julio's shirt where he'd soiled it, "A man can take his son out for ice cream, after all. And show him swans." He handed Julio the Black Magic box and took his comb to his hair. Julio cradled the box as he would a kitten. It felt heavy to him, heavier than he would have expected.

"What if—just today—*you* surprise Mama with the chocolates? I think she would like that." Papa always had a trick.

"No." Julio shook his head. "No."

"Never mind then."

Halfway up the steps, though, Papa turned. "Julio—" All the colour had gone from his face and lips.

"Julio, I—. That lady—" Julio had never seen Papa like this, with his hand pressed so against his chest, as though something pained him. *How would it be for a man in my country, if they found him weeping?*

He stood without moving.

"No. It's nothing. Promise?"

Julio's throat trembled. "Yes, Papa." He tightened his arms around himself and looked away towards the corner. "I will pretend to be a mute."

He kept his promise. Even though, not one week later, his father went out, perhaps to the same park of the swans, perhaps to the same bright lady, and forgot to come home.

INSTEAD, JULIO SAT WITH HIS MOTHER in the shadowy attic room night after night as she ironed. When she slammed the iron down too close to the end of the board and his unslippered feet, he drew them back quickly. He listened without speaking as she told him what men were. She was only a woman and couldn't help herself. He would soon be a man. As her words hit him like spray, he let the pictures come. He followed his eyes back, and was a boy.

LISTENING TO THE ANGELS

hen he comes back at last—his body simply unstrung and shivering with weakness—his eyes are the clue. Oh, they've always been blue, against all odds and theories of heredity, bluer than Lake Huron on the kindest of days, and brighter, so it isn't the extraordinary colour or even the light in them that tells me. No. It's the misleading absence of light. Stephen's been listening again.

He's listening now, the rattan settee creaking and groaning as he rocks himself. One hand grips his hair as though presenting it to someone for inspection, pale curls snagged like a fleece on his fingers. His other arm wraps his head, stopping both ears. His knees meet his brow. He's a curve, a bow, quivering with oblivious concentration. Within the circle of his bent form, within the silence of his muffled ears, whisper angels exclusive to Stephen. At least, that's what I think.

It's his knees that bother me most, drawn up like that. They hide his face. I want to see even his shuttered eyes, his intent chin, to read something there. Some tiny thing.

Our parents don't believe there's anything to be read. As always, Mother has fled the room, espadrilles flapping.

Her exit was followed almost at once by the squeal and clatter of the drawer under the oven, where the pans are kept. She needs to bake. I can picture her out there, in her gingham apron, puzzling, running through the list of what's already on hand, what we could do with. She's stingy with goodies, preferring to serve up a pair of ginger cookies which have lost their snap, than to recklessly give us three fresh at one sitting.

Wait, she's calling me.

"Ireeene, honey! What was that pie your father was asking about last night? Peach? Coconut cream?" A panicky edge to her voice. He does that to her.

"Lemon chiffon." She'll fuss and fret over the meringue, trying to get it perfect, even on an afternoon like this. First week of September, wilting weather; until the breeze quickens off the lake, I've abandoned my packing.

Packing—I fret over Stephen. Who will sit here with him when I'm back at Carleton? Who will make conversation—*milk* it out of thin air—at the dinner table? Mother and Father don't speak much to each other. To Stephen, either. Mother saves her comments for her wheezy Electrolux, for the cantankerous washing machine, for Alex Trebek on the television, and for me, when I'm here, because she thinks I need to master domestic dialect, being female. (She's wrong. I will never, never. Never. I will elope with a boyfriend and plant aspen on the Kamchatka Peninsula first. I will pitch a nylon dome tent on the blistering slopes of K-2. I will barter for goat's cheese and black bread with elaborate pantomimes in a Turkish bazaar. Anything.) But what about Stephen? He may suffocate, wither, become a mute, alone with the two of them in this house.

Technically, the angels are only conjecture. My own. I

21

invented them in sixth grade, when one of my classmates came across Stephen in action. A cover story, created on the spot, without a moment's thought, launched into the shocked silence like a comet. But in its wake, seeing my little brother through my friend's awestruck eyes, I started to think that maybe I'd had a brush with Mystery. Ten years later, I'm a true believer. Though Mother is forever warning me that my overactive imagination will be my downfall. That, and my saying whatever comes into my head.

Stephen has never said a word about what's in his head when he leaves us like this. Everyone else assumes he's in limbo: unconscious, lights out, lost. But no. Definitely, no. It's to presence, not absence, that he relinquishes himself, his interest in the outer world suspended absolutely. You only have to watch him.

His body moves, there's a current in his limbs, you can feel it lift the hair on your arms, if you sit tight beside him. His head stirs ever so slightly as in answer to a delicate cadence. If he isn't trying to hear something, why that arm thrown up around his head, fiercely guarding his ears? He's listening for a voice in his inner ear.

And the squeezed eyelids? A screen that from the inside becomes a window for him. A well-lit window. Does he step through it? I can't say. But he *sees*.

My brother's eyes afterwards are opaque and sad in the way of clear water inadvertently muddied. He's reluctant to look through them. After whatever he's been seeing, we must present a bleak vista. I want to whisper, sorry. Sorry, Stephen. Because I'm part of the everyday world he has to deal with, a world diminished and diminishing. Dimin-ishing in part because, at eleven years old, my brother doesn't write. He won't write. He could get all of them—a pretty substantial them—off his back with one paragraph. He's never written a paragraph, though. Has yet to produce a sentence. And he's not dyslexic.

Reading is nothing to Stephen, he's prodigious. Since I've been back here this summer, he's borrowed Chekhov, Dostoyevsky and Turgenev, Bulgakov and Zamyatin, and the twenty-odd novels *(Monsignor Quixote, Henderson The Rain King)* I picked up used along Bank Street. When he was just five, he worked his way through one of those children's series which torque reality to teach kids their place in the world. Mother couldn't help quizzing him afterwards about what he'd learned. Stephen told her, "Books are like yoghurt. You have to get through all this stuff that doesn't *taste* good before you get to the fruit at the bottom."

Intrigued, I asked, "What fruit?"

Stephen blinked at me and whispered, "Cantaloupe." Melon of any kind nauseates him. "*You* know, Renie—the message."

"Message?" He was a pre-schooler.

"Kid stuff." He left the room.

School has been a crucible for him; he's hardly die-cast, reading like a whiz but not writing. They can't help speculating, wielding verdicts. "Hand-eye coordination," one theory went. (Had they ever seen him draw?) "Compromised linguistic connections." "Highly function-ing autism." (Heard him talk?) "Repressed psychological trauma." That last one got my attention. But in a house where everything is *suppressed*, there'd be no trauma to *repress*. Would there?

The truth is, he confounds them. By Grade Five they had him inscribing spirals and loops and uncrossed t's for a Hungarian tutor of penmanship who finally threw up his hands in melodramatic despair and consigned the child to a life of mock illiteracy. Officially, Stephen's an unclassified *Special Ed.* (On the school bus, a *Sped.)*

He must hate the label, for its vagueness as much as the stigma. He's dismayed by imprecision. That may be what prompted his conscientious objection to inscription in the first place. Grade One, those blunt ball-and-bat consonants and vowels. The pencils thicker than his thumb. The words themselves—the *at bat fat cat that sat* on a *mat* in a *hat*—between lines a *pat* inch apart. No wonder he resisted. And once he'd taken a stand.... He's stubborn. Implacably stubborn. Always has been.

Still, I say hats off to him. How dextrous does a kid have to be to spend years in directed doodling, in creative ciphering, without one lapse into a recognizable character? Pretty dextrous. He will write when he feels the need. I can just see him nonchalantly penning uncials, upper case and lower case, each letter round and satisfying and perfect. He did serve that time as a calligrapher's (albeit uncooperative) apprentice.

His standoff is awfully hard on Mother and Father, who hunger for public proof that their boy's not stupid. Stephen recognizes their predicament with small kindnesses. A portion of breaded liver eaten without ketchup. Dandelions, bluebells, and cornflowers with Queen Anne's lace for the breakfast table, after one of his sunrise rambles. (He wanders off regularly. At sunset too. Like Father when the fancy strikes, there's no keeping him.)

Then, his pictures.

He makes pictures with pastels. Not tawdry sidewalk portraits, enlarged eyes brightened by two starpoint dots of white. And not a child's ball on a stick tree, apple-studded, immobile under a tentacled smiling sun. No. No approximations. What Stephen draws is awesomely observed. He gets it right.

His landscapes are recognizable at once. As Lake

Huron in certain weather from a particular gap in the screen of trees across the Bayfield bluff. As the hedgerow with blackberries on the way to the Rasmussens' run-down A-frame. As the spot on the breakwater where we're convinced one of the boulders, metallic and mysteriously scorched, is a meteorite.

Recognizable, that is, as minutely observed *strips* of Lake Huron, or the laneway or breakwater. Tantalizing slices, fourteen-by-three inch *vertical* strips, always. Why Stephen sets himself these boundaries, works within these parameters, I can't say. No one can. He lets me watch him, though. Like yesterday.

"RENIE," HE SAID QUIETLY, standing just outside my bedroom door, "I need to work. Coming?"

Work. He's eleven. I was glad to go, though. My room a sweltering warehouse of heaped clothes and so-called essentials for off-campus housing.

"Where's—"

"She's out back," he said gravely. "Getting a zucchini and tomatoes for supper."

"Okay, give me five minutes." I had my hair on top of my head in a plastic banana clip. I'd stripped down to camisole and cut-offs against Mother's indignation. (Is it my freckles or exposed flesh she so objects to?)

Stephen nodded and retreated to wait as I dug for a T-shirt I wouldn't be taking back to school.

Quickly, I packed along something to read. I put almonds and raisins in a Zip-loc and towel-wrapped two cans of (Father's) Pepsi. Threw sunscreen into my sisal tote in case Mother caught us. Hurried to join Stephen.

He was crouched out here, on the veranda, watching a pair of ants hoist a crouton. I tossed his Blue Jays cap at him like a Frisbee. "Ready?"

He grinned and ducked. "All set."

With his oversized sketchbook under one arm, and a fluorescent fanny pack full of pastels, he whistled a bit while we hiked to wherever it was he planned to draw. Good, towards the lake. Turning off the gummy road, through the bit of meadow, the woods and scrub bush before the beach. Our beach, more rugged and breathtaking than the summer people's.

We had it to ourselves. How did he always seem to manage this?

The lake was spectacularly blue. I dropped to unbuckle my sandals. Winced and counted to ten. The sand was a kiln.

"Over here, Renie." Stephen had skipped ahead in his runners. Was halfway to the breakwater that girdled the curve to the point. "You know where we watched the meteor shower that night? Those rocks."

Bone numbing, they'd been. Ankle wrenching (or jean drenching) to get to. But the waves at two AM like glimmers of mother-of-pearl. The sky like glimpses into a vast Pandora's box, intermittent jewels, gemstones thrown across the velvet haphazardly, trailing stardust. It had been worth creeping away from the house like cat-burglars. Worth limping home afterwards in damp, wind-stiffened denim. Because Stephen was incandescent. Ecstatic.

"Sure, wherever," I told him, "But give me a second to get wet." I waded out thigh-deep to splash my face and arms, blessed cool, then followed.

Even in full daylight, with bare feet, the rocks were a challenge to negotiate. No point arguing, though. Stephen never headed out randomly to sketch, never took my suggestions. He scouted, I guess, on his dawn and dusk rambles.

I stepped carefully into a tepid pool between boulders. Felt for a bit of roughness to give me purchase.

"I'll wait for you to catch up, Renie." His feet swinging over a four-foot granite drop.

We scrambled on together. Next week, I couldn't help thinking, he'd be doing this alone.

When we reached his spot, Stephen climbed up to the inner edge of the rocks, where they met the low bluff well back from the water. Then he sat for the longest time, just looking. Not a fixed gaze, but this horizon-to-horizon, earth-to-zenith sweep, dreamily intent. Next he felt the wiry dune grass. Poked at the nubbled dirt, ran his thumbnail over the ridges of a clam shell. Baptized his hands and lips with sand, both white-hot and damp. He sniffed things, and got me sniffing too, in spite of myself. A bit of purple crown vetch, the wind full-face from off-shore, a licked stone with green indications of the lake bed in its cracked marble surface. (He always does this. What is it he's after?)

Then, propping his sketchbook on his knees, he unzipped his pastel pouch, sighed—and settled down to study the sky and landscape all over again. As though he were about to sketch a Grand Canyon of a scene. But, inevitably, a three-inch slice of what's out there.

I squinted, panned for an invisible seam, a strategic shimmer, even, in the atmosphere. Nothing. I scanned what he'd drawn in grids, casual about glancing from paper to panorama, so as not to alert him. Then I sat asking myself: Do his eyes have a frame I'm not seeing, is this the most he can take in? Or is he trying to enlighten us about something with these fastidious cross-sections? Offering us an angel's-eye view?

I thought suddenly of the print I'd bought for my dorm room last fall. "Wounded Angel," Scandinavian, turn of the century. It reminded me somehow of Stephen. Two boys carrying an angel. Young boys, one dressed like a sombre Lutheran pallbearer, black-hatted, plodding eyes-ahead-stoically, old before his time. The other taller, more graceful, a close-cropped blond farmer's or fisherman's son, but troubled, frowning inscrutably out from the tableau. Seated suspended between them on a wooden-poled litter, the wounded angel. Girlish, a few pale field flowers in one hand, her head and body bowed a little despite her radiance. And across her eyes, tied around her corn silk hair, a strip of dazzling cloth, a homemade bandage. One wing seems bent slightly, torn as though she'd snagged it. Beyond the little procession, tundra-coloured flats and water, a listless lake or river.

That enigmatic blindfold, about three inches wide. Stephen's luminous three-inch landscapes. Did he see the painting somewhere when he was small, before he took up pastels? Or was there another, more tangible, connection?

My brother was a boy full of secrets. I knew better than to trespass by asking. Leaving my book in my tote bag, I watched Lake Huron swell to vibrant life under his hands. Wondering when I would have the privilege again.

NOTHING BUT NOTHING WILL TEMPT HIM to expand his vision. Teachers have tried laying in reams of good-sized manilla paper, bristol board, even quality watercolour stock with the offer of a matte thrown in. Stephen says no thanks and negotiates access to the paper cutter.

At home, Mother has ventured roundabout remarks with Father or me in attendance. "Oh my, from the back, honey," she'll say to Stephen, "your pictures could almost be taken for flypaper! Who would guess they're so lovely?" (Flypaper—even Father snorted at that.)

"Just look at this little *bit* of the lake, Irene! Imagine if your brother drew the *whole scene!*" At least she dutifully hangs them from the kitchen ceiling with thread. Like fly-paper. (Or like tubular wind chimes, like parchment Haiku). They rotate, slowly, shivering with the seismic pressure of our footfalls. Poor spick-and-span Mother. Her primrose kitchen's festooned with her son's anomalous impressions of the world, each proportioned like the satin Miss Huron County banner of her glory days, but infinitely more provocative. Earth and sky and water between them, stunningly rendered.

Adjusting his perspective is a dead issue with Stephen. Like the fixative.

That was one of my blunders.

IT ISN'T OIL PASTELS HE USES, but the other kind. The chalky, crumbling ones, which have a tendency to smudge. We drink a fair bit of tea in our house, and the warning whistle on the kettle isn't what it used to be: those meticulous, multi-coloured fronds suspended from the ceiling. The surreptitious steam. Mother and Father's inattention. Stephen has suffered losses. So last Christmas morning he unwrapped what I'd thought would be a wonderful gift—a can of fixative.

As he sat dumbly holding it, rigid as a Lego chevalier, I sensed I'd gone over the line somehow. But how? I tried to dredge up enthusiasm.

"Stephen," I exclaimed, "you know how much we love your pictures. This will preserve them!"

Nothing. He set the can down on the neatly folded reindeer wrapping paper. Tucked his hands into the sleeves of his pyjamas (reindeers, too: Mother takes the festive season seriously).

I nodded at his most recent landscape. I'd hung it on the Christmas tree the night before, anticipating that he'd be eager to try out his present.

"Think of the kitchen, Stephen." Complicit noises from out there, where Mother was whipping up eggnog and waffles to justify waking Father before noon on a Holiday. Now I gestured at the blue and yellow aerosol cylinder. "The man at the store told me this will keep your colours from running even if moisture gets at them. Wouldn't that be great?"

Stephen heard me out, wide-eyed and silent. What was he thinking? Afraid of? I picked a strand of tinsel off his hair, felt him flinch and withdraw a bit.

Trespassing further, I reached for the fixative. "Just watch."

I uncapped and shook it. Then boldly sprayed his work of art where it hung: "Un, deux, trois, Voila!"

With a flourish, I let him see how natural it still looked—snow still boot-deep against the Wilson's rusted gate, ochre corn stubble bent under the white weight, sky opaque and placid as Wedgwood.

Still nothing from Stephen.

I demonstrated with my terry cloth cuff how not even rubbing would efface the pastel now. (Maybe it did look a little flat, though, on the paper.)

He cried. Covered his face and cried. Fiercely. His shoulders shaking, his legs pedalling against the floor. Maybe it was because the first gift he'd found under the tree earlier had been a five-year diary from Mother. Maybe it was because the spray smelled like death by ether. Maybe—Mother's guess—he had simply eaten too many Christmas candies before breakfast. He didn't say what upset him. Wouldn't say. Ever. Though I asked and asked him.

The can sat on his desk, unused, with the diary, for the rest of my Christmas break. It was still there when I got back in April. Victoria Day weekend, though, just in from a morning walkabout, Stephen announced that he had permanently—and conscientiously—disposed of the aerosol. Mother's hapless gift, more volatile even than fixative, evaporated about the same time.

HE'S LONG SINCE ABSOLVED ME. At least, he's never mentioned my mistake again. Nor have I. Even when a picture's been marred or rippled.

Well, this summer we're all suffering from humidity. Up away from the water the heat can hang like a vapour, barely stirring. It saps you, you go around with your face and feet bloated, feeling pregnant with fever. The fields hum. The ditchwater stinks and disappears. The house smells of mildew. Father gets snappish and sarcastic. Stephen and I, lethargic.

But Mother, in a haze, soldiers on. Like this afternoon. It must be thirty-five in the kitchen, a steamy, sticky thirty-five, but she's got the oven pre-heating and the Osterizer whirling. To keep her mind off Stephen's spells. I think they terrify her.

"Aren't you worn ragged just watching? Where does he find the energy?" she asked guiltily from the doorway as she left me with him. We'd been sipping icy grape juice and trying to catch a breeze out here on the porch. It's all screens.

Where, indeed? He's still off. Head pulled down, quivering, oblivious.

I feel sorry for Mother. Her life hasn't worked out as she'd been led to expect, and she has no faith in Mystery. Here I am going into third-year Russian Literature, a choice unfathomable to her, but one she feels duty-bound to defend in the face of Father's hooting, and here is Stephen. Still inexplicably rocking.

For the longest time, she kept hoping some medical

wizard would unravel the enigma of his silences and dispel them. Surely he'd be scribbling his alphabet in short order when his spells stopped. I think she's losing hope now. That pathetic diary.

But to satisfy her, poor Stephen still gets carted off periodically for testing. Over the years, he's been to University Hospital in London, to McMaster in Hamilton, even, after a seventeen-month wait, to Sick Kids in Toronto. They've done CAT scans and echograms, magnetic resonance imaging and electro-myography. Monitored him waking, sleeping, talking, walking. Even half-heartedly sketching. Yet after all these years, sheer guesswork.

Because they've never caught him *listening*. Not even once. Which all the more convinces me.

No angel would be compromised like that, apprehended on electrodes or scanners. So, of course, they abandon Stephen when he's under scrutiny. He's a shell which doesn't whisper when held to the ear. A ship standing by on radio silence. He is unflaggingly present as long as the physicians observe him. No extinguishing himself, no reverberating arc, shuttered eyes and face. Poor doctors. (No summons to the holy mountain, no unseen afterglory. Poor Stephen.)

LAST TIME (THIS PAST JUNE) he came back from the hospital contrite, exhausted and guileless, in clothes that smelled toxic. Still undiagnosed. Mother slumped on arrival, grey and frazzled from sleeping in armchairs, from facing incredulous specialists at yet another failed Mecca. She needed to slip, bathed, into Battenburg sheets, for a good sixteen-hour sleep. I promised to take care of things if she did. She was too worn out to argue.

Father, mercurial, headed straight for the bluffs. But

not before announcing (as he booted the overnight bags down the hall): "Told us nothing we didn't already know. Do they take us for morons? Does that kid?"

He needed to stump, stew, smoke. I knew he'd slam his way back into the house late, to do some serious drinking. Understandable, I guess. Back when, he must have had visions of fishing trips and coaching his son's hockey team. Instead, humiliation and hospitals, extra billing. He gets more embittered and sullen every time he's dragged on one of these pilgrimages. (He often sleeps out here on the settee, homecoming nights, where, if the wind is up, you can hear the pounding of the lake against its moorings.) I checked to be sure the ice trays were full.

Stephen was on his rug dismantling a Lego castle. I closed the drawbridge gently and sent him for a shower. Headed for the kitchen, tripping over one of the bags Father had unceremoniously left. From the look of things, the ride home had been as much an ordeal as the medical gauntlet. So when Stephen reappeared at last in fresh pyjamas, I fed him home-made French fries and two slabs of carrot cake with praline ice cream. He said, picking at crumbs with his finger, "Do you know they make cream of carrot soup? It's gross. And watermelon Jello?"

I made a face. "Sounds awful." I twisted my neck and began to study his delicate slices of life, one at a time, to keep from quizzing him. If he had anything he needed to tell, I'd hear it in due time.

All he said was, a few minutes later, in a small voice, "I think they're really mad at me this time, Renie. They wouldn't even stop to let me use the bathroom. All the way home." He had his head in his hands.

"It's not you, Stephen. It's the doctors."

"Then how come Dad asked Mom to sell tickets next

time—ringside seats—" his face was tragic, "then maybe I'd perform."

"He's just blowing off steam." My hands shaking, I grabbed the ketchup. "Better put this in the fridge before I forget. Don't want to give Mother conniptions."

I sat beside Stephen on his bed, reading Tolkien, until he was asleep. Then I retreated to my own room. My own book.

Stephen seems to be slowing a bit now, his fingers loosening. Soon he'll be back, his face and body blearily tentative as on first waking. He'll look at me with these disappointed eyes and this mouth wavering like someone had smudged it.

"Ree-nie?" he'll murmur, and I'll ache. He may let me take his hand, then. Sometimes he even lays his hot head in my lap. (His hair is dewed—smells sweet and sweaty as a toddler's, is just as fine and fair and tousled.)

We won't speak much. To soothe himself, he'll rock a bit, while the little tremors diminish. Weary as he is, he'll let me touch his cheek. And I'll do it, shyly, to feel his goodness. He has this goodness you can't get at. Sometimes I think he wraps himself in it, it's that impervious. Other times I'm impressed with the depth of it, the bottommost part of him, and the uppermost.

"Irene? Everything all right in there?" Mother. She's got the lemon simmering and the pastry shells in. The whole house shimmers with the fragrance and heat of the oven.

"We're fine." We are. Fine without her.

Yet I don't blame Mother for retreating, finding what passes for sanctuary in the mundane, in her baking and bustling. Her son's read more books than she'll ever read, but he's never signed his name to a Mother's Day card.

She's had to face all those doctors and teachers. To appease Father. About his silences—what he's seeing, what he's feeling—Stephen's disclosed nothing. She's surrendered her faith in miracles. These things take their toll.

Almost time. When the angels are finished with my brother, he'll be turning shivery and wall-eyed toward me. If he's up to the walk later, if the sunlight is not too belligerent, a long float in the lake should cool him. Cool me, for another stint of packing.

THE LESSER, THE LARGER

ut beyond the light cast from the windows, Noelle could feel the night come solidly down around her. It was too cold, biting into her, but she welcomed it as something real, without artifice. From across the snowy lawn wafted giddy voices and laughter, vivid and overheated as the cottage and clothing of the guests. She should have been inside—they'd come all the way from Toronto tonight to see her. Instead, she moved closer to the trees, screened from the party, but not from the sky or the slope to the water. With no wind, the frosted air was delicious.

Driving out this afternoon with Karl, she had been astonished by the colour of the trees, the bare branches showing ginger and burgundy, pewter and taupe against the snow and muffled air. The woods were like a sketch in conté crayons. In that delicate balance, she'd observed through tears, leaves would have been an intrusion.

Transformed now by the hour, they were limned charcoal against the midnight sky. The wide crescent moon and the stars hung low, brilliant and perfectly placed as in a child's book of verse. There was an illusion of intimacy in the subtle silvering of everything she could see—as if it were all drawn wonderfully close, and she might walk with no effort in any direction and find herself miles away, beyond the reach of everything familiar. Beyond the reach of the past twelve months and the ruin that she'd become.

How long had it been since she felt fully herself? Three years, four? She remembered suddenly a disquieting student trip to the Fine Arts Library—had she sensed this coming, that far back?

A FILM ABOUT THE LIFE OF EDVARD MÜNCH had unsettled her, like a message half received. By looking at his works, she'd hoped to efface pervasive images of his days. So, on the worn oak surface of the very last table, where the artificial brightness of the library was tempered by the dull light from the window, she arranged the books. The covers were rough as canvases; she closed her eyes to imprint the texture on her hands. The pages would be glossy; she suspected Münch's paintings were not. In the film, he had laboured with oils and acids, thick brushes and knives. Had used paint courageously. Made etchings by gouging and burning; as he bled life from a stone plate, from scorched wood or metal, she had almost sensed his sweat rising sharp with the stench of the inks. She, too, was coming to know the heady drag of roller across a beautifully scarred surface. Cautiously, as though she were lifting a fresh engraving from the block, she opened the book to the first print.

In a room gentled by the play of sunlight with lace curtains before an open window, a young woman was dying. In a chair ribbed strong as a boat, she sat tranquil, her cheek resting on a pillow handworked to give pleasure. Beside her, her grey mother's hands were still busy. Her own, translucent, held a blood-flushed handkerchief in an empty lap. On her face was neither fear nor shame, only regret that there was no child to warm her dark dress, or the empty chair when she was gone. She was forgiving the world for withholding itself. Her shoulders were slight, would travel well, Noelle found herself thinking, because the years had placed on them nothing more weighty than a crocheted shawl and her own leaving. She would probably touch the embroidered pillow once more, then slip the room off as lightly as the shawl. At the window, the lace billowed.

Involuntarily, Noelle reached to brush the luminous folds; met the cool sheen of the page. She felt bruised. This painting; this girl seen through discerning, tender eyes. The artist himself so young. Scenes from the film came back: Losses. A tall house with many doors quietly closed. Helplessly, in small rooms, people choking up blood. At night, the sound of tuberculosis in Edvard's ears, the colour behind his eyes. Just viewing the documentary, Noelle had been engulfed by the encroaching intimacy of death. Of northern life in those narrow Lutheran years. Had felt his paramount need to paint. To preserve. To evade. But had painting saved him? She turned the page, slowly.

Here, promenading on *Karl Johan Gade,* were homburged men like ghouls, and women with haunted, unlit eyes. All strolling to hell under the benevolent yellow light from the windows, along the dusky familiarity of the street. And in the next work, *The Tempest,* a woman in a sheer dress, almost a wraith, distancing herself from a house solidly illuminated on a hill, a knot of people halfway down. Only a wind-whipped tree sensed that their number was diminished, caught the glimmer of her gown in the darkness.

Overleaf, Münch's signature piece. A man on a pier—

shrieking. The impact was immediate—Noelle was dragged through seas and sky striated in bands of colour. Orange and scarlet and indigo. The jetty surged, enveloped in the hues of an angry sun, of lifeblood poured out, in the colours of a night sky shattered by flares. With a shudder, she tried to reorient herself. Then, palms flat on the oak table, framing the picture, she looked again. The man was carried somewhere against his will, trapped against an endless gleaming rail. So he screamed. His hands pressed to his head, his face contorted. Bending all light and time and sky with his rage.

He accused her from the page. Accused everyone. Everyone was the unheeding party along the dock, watching the sun set gaudily on the water, waiting with a wish for the first twinkle in the darkening sky overhead. Everyone refused to bear witness.

Shivering, Noelle closed the book on him. She was not guilty. It was the closeness in the library that made the room waver momentarily, her heart race. In her own life, nothing had been decided yet. She was only just learning to paint.

Outside she took to the sidewalk, red coat buttoned high against the late September gusts. The leaves underfoot were like Japanese paper, the sky opaque. She walked more quickly. When she still shivered, she moved her mind deftly from the chill breath of the paintings, the dying girls—from wherever that man was headed. Her emotion was absurd. What had she in common with a dead Norwegian painter? She was nineteen years old. A vigorous girl with many friends.

NOELLE HUGGED HERSELF HARD NOW, shaken anew by the power of those paintings. It had seemed deceptively easy, then, to elude them. She'd simply lost herself among the living.

But she was no longer invulnerable. The illness had robbed her. Aged her. She was weak, her back and shoulders curled defensively against the pain in spite of herself. She'd tried to contain it, keep it penned up in her blood, in her hollow bones, where no one could see. But eventually it had outmaneuvered, overpowered her. Now, whenever she began to shiver, the fear stalked her that the pain would break out, that she'd be shuddering again uncontrollably, her body trying to shake her loose.

A swell of sound from the festive crowd—smoky jazz—Karl must be playing them his new Wynton Marsalis. Darnel would be keeping pace uncannily on his invisible horn, a few of the women dancing with intensity, now that their drinks had had time. Did any of them realize how lost she was?

First, she'd been treated to chaotic fancies at night. In her dreams she saw herself functioning, laughing, inextricably bound up in the lives of others, even her studio improbably abuzz. Then abruptly, inexplicably, she would be wearing a backless cotton gown, two ties missing, and the floor under her feet terrazzo-stone cold. The studio fell away and she'd find herself on a bed. The bed was an ice-white slab and she on it, almost one too. Very much alone.

She had kept these dreams to herself, even from Karl. They'd recurred. At some point, ceased to be fancy: she was disrobed, laid out on a table like granite. A shawl of lead lay heavily across her bare shoulders, her breasts. Footsteps receded; suspended a scant inch from her flesh, a machine murmured and clicked. Light flickered somewhere brief as heat lightning; the room seemed colder. The technicians came back. She could feel her sharp hips as they turned her, tried to impress the lines of her body onto the plate. Understanding the difficulty of printmaking, she tried to be helpful. She apologized for the uncouth trembling and they, with their gentle hands, apologized for being so very much alive.

There was no waking up. Her life had been given into the hands of physicians and technicians, professionals who, in the chambers of nuclear medicine, worked at projecting her days in inky images that said nothing of her own plans. Although they were careful to keep her informed, what they held up to the violet-lit panels remained as opaque and indecipherable to her as microfiche. Waiting for them to finish, she tried to conceive paintings, but colour and perspective were swept away in the chill tide of loneliness that washed over her in those unlit metallic rooms, in the nausea that came afterwards.

More and more it was taking her unguarded even in the studio, making the weight of a brush beyond bearing. She knew this worried people; it worried her. But the disease was carrying her with it. Like Colville's *Swimmer,* she was a woman moving through steel-dark water, caught by some trick of timing or current in a course parallel to the jagged shore. There would be no resisting the swell that gleamed a long way out.

Tonight, she found it impossible to pretend otherwise. Tears of desperation came; she tugged off her gloves and covered her eyes with cold fingers. She could scream, she wanted so to survive. Scream. What was wrong with her life? Had she done something? No, she had to stop. She'd get feverish and have to go in. It'd been forever since she last went walking alone. Taking a stiff Kleenex to her face, she worked at calming herself. The tissue smelled of mint—a piece of linty candy cane stuck deep in her pocket. The tightness in her chest began to ease.

She concentrated for a moment on the terrain. Should she try for the lake, or simply follow the laneway up through the trees? The grade was gentler uphill, and the cars had been through. Still, if she could make it down to the waterfront—she turned to look, and was caught again by anguish.

This scene. Austere, unspeakably lovely. Suppose she were to paint it, a study in solitude under the night sky? The shrubs over against the cottage squatted indistinct as clouds, heavily blanketed with snow, while here the trees which stood up to the winds were bare or glassy, more line than colour. Would catching them on canvas as they were tonight say anything about how they'd beguiled her this afternoon, or hint at the green explosion when they came to leaf? How could she live on herself in her art, as everyone assured her? The truth was, she couldn't even capture trees.

Not to cry again, she stooped to examine the track of a rabbit in the snow, found finer tracings where birds must have come for berries. Her husband might be able to say which birds, Karl had that kind of knowledge. It'd been his idea to come out. AWOL. She'd spent a month in the hospital this time, and he wanted to take her beyond the reach of doctors for the weekend. A risk, but at this stage of the battle, three days' peace would be a major beachhead. She hadn't felt up to it, but Karl had been right about coming.

The day had been splendid for getting away from the city. As they'd backed onto the street, she was suddenly comforted by the sunlight on the softly mottled brick of their home, by the glazed houses huffing in the chill air— her community, all intact. At the hospital it was easy to lose her bearings.

For a time, Karl drove silently, letting her watch the

play of light and cold. She noted the crenelated drifts like a frozen wake, marking the passage of traffic close to the limits of the roadway. Traced with her eyes the padded movements of rare pedestrians, the collar of snow which had taken the place of birds along the power lines, transformations of winter.

Then, turning to watch him instead, Noelle thought how young Karl looked. His hair was still silvered with blond, not grey, and his body several years from softening. At the hospital he seemed older. His movements hesitant, almost perplexed. Never speaking of the sentence she'd been given, he seemed to approach everything obliquely. He had even developed an amazing resistance to provocation, utterly out of character.

Maturity, she wondered? Or simply that the visitation of dread disease in their lives had knocked the spontaneity out of him? The first time she'd ever seen Karl he was fervently calling up Hamlet in an empty theatre, his words and hands arcing, conjuring—until a set shimmered almost visible on the bare floorboards at his feet. His pale hair, passion, black turtleneck were numinous. Smote her at once. On stage, he was still more alchemist than actor.

With a rush of gratitude, she reached over to poke the side of his knee, a trick she used to keep him awake on car trips at night. The gentlest jab made his leg jerk up and smash the underside of the dashboard. He pretended to swerve and they laughed, remembering how she'd forgotten and done that just a few weeks after his cartilage surgery—they nearly had crashed, that time. She kissed his ear, tugged her seat belt loose and moved close, absorbing his warmth and the slight flexing and easing of his shoulder as he handled the steering wheel. The fragrance of his light aftershave was wonderful.

Fields rushed by, deeply snow-covered or punctuated

with broken corn-stalks and rocky hillocks. Farm buildings clustered far back from the highway were flushed out
of the landscape, ruddy or stone faced, vanished again.

An hour from the lake, Karl startled her. First, he told
her about the crowd he'd invited out to join them for the
evening; as he put it, their whole rogue's gallery of
friends. Then he told her that he had begun to make
plans for the summer. He thought they might fly out to
Victoria and drive to Pacific Rim Park; they'd always
meant to go back. Hike, sketch, watch the ocean—they
could do whatever she felt up to. He'd already looked into
accommodations. What did she think?

Noelle felt herself sinking. Pacific Rim Park. Their
honeymoon trip came back, washed over her. Days
passed on the wind-swept beach in a kind of reverie.
Feeling no need to swim, they had slowly traced the
wavering line where the land and their footing dissolved
into the Pacific. Retraced it. Wordlessly watched the luminous swells roll in and in, until their eyes were burnt by
the dazzling play of light and dissolution, trying to take in
that out there somewhere was Asia. Every day she'd filled
her pockets and Karl's with pebbles. The green she called
jade.

She remembered how, wrapped in layers of clothes
that flapped about their arms and thighs like gulls trying
to take flight, they went looking for shelter. On a granu-
lar bed, amid a drift-log tangle of massive proportions,
they'd huddled together to eat sand-encrusted Brie and
sticky buns, biscuits and peaches bruised from Karl's
rucksack. In those days he carried a blue thermos bottle
almost two feet high, which she said should be restricted
to workers on high steel. Curled up exactly at sea level,
they'd sipped scalding tea at wide intervals between caress-
es, as though they were Afghans marshalling kafir and

warmth at the end of a day's frigid climb.

Afterwards, gritty and stiff, they had sat up in the fierce light and read to each other, one holding the frantic pages as doggedly as a halyard in a squall, one shouting poems into the torrent of air off the ocean. They'd read until the thermos was spent and the light began to fail. Then watched, silenced, the poetry written across the water and sky in a requiem for the day.

Four weeks, almost half a summer. They had imagined then fifty summers to be spent or squandered together; inconceivably, that was not ten years ago. Karl still carried in his pocket a tiny stone, as meticulously curved as a mermaid, and banded like malachite. Her gift to him for remembrance, the exact shade of her eyes. He called it his Jade.

What she had culled from the wind-strafed beach, from their reading of Rilke, was a sonorous truth. Through all the years of painting, it had been both touchstone and calling: that works of art are of an infinite loneliness, to be approached only in the opening of oneself, which is love.

This past year, she had been discovering that it was true also of persons. In the unravelling of her life, everyone, even he whom she most loved, who most loved her, was receding. Closing themselves to the hated illness, shielding themselves from the suffering which increasingly defined her, everyone had begun to take leave of Noelle. And she, of them. Was this a failure—or a corollary—of love?

Either way, the distance remained. Sadness spreading through her as irresistibly as unwanted sedation, she turned to watch the winter-blitzed fields. Let Karl float plans, try to tie their futures together. Apart from the knee repair, he'd never been hospitalized. Had he been the one lying all those nights between stainless steel rails, next summer would seem as elusive to him as had the sun, in its incandescent procession across the Pacific.

Tonight she was sorry she'd given Karl no answer about the summer. Her silence through the rest of the drive must have been disconcerting. And she'd further abdicated now, by leaving his gala gathering of friends.

Snapping an iced berry from its branch, she held it until the slight heat of her hand melted it down to the creased waxy surface, then reached for another. They were hard as cranberries, sank out of sight when she dropped them into the softer snow under the bush. She looked across to the cottage. There, where every window was a yellow beacon in the night, the tone was too bright for her, almost surreal. She'd felt like an interloper, the only one who had lost faith that there was safety in numbers.

Letting the berries fall, she straightened and gripped her ribs fiercely. Was she dreaming all this? Or was it possible that the doctors were right? She hooked her hands over the blades of her hips. Yes. Even through the heavy coat her flesh was defeated. It was inconceivable. She, Noelle, would pass on. Soon. But to where—as what—if she outlived the tenuous hold of the flesh? As spirit? Not good enough.

She spoke this word out loud. "Spirit." It hung, a minute trail of exhaust in the air. From the violet-sheened snow, no answer. Again. "Spirit!" The night was unshaken. She intoned it a third time, quietly. "Spirit." Gave up and began to move with the plane of the land towards the lake.

The crust glittered, fragile as a meringue. With each step she had to choose between letting herself skitter slightly along the surface, or shattering it with the heel of her boot for footing. Where the ridge on which their cottage was set dropped away, she slipped more seriously. Slid for a few heartstopped seconds.

She didn't cry out, even when she came to rest with throbbing hip and scraped cheek in a bramble. She sat very still—the numb face, chafed hands, were remembered sensations. Even the icy trickle where some snow found her neck reminded her of something. Of another time, very remote. As she reached to wipe at the wetness, she suddenly missed her long hair, as though she should be stuffing it back under the collar of her coat. And what was she listening for? Water? She shook her head. Still nothing. Whatever the memory, her senses wouldn't share it with her mind.

She unfolded herself, massaged her hip and got to her feet. Her legs were quivering. Continue down? Suppose she fell again? She had so wanted to walk alone. Incidents like this became crises, though. The devastation of her whole life was not enough for the disease, it imposed a vigilance in small matters, too. She used to take it for granted that adversity matured a person, that suffering produced wisdom. That seemed aeons ago. She would have liked to believe it still—to become wise herself, to handle this immensity with grace. But the effort was enveloped in exhaustion, the toll of petty decisions and griefs. If anything, she tended to be more truculent and territorial, more easily intimidated. Tonight she didn't want to give in.

She tried a few steps. For now, the trembling felt manageable.

The hill was becoming trickier; she guessed it must be where the grass ended in a soft bluff before the shore flat. The fall had left her shaky, so she moved tentatively, concentrating on her footing and the sound of her progress. Almost to the lake. It seemed uncharacteristically silent;

she had not been here since the summer. Finally, level ground. Her feet found the track, beaten still under a foot of snow, which led to the landing. It would keep her clear of the rocks and the water. Passing the far end this afternoon, she'd been surprised to see the ice already heaved up in places, looking uncannily like the shale flats on Georgian Bay, where she summered as a child.

Georgian Bay. She'd made her first primitive prints there, the year she was twelve. Had passed most of that summer on the rocks with a mallet, splitting the monotonous shale plates to expose the blacker fossils within. Dragging her best finds back to the cottage, she'd lay onionskin over the washed stone and rub with a soft leaded pencil until the image emerged. When she held the fragile paper up to her lamp at last, there would be a marvellously tiny marine animal, a shell, or a fern. Evidence of life past, preserved. She remembered making dozens. Where were they now? The collection must have been lost, like so much else, when her parents' household dissolved the next spring.

She looked up. The stars were even lower here, the sky seemed to breathe with them. Involuntarily, her eyes found the Dippers. To her, they'd always been Jewelled Chairs—the Lesser, the Larger. It had been her intention, as a girl, to ask whoever ran heaven to let her sit in them as soon as she arrived. She'd estimated that a hundred years in each would suffice to give her a good look at the world. From that exalted vantage she'd come to understand everything.

She was saddened to know now that she'd have to travel almost forever to reach those chairs. And to think that the earth, no more than a chance mirror for its star, much as a puddle burns for a moment with sunlight, would have long since been lost in the heavens.

Cassiopeia, Orion, The Pleiades, planet Earth...the scale of things had changed, become inconceivable.

Yet, out of childhood, it was easier for her to think of the heavens, than of heaven, which had somehow been left off the celestial maps. Her own maps. She regretted that, now.

Back when she was first diagnosed, Karl had taken her to hear a lecture on contemporary metaphysics. Desolate, she'd been ready to consider anything. But the gist of the message seemed to be that death was a passage from the lesser, physical realm, to the greater, spiritual realm. Her real self was eternal, pure spirit. In breaking out of the confines of the body, she would be elevated from the carnal, into the realm of infinite light.

Her reaction had been volatile, shocking her. On the drive home, she'd lashed out unfairly at Karl. He could embrace metaphysics if he wanted to. But she could not see her body as a mere casing to be discarded. Found no consolation in the prospect of an interminable half-life as some kind of conscious shadow, incommunicado. It was utter hypocrisy to pretend that disintegration into two halves, with only one of them surviving, was preferable to her current situation—or to oblivion. Better nothing, she told him, than a sham immortality. Then she'd wept, so desperately that Karl had to pull off the rain-swept road to comfort her. He had held her in the streaming car for an hour. They'd never spoken of it again.

But the episode had disclosed to her both disabling rage and a paradox. Rage, that she'd been robbed of her right to another half century of growing into her death. That she had no control over where she was headed. Had given Karl no child. Paradox, that flesh was as the speaker had described it—fragile as grass, momentarily touched with glory, then as quickly withered, wind-borne and gone. Yet the body, even in extremity, resisted death as unnatural. At the hospital she'd seen both the remarkable frailty and resilience of physical existence.

She tried now to rub some feeling back into her numb hands. Blew into her gloves before pulling them on, wishing the ornamental rabbit fur went deeper than the wrists.

Barely audible, the lapping of water. She turned. There, a dark tongue where the point arced out around the marsh. She picked her way over, crouched to watch the play of moonlight on the narrow current. The cold rose off the frozen lake as from dry ice. This close, she could hear the tentative swelling and creaking. From the hill this afternoon, there had been a few resounding rifle shots as cracks spread like lightning far out across the surface. The overhanging trees were glass-sheathed, but the lake would break out soon at this end. Widening channels and dusky patches testified to the waning of winter and the lengthening days.

She was still preoccupied. In her weakening state, she was finding that she could no longer sustain her anger. Besides, in the end it wasn't enough. The progress of the illness seemed irresistible, and rage was no antidote to fear—or the questions that visited her through the long hospital nights. Lately, she was vacillating. Sometimes it seemed obvious that the only way to serenity was acceptance. Yet, however she tried to reconcile herself to dying, she found she could not relinquish the hope that she would go on being. She was still hoping, absurdly, for a permanent fusion of body and spirit. A simple reversal of the order of decay—was that so fantastic?

Less so, out here. The light was obsidian on the strip of black water, reminding her of the stream in an underground cavern she and Karl had explored. Tonight the icicles, too, seemed to reach down geologically, from the petrified grass to the water. There was no hint of the ferment that made the bog fetid in summer, so that canoes would negotiate the reedy narrows quickly, pausing for lilies only above or beyond this point.

As so often these past weeks, she found herself wondering about God. She was illiterate in matters of religion, a legacy from her parents. The one provocative story she had picked up was that even Jesus Christ wasn't content to dismiss his body and live on as pure spirit. Somewhere she'd heard that he insisted friends touch him after his alleged death, to acknowledge that his re-animated flesh was real. Whatever lay behind it, the story gave her an obscure sense of solidarity with him. She had always meant to view Kurelek's Passion paintings, the collection a few hours drive from the city. But could she ask Karl to take her, now?

Enough musing. Since childhood, she'd known the value of small distractions from great dilemmas. Still crouched, she cut a star into the wafer-like surface of the snow. The edges were a blade against the skin of her glove. Strange how irresolute the snow was underneath. With a movement of her wrist not unlike skipping stones, she set the sheer fragments afloat on the dark current, where they were lost. She cut another star, then one more. Rose when the Chairs were roughly outlined at her feet, shadows etched into the shimmering snow.

Probably another dead end. But what if, out there—she turned to follow the curved parameters of the impassively beautiful night—beyond her field of vision, someone was watching? She caught herself scanning for a shooting star. Something.

It was time to head back. She'd have been missed by now, and with the overheated tone of the festivities, it might spill out into a general alarm and search party. That had happened at a Christmas get-together when, disconcerted by the words of a carol, she'd gone out unnoticed to her host's garden swing. She made her way to the path.

The hill looked treacherous from below. Resined and slick. She would have to tackle it sideways, wedging her boots into the slope, staying over by the bushes. She turned for a last look across the ice just as something gave way with a great snap south of the narrows.

Climbing took even more energy than she'd expected. She became intent on the placement of her feet, on dragging air into her lungs. She was conscious of leaving a broken wake up the smooth face of the hill, but couldn't turn to look, break the rhythm of her ascent. Her boots reached, and passed, the spot where she'd slid into the bushes earlier. With tremors now in her legs, and jolts of hot pain from the small of her back, she had a brief image of herself bivouacked there in the softened snow. Felt tempted to turn back, to rest. But just as suddenly, the climb was behind her. She stumbled, leaned weakly against a tree, a metronome in her head and chest, her hip.

Music usurped the solitude here, but pleasantly. Voices curled out from the cottage, pervasive as wood smoke. She whispered, "Thank you." She had not ruined Karl's party after all. Alarmed her friends. She'd made it down to the water's edge and back. In a moment, would go in and make merry.

Staying out too long, straying too far, she might have given the illness the upper hand again. She hoped not. It seemed a great silvery distance across the lawn to where the snow shone topaz under the windows. Not so far as the constellations overhead, but a very great distance. She felt almost ready now to cross it.

BLACK LANCASTER

o street lights out this far. Just the shapes of trees, blacker on black, and the arcing gash where the road cut through. Graeme edged crab-like toward it, listening. It was past mosquito season. Nothing but the whine of blood in his ears, his jagged breathing, and the stir and rustle of leaves overhead and underfoot. Autumn. A moldy, sulphurous smell hung like a net over the knotted underbrush, rose like a lifted veil off the dark slough.

He was taking exaggerated care to keep clear of the muck. Habit. As though clean shoes mattered any more. In fact, it might be better to muddy them. He ploughed his way over to the slough to cake his rented pants to mid-shin. There.

Gestures had become inflated somehow, looming up suddenly and insisting themselves. Maybe this was drunkenness. This and the sluggishness of his limbs, his head's balloon-on-a-string-indifference to his body. He was dazzled, too, by his furtive, minnow-like thoughts. Champagne, a whole bottle. Brandy, a few belts. His first, ever. Of anything alcoholic.

A set-back as he reached the highway. He staggered.

The lines on the road as they spilled around the blind curve were solid as a yellow tape. An unbroken tape. His plan called for a single dotted line.

He stood stupefied. Sank to the oiled shoulder. What a dolt he was. Of course the centre line would be solid here. The switchback was less than a minute from the edge of town, on a provincial highway. To pass here would be suicide; he had picked the spot deliberately for the hairpin turn. The scenario had seemed failsafe. Easy, almost innocent—but fatal. Now this.

The resolve to act had solidified yesterday at the wedding, when Peter and Natalie's vows named death the only amnesty from love. Mute with loss, Graeme had gazed over the minister's uplifted hands and asked himself, *What now? Annihilation or anguish?* No contest. In a charged instant, he'd made up his mind. Now, to accomplish it with minimum fallout for his friends and students.

The reception. *Liquor*—key element, he'd realized, watching people become giddy, uninhibited. He'd need that. He swilled toasts in his customary Canada Dry, but kept his eye on the bar until festivities flagged, the bartender stepped out for a moment and he was able to make his move. The Freixenet Cordon Negro, for its elegant ebony bottle. The Napoleon brandy as back-up. He smuggled the bottles home, then let them sit unopened while he reconsidered through what was left of the night. Sunday morning. Afternoon.

Still no contest. His mood rocketed between misery, black apathy and rage, as it had for months. And still no one to ease him. No one, ever and forever now, amen.

But he had to devise a plan. Something that would leave his intentions unimpeachable. Get drunk and do what? He didn't own a gun, to stage a cleaning accident.

And he didn't like the thought of his house becoming the scene of—too grisly. Drive his car? He might maim someone else or leave the job half-finished. But the highway—he could overindulge, go for an inebriated stroll and fall asleep strategically. Odds were anyone out with a car past midnight on a Sunday night around Sedayko would be joy-riding, a little the worse for drink themselves. They'd never spot him in time.

Sunday night. Years of Sunday School, trenchant sermons kicked in. He vacillated. Agonized. Maybe if he fudged things somehow, so that it wasn't an absolutely premeditated act. Some form of a gamble, a lottery, the element of chance.

By late evening he'd made headway. Talked himself into at least fuelling up. Bitterly calm, he collected what he needed, and sat at the table to throw the dice and tally. Contrived, quasi-fair, a patient inventive game—patient *end*game—of numbers with diminishing returns. He lost, repeatedly, as he'd hoped. So, shrugging off his threadbare quibbles about drinking, he began to choke down the effervescent painkiller a single egg cup at a time.

He didn't rush things. Couldn't. The lack of sleep had made him sluggish.

He inspected the bottle of Freixenet. Scrutinized under the light, the black of its lip showed a festive chocolate tinge. The label looked heraldic. He poured ceremoniously. He paced a little between rounds. Called Environment Canada to check the overnight forecast. Cooked and ate an omelette, mushroom caps, rye toast, chasing each course with a breathtaking slug of brandy. Intermittently tidied and sat.

All the while refining his plan. Choosing the spot for maximum impact, minimum risk of being detected before the fact. Planning the most plausibly unstudied route.

After the third dose of brandy, a moment of heady clarity. *He could connect the dots.* A double-dare-you game with deadly results for two partying graduates a few years back, out the other end of town. Even if Graeme played it solitaire, someone would draw the parallel. Especially—another moment of illumination—if he was wearing a *tuxedo.* Destiny. He still had his wedding gear. And at his end of town, a notorious switchback.

Energized, he hustled to change. The shirt studs almost did him in. His fingers behaving like palsied marionettes.

Back to the dining room for further fortification, token tosses of the dice. Playing and rescanning pictures of what came next—himself on all fours scrambling, stretched out, scrambling, stretched out again, never looking back—in drunken apparent innocence measuring himself against the dashes on the unlit highway. Connecting the dots, waiting for a lone car. Dots and dashes, an encrypted message, brilliant. Truly, a brilliant, brilliant scheme. With each belt of bubbly more brilliant still. Fail-safe. Except for the car, which would have to materialize before he lost his nerve.

And the dotted lines, which had never been here. Graeme slammed his palm into the dirt. Connect the dots? How could he connect the dots? There were no dots. Had never *been* dots. He began to cry. Brilliant? He was a buffoon. A harlequin, a joke.

A whiff of swamp stench, as good as smelling salts. God, look at him. Whimpering. Sulking. Pathetic. Pull himself together. He rubbed his hands and arms. He wiped his face and took a swipe at the ruined trouser legs. Too late for them, let the store suc. Sue Peter, whoever. He took up a handful of gravel and let it winnow like seed through his fingers. Heavy seed, sown on the rocks. Like him.

Cut that out, he told himself. Counter-productive. The big question was, *Now what?* Follow through some other way? Or turn back? He shook his head, trying to clear it. He didn't trust himself. His predicament here went beyond oversight. Beyond a half-cocked plan. He'd betrayed himself. Must have. Staged the march through the bush *knowing* the road would provide a freak rescue, a chance to reconsider, knowing he'd be left a near miss.

After all, he'd grown up on the story of a miraculous wartime reprieve which had changed everything for his father. Grounded on a technicality the night his bomber crew was blown out of the sky, R. Scott Thayer had been carried through life on a boundless surge of hope and self confidence: if Someone intervened from on high because a man's number wasn't up, that gave weight to whatever came after.

So where was his own surge? Sprawled on the edge of the tarmac, he concentrated.

Harder.

Willed it.

A rush of goose bumps, the sense of being brushed by a dark wing, overshadowed by something massive. Something...

No, not a hovering angel. More like a Black Lancaster. He felt the small quickening of hope subside. He was on his own here. Melodrama, manufactured grace—what had he expected? His father had despised bottled courage. And so had he, before tonight. His father's son that way, at least.

He scattered more gravel, this time pelting it toward the undergrowth. Grapeshot. *Wait.* He sat bolt upright. Forget the game. Why become fixated on the game? It was peripheral. Another of those inflated gestures. Like Russian Roulette with no witnesses, the details obliterated in the outcome. Back to plan one. If he just lay down someone would run him over sooner or later. They'd find the bottles at his house, blame the unaccustomed booze.

Enough sitting around. His haunches hurt. He pushed himself up and stood letting things right themselves. His palm stung. After rubbing away the grit and adjusting his cummerbund (frosted melon, Natalie's doing), he moved to the middle of the highway.

There! He bent to feel the surface with his hands. The pavement was glacial, cold as a crypt. Appropriate. When he was a boy, this stretch had been the feared highway of his mother's morning litany. "Graeme. Don't go near the highway, now. Never mind making that face. Remember what happened to Sparkie, and the Hryluck's cat. You keep well away." *Sorry, Mom.*

He sighted back toward town. From his crouch, the curve really did look deadly. A rare prairie switchback. Something to do with the marsh, a waterfowl habitat which had seen better days. Pickups and cars accelerated at this spot, aiming for Saskatoon. Over his left shoulder the asphalt pulled around to pour straight across the land for eighty kilometers. No need to turn for a last look. He'd driven it a thousand times. Could summon without thought the slipstream of fields, spent outbuildings and dugouts that ended in the city. Nothing for him that way, or he wouldn't be here.

As though it were a perilously skittish canoe, he lowered himself onto the pavement. The cold found him instantly through the tuxedo. His bones were unpadded and the fabric fine. He turned face down. Awkwardly maneuvered himself until he was aligned over the sweep of yellow paint with his head pointed toward Sedayko and his unknown deliverer, his feet toward Saskatoon. Or maybe his feet toward his—impossible to predict. But from here he could roll into either lane, launch himself sideways. Whatever it took.

He lay still. Time for reflections about becoming one with the earth. Or resurrecting a prayer. A bit of a retrospective at least, reliving his best moments. He shuddered, hardened himself. Which moments? Which prayer? Yesterday's event eclipsed things.

Peter, the thought of Peter and Natalie, Peter *with* Natalie, made him suddenly reckless. Reckless and giddy. He balled his hands into fists. Felt his jaw cramp. *Brrmmm.* He mimicked a car. *Brrmmm!* Mimicked louder. And louder, until he panicked himself. He smirked at the frantic floundering of his heart, a hummingbird caged in sudden ribs. Scare the life out of himself. Why not? Flush it out before the thrum of tires on the icy tarmac, before the startled flight of headlights across the black wall of foliage. There were no rules about how he finished this, now that his game was off. He grinned, clever. More clever than Natalie. He'd outmaneuvered her. Would never have to see them together again.

Brmmm. He must be very drunk.

Or was he?

He pursed his lips and pondered the question. One bottle of Spanish champagne. A few inches of French brandy. Would that do it? Get him drunk?

Was he?

Blitzed, smashed, blotto?

No. *Rational.* He felt as though he'd become supremely rational, had been initiated, in fact, into arcane rules of logic previously inaccessible to him. A whole new modus operandi. Wider. Deeper. Colder somehow.

That was what the alcohol had done. Changed the governing principles.

Wait. Changed or suspended?

Suspended or expanded?

Expanded or—he yawned, arched his back and

reached under himself to smooth a ridge in his jacket. Gooseflesh. That really was pavement under him. He really was on the highway.

Return to the question.

The rules.

Forget them. Rules, questions, mental breathalysers, he was only confusing himself. The alcohol had animated him, had got him out here, that was enough. Take a sabbatical.

Some time later his watch played a tinny *Für Elise* (Peter's needling gift, when he suspected Graeme of brooding over a community health nurse). And again. Two o'clock! He broke into a sweat. How much longer? He was clammy and half frozen. He could use a hot coffee, a steaming hot coffee. *Stop, don't weaken.* Think about what lay ahead if he backed out. Desolation. Peter's obtuse confidences about wedded bliss. No thanks. He sat up to remove the watch and send it skidding across the road. Lay prone and realigned himself. That should solve the time issue.

The minutes continued to pile up. Perversely, he thought.

Relentlessly.

He was starting to feel nauseated. Despair threatened again like clouds boiling up at the horizon. Cumulonimbus. He fought it. Tried to recap Sedayko's marital history from memory. Naming the families, the lonelyhearts like himself, the aging widowers—scanning back a generation, then projecting forward—pairing the teenagers off as though a deluge threatened. Not much to work with. Sedayko being Sedayko.

Now a troublesome worm of boredom. He began to list aloud the properties of an acid. A base. Of liquids and solids, of gas. His teacherly sing-song comforted, kept the thought of retreat at bay. He tried to pick up the tempo. Rapped through the chemical valance tables, boxcar rhythm. MO A-G K L-I N-A. *Molybdenum, Argentum, Potassium, Lithium and Sodium.* Was that right? *Fluorine Chlorine Borine and Iodine.* Iodine, the perennial rhyme wrecker.

A necessary element, though, Iodine. Essential.

He must be losing it.

So?

So *Iodine, iodize.*

Iodize, ionize.

Ionize... ionized particles. Aurora Borealis—*Ghost dancers.* That was a thought. Were they out tonight?

He rolled to look.

Overhead, dramatic wisps of cirrus in a starred black tapestry. The roadside trees a frame. Spectacular. But no phantom dancers. No—what was it?— *heavenly curtains rent and rehung, rent and rehung across infinity's darkened window.* Peter's words; sweet Peter, the poet. And Graeme a heartless redactor of phenomena; Natalie's verdict. He shut his eyes hard. What did she know? God, tears again. Self-pity. Was love—a shared life like anyone's—too much to ask?

Too terribly much?

Apparently. He curled on his side, fetal, with his back to the marsh.

⁂

"GRAEME! IS THAT YOU?"

Monumental stiffness. Cold. Someone touching his shoulder.

"Graeme?" Another tentative touch, moving his hair.

He pulled himself back from the edge of a dream, into

what must be another. Pavement against his cheek, swamp gas. Streaky darkness. He was outside, had apparently slept. Someone close, breathing on him.

He groaned.

"Sit up, man, if you're alive! What on earth are you doing out here?"

Sudden warmth, panting, wet pumice on his knuckles, dog stink. He gagged, kicked at it.

"Off him, Brandy! *Brandy!* There, keep back, you'll smother him."

Brandy?

Focusing now, vaguely, on someone reshaping the strip of sky. A woman. Big woman. Edith Schellenburg. Crouched, almost on top of him. His neighbour Edith and her sheltie.

"What in heaven's name—"

"Oh, God." He started to shiver violently. On top of everything else, a good Samaritan. The whole thing had miscarried. He was an idiot. "Oh God." Sick, a wave of it.

"Man, you've puked yourself. You sick here, is that it?"

He gagged again. Wanted to die. Helpless tears.

She half-dragged, half-shoved him off the road, moved to a discreet few paces and squatted. Watched covertly, picking at the dog's snarled coat.

He retched and apologized, retched and tried to apologize again.

She exclaimed, "Lord love us, man! What are you apologizing for? Just get it all up while you're at it."

The rank wine was bad enough. But those eggs, garlicky mushrooms, bile.

His stomach quieted at last. He nursed it for a few minutes, tried to sit. A queasy equilibrium. He stole another look at Edith.

She'd nudged the sheltie away and was sizing him up frankly.

He should concoct some story. She looked about to ask.

She nodded, though, and straightened. "That's better now. Let's get you home. Wonder you weren't killed, laid out like that." She was coming at him. "The shock! Couldn't tell whether we'd stumbled across one of the quick or the dead!"

Tell her to get lost. That he would be all right. Just fine.

But his tongue had gone sluggish. His whole body quivery. He didn't stand a chance. The woman had wrapped her arm around him now, was lifting and forcing him to his feet. His legs felt akimbo, two pick-up sticks. He wobbled, and the tree line opposite with him. She gripped his shoulders more adamantly.

Brandy rubbed against him, hard, trying to get at his hands. "Lay off him, you brute!" Edith pushed the dog back. Graeme staggered and let her prop him. She was built like a Clydesdale.

"You're no heavier than a boy," she fussed. "We've got to get you inside! Shivering like that—puking yourself— how long you been out here? You after pneumonia?"

He tried to wrench himself away, but she had him clamped. Unnervingly close, she scrutinized his face. He considered the sky, his shoes, the agitated sheltie. Her grip and tone softened. "Never mind. Been out here half the night, from the feel of you. Good thing we didn't get that frost."

He cleared his throat. Cut the conversation and see him home, if she must. Leave him to work out his next move. He shuffled his feet.

She nodded again and began to guide him back across the road. "All right then, so you're not talking. I imagine the story will keep. We'll get you home and cleaned up first.

"You're damn lucky. You were about one moan away from a CPR attempt. And I'd likely have collapsed your lungs—don't know the first thing about it."

The nearest hospital was in Saskatoon now. Almost an hour's drive. He'd toasted the government for that earlier. Rural health cut-backs.

Stopping for a moment to catch her breath, Edith indicated his formal suit and bow tie. She wore a man's plaid flannel jacket, with jeans. "Quite the duds."

He scowled down at the evening wear. Tricky. Half the community had been at the wedding yesterday.

"Going dancing, were you? Just where would that be, at three o'clock in the morning?"

He felt himself blush. Shrugged. They both knew better, knew Sedayko. And every other town this side of the city. He had to shake her soon.

He coughed up phlegm and jerked his arm free to whack his chest. Became acutely aware of his bladder. "The bushes!" he gasped.

They hobbled double time towards the break in the trees, leaving the highway behind.

"CUTE, IF YOU DON'T MIND the boneyard out back." Edith spoke as though she'd never seen the place. She lived one grid road over.

Graeme turned from the steps to look dully at his property. He'd sold his parents' fussy Victorian three years ago to buy this one-of-a-kind house just beyond the town limits. It had been a church once. Presbyterian, casualty of Sedayko's haemorrhaging. His decision to jettison the Thayer home to fix up his own had caused a bit of a stir. Peter had encouraged him, though, so he'd bequeathed it to him, unbeknownst. Pre-Natalie.

He pulled the heavy door, an effort. He was close to collapse. How was he going to brush this woman off?

"Never been inside since that young couple converted it. Not much before, either," she admitted.

Maybe he could throw up again.

"Be nice to see it." She was crowding him, making sure she got past the threshold. "Since I'm here."

Defeated, he led her through the chilly vestibule. At least she'd left the dog outside.

She stopped just through the inner door.

He sighed, hit the light switch.

"Goodness! Will you look at this!" She stood gawking.

The vaulted central room always took people aback—the space itself, his furniture. Harp back chairs, re-cushioned deacon's benches for sofas, bookshelves which had held hymnbooks. Curiously bevelled coffee tables cut from sacristy doors, wall lamps and fixtures made by a stained glass artist to complement the spectacular windows. The cedar-panelled ceiling. Plank flooring with the dark lustre of age; Peter had talked him out of brightening or Varethaning it, and he'd been right.

He crossed his arms and rotated his shoulders to release some of the tension in his neck. He loved the place. The previous owners had run out of money before they could do much beyond dismantling the church fixtures, reroofing, and replacing the duct work. So much the better for him. He'd run giddy on adrenaline for more than a year while he worked on it. When it was done, an incredible sense of sanctuary, of having built himself an ark. *A benevolent pavilion under the fathomless firmament:* Peter's housewarming paeon.

An air of the sacred lingered still, especially after dusk. Maybe nothing more than old beeswax and oil soap, or the residue of fragrant smoke released from the wood by humidity. But he'd favoured the plan to expire on the road tonight partly because it would leave the house inviolate—and leave him unmoved by its associations. Now here he was, back. Unsettling.

"*Man.*" Edith shook her head. "For a fellah, you've done wonders. Put the rest of us to shame." She reached her hand to touch the nearest lamp. Emerald and citrine foliage in old-fashioned lead solder.

"Now, how about you go wash up and I'll put the kettle on. You're no rose."

He went.

"That's more like it," she told him when he rejoined her. "I'm just pouring." She'd taken over his kitchen and dining room, a one-woman invasion. He felt displaced.

"Hope you don't mind my nerve, helping myself. I'm no great sleeper to begin with," she explained, pouring Earl Grey into a mug. "So after supper I generally stick to tea. But it's black coffee for you—I figured you could do with a transfusion."

He accepted a mug and napkin without comment, although the coffee looked like sludge. Maybe she'd passed on the paper filter to make it more sobering. Needless. Standing under the shower seemed to have flushed the last of the fog from his head. Vomiting aside, he might have made a heroic boozer.

"No shortage of elbow room." She gestured along the dining table, an oak trestle seating ten.

He winced. The wine bottle stood prominent, capped by an inverted egg cup of stainless steel. It looked like an irreverent bell tower. Worse, there beside his students' latest quizzes, were the dice and memo pad which had figured in his game. The brandy, too, would be out in full view on the kitchen counter. Gingerly, he pulled up a chair.

Edith stirred sugar into her mug, sipped thoughtfully and began. "It's an unearthly hour, Graeme, and I'm not one for visiting at the best of times." He nodded. "So I can't pretend to know you real well, neighbour since the Great Flood or not." She drank, cleared her throat.

"But from where I sit, you'd be about thirty years old, a decent-looking man with your hair, teeth and good name intact. Steady work, your own house and a bachelor to boot. While I'm pushing sixty and almost one hundred and sixty..." She ran her hand along the grizzled braid of her hair, then down across her flannel bosom and belly. He watched, recalling one of his mother's phrases. Farm stock, she would have called Edith. Prairie farm stock. The plaid workshirt was probably her husband's once, grey and black, generous even on her bulk.

She winked and continued, "...with one nuisance of a disposable breast, varicose veins, and a husband who ran off with a bingo caller after cashing in our RRSP's. So—" she hesitated, "how come I pick you up off the highway, and not the other way around? You might fill me in."

He caught his breath. Glanced at the Freixenet. Witness for the defence, his alibi. Along with the brandy.

"Carelessness," he murmured, gesturing evasively towards the bottle.

She frowned, unimpressed. "Oh, no. You don't get off the hook that easy." She shook her head and squinted at him. Her eyes were frank, blue, quick. "You must be forgetting I know you for a Thayer. For your father's son. You wouldn't have been putting that stuff away for nothing."

His father had been a Baptist and a militant temperance man. All Sedayko remembered old R. Scott thundering against the local billiard hall's liquor license. Graeme had put up with merciless hazing, but stayed dry himself even through university in Saskatoon. Safeguarding himself against indiscretions, and compensating, maybe. Powerless to meet more fundamental expectations.

To avoid Edith's gaze, he began to draw on the little note pad. Molecular structures. Wavelength patterns. Higher frequencies.

She gripped the paper and blurted, "You weren't hoping to do yourself in out there, were you?"

He shielded his face with his left hand, held the ballpoint poised in his right. The air in the room had evaporated suddenly.

"Looked to me like you might have been lying there in the dark waiting for some poor devil to run you down."

He collapsed and buried his head in his arms.

Why hadn't they? Why not one single car?

"Lord love us—so you were! You didn't seriously think—"

Yes. He'd thought.

Edith was touching his elbow, "It's all right. There, now." He hadn't cried in front of anyone since he was a boy. Not yesterday. Not when cancer took his mother. And not when his father's heart gave out. Tranquilly, in his sleep, at the proverbial three score and ten, his father had had the best possible death. Vindicating. Whereas Graeme....

Several minutes passed before he dared look up. Edith had left the table, at least. She was in the kitchen tactfully fussing with the tea. Topping it up, replacing the lid, refilling the kettle—did she plan to stay all night? He felt raw, defenceless. The skin of his life had been peeled away somehow. A woman, this interfering Edith Schellenburg, was going to see in.

Never. He folded his hands to hide the tremors. Set his face. Never.

She came back to her chair, unhurried. With a sidelong glance at him, she uncapped the pot and restirred the tea. He inhaled the fragrant steam to calm himself. Oil of Bergamot. Sweet. For him, too sweet, almost soapy. He kept it for Natalie and Peter—she'd weaned him off coffee. Carcinogenic. As if.

Edith poured, then sipped quietly. He tried to keep his hands still. And to keep his eyes away from hers; she seemed to be sizing him up again.

"There. No shame in a real good cry." She cleared her throat, said matter-of-factly, "When you've got cause."

He held his breath.

"I'm guessing that wedding Saturday comes into this?"

Damn her! He shook his head with vehemence. Too vehemently. The room careened, listed, righted itself.

"Sheer coincidence?"

She must know he'd been best man. Best *friends* with Peter. She placed her hand over his. Stung, he shook it off. He couldn't speak. Think.

"Look," she persisted, "You're in a bad way here, Graeme. That monkey business on the road. That's not behind you yet. Whatever's eating you—"

"Leave it!" Leave it, leave it, leave it.

For the moment, she did. She nodded, shut up and finished her tea.

The kettle lisped weakly and gave up the ghost. The house became unnaturally quiet around them. Stiflingly quiet. A good minute passed. Two. Her patience was unnerving.

Brandy sounded off frantically, startling him. The whole town would be up. He felt his keys against his thigh.

Edith dismissed the noise. "Ignore her. A gopher."

The kettle was rallying. How could he end this?

She unseated his makeshift shot glass and set it on the table. Clinked it with her spoon, as guests had tinkled goblets *ad nauseam* yesterday. Stainless steel on stainless steel, unlovely; she dropped the spoon. She took the bottle, read the label and frowned, "Wonder you could pronounce this. Freaksenate? Fricksy-net?"

He couldn't.

She wiped the rim, tipped the bottle into a napkin, then lay it on its side and gave it a spin. It came to a stop pointing noncommittally toward the living room.

"Natalie, was it?" Another spin. This time, directly at him.

"Certainly not!" Scalded. Terrified.

"Must've been." She set the bottle upright. Recrowned it. "The truth now."

"I told you no!" he cut her off.

She stiffened in the chair and studied him.

He should throttle her. Now. He gripped his wrist, handcuffing himself. Better to go for his keys.

She began again stubbornly, "We'll let that pass. Say your half-pickling yourself and bedding down on the highway had nothing to do with young Natalie's getting married to your buddy yesterday—"

He was boiling, trembling.

"Then why the fancy getup? Why deck yourself out like a thwarted bridegroom?"

Thwarted bridegroom? "It was *Peter,* damn you! Not Natalie! *Peter!*" The name was an ejaculation, an eruption.

An evacuation order. He leapt to his feet, knocked the bottle flying and bolted for the door. He was out, across the drive and into his car in a moment. A blur streaking out of the graveyard—the sheltie, frenzied, coming at him. She took a yelping run at the headlights. Gunning the motor, he slammed into reverse.

Peter! Had he named him?

Forget the shimmy, he floored it.

He was horrified. Why couldn't he keep his mouth shut—after all this time! Make up something. Anything. Let the damn busybody think it was Natalie. Exit with at least that much dignity.

He roared past the Schellenburg acreage, watched for the turn north. There.

A fishtail turn. Buckshot backwash. Ease off.

Would she tell?

A wash of realization—even if Edith took her dog home right now and forgot she'd ever run across him, he'd left the muddy tux, left the whole place lit up and open. The school would call when he didn't show up to teach first period. When they couldn't raise him on the phone all day, they'd send someone over to check. By tomorrow the RCMP would be questioning everybody in town.

He was having trouble seeing. Steering.

Edith would have to give some kind of statement. By the time she finished, Peter's name would be dragged into it. He'd be stunned, coming home from his honeymoon to this. Malicious talk about him—insinuations in class, in the teachers' lounge—Natalie would be livid.

He groaned. *The will.* That would cap everything. Stupid, stupid, stupid. Peter wouldn't miss him. He'd end up hating him.

At that, he had to fight to keep from running off the shoulder. He slowed the car deliberately.

Maddeningly.

Made himself concentrate. Grimly tightened his grip on the wheel. No point taking chances the next few kilometres. Curves and dips. If he rolled over he might wake up in some rehab centre. In a wheelchair, having to face people. Having to face stupefied Peter. Think about *that* scenario.

He eased off further on the accelerator, put on

Shostakovich's Eleventh and turned up the speakers. Perfect. Soothingly apocalyptic.

Cresting the hill just beyond the Piebald turnoff ten minutes later, he took a sharp left. A kilometre in, the gates stood open and unattended. The remote air base tucked into the highlands had been shut down for about a dozen years. He should have come here in the first place.

He bypassed the main thoroughfare. Looped away from the barracks, PX, and Quonset rec buildings. The surface of this secondary drive was badly crazed and rutted. Taking a rattling, he eased up on the gas. To his left were the old RV sites where kids came to park. He was always warning his students about the transport trailers beached behind the windscreen of elms. They held PCB impregnated plastic jugs, deadly stuff. Sooner or later some curious teenager would get at them. Government—he'd written a fistful of letters.

The pavement climbed toward a plateau, then dog-legged to pass behind the complex. It ended before a barbed wire-topped Frost fence enclosing a radar tower. He braked, parked, flicked on the dome light and rummaged for a flashlight in the glove compartment. Success. Catching sight of himself in the mirror, he was still for a moment. His face was bleak, drained, already dead. How long had he looked like this? Had no one noticed? Not even Peter?

He abandoned his car.

In no time he'd breached the compound, despite a bit of grief with the lock. His shaky, overeager hands. He had keys mislaid in the lab by a student who patrolled out here summers. He'd kept intending to "discover" and return them, but four times in recent weeks he'd broken in like this, instead. Mr. Thayer, teacher extraordinaire, exemplary citizen, mocking his own code of ethics. Maybe he'd been unconsciously working up to tonight. Worse luck, the *unconsciously* part. What he had in mind now would have preempted that farce on the highway.

The radar structure loomed. Unremarkable, up close. Fashioned of corrugated tin like a farm outbuilding. Battered Robin's egg blue. And held by a padlock he wouldn't trust to secure his mountain bike. Yet the Pine Tree Line, along with the DEW line across the far north, had been a crucial gauntlet, an electronic bulwark against the Russians. Laid waste by history, this and all the other outposts. Twice, actually. This one had been an RCAF flight school in its heyday. Active, not passive engagement.

The door was one thick sheet of rust. He butted it ajar with his shoulder. Braced himself to enter. His first visit in the small hours. First visit post-daylight–*pre*-daylight. The interior looked unfathomable. A flutter of nerves.

Switching on his flashlight, he inched forward. The air was putrid. He kept the torch trained on the floor, making his way over fallen crusts of drywall, decaying newspaper, flakes of oxidized metal, a telephone receiver. Flushed out by the inadequate beam, the debris seemed grotesque. It broke and gave underfoot like small animal bones. To dispel that impression, he tried to visualize his passage by memory. On either side of him was a warren of rooms which could have been in Dresden.

Exploring these in daylight, he'd been astounded by the deliberate mayhem. Some of the walls had ragged, door-sized holes knocked out six feet off the floor. Tracer fire patterns–the work of bored smokers–puckered the surfaces of linoleum which hadn't been torn up altogether. Duty stations were personalized with the ballpoint character references and phone numbers of girls kind to airmen. Dilapidated farm wives now, probably, all of them. In a vaultlike room housing a bank of dire electrical boxes, a yellowed MacLeans ad offered perpetual security; the pert family flanked by a Monopoly house, like the insurance company, long since defunct.

He stumbled and shuffled past all of it tonight. Was drawn on the wan rail of light through the ruined hallway, a further locked door, and into the tower proper.

It was an abyss.

One which opened up, though. Not down. His stomach lurched. Could he do this? Pigeons and bats whirred and fled in the dark. Smaller birds—swallows, sparrows? Droppings fouled everything. The shaft might as well house a dumbwaiter; it was suffocatingly narrow for a stairwell. Twice before, he'd backed away from it. The whole place reeked of moldering filth, oil, and corroded metal.

He shone the light up. From below, weirdly lit, the hanging stairs were footholds across oblivion. Insubstantial footholds. No risers. He'd never been great at heights. One misstep and he'd end here. Here, in this squalid box. He blanched. No thanks.

So dedicate the beam to his feet and grope for the handrail.

How many turns? Impossible to tell. What difference, anyway? He was committed.

Now. He shuddered, wiped his forehead—sweat and what might be cobwebs—and started up.

Why metal mesh steps? Hanging stairs were bad enough. But having to look right *through* them.

And they were encrusted, a honeycomb of excreta. That much showed in the wash of watery light. Worse, so was the handrail. Guano and grime. He had to force his hand over it. To will his nausea down.

The third revolution was behind him, the ground floor swallowed again in shadow. Fifth revolution. Sixth. He held the railing weakly for a moment. These turns. The disorienting blackness, the murky sweep of his light. Which was worse? The dark—or suggestive glimmers?

He forced himself up and around two more twists of the screw.

Three.

Had to pause. Had to. His head was afloat. Heart hammering. Like earlier, on the road. His body absurdly preoccupied with his safety. When the moment came, would it let him go?

Keep climbing. Don't think.

Keep climbing.

Thank God. He stood gasping on a miserable landing, three feet square. The interminable steps had ended. Abruptly, just when he'd become convinced he was on some perverse Jacob's ladder.

A gift of air. A door, propped ajar. What if it had been locked?

He trained his beam back down and shuddered. Poor saps who used to be stationed here; no wonder they'd trashed the place afterwards. Nothing imaginable could have induced him to descend, even once. His die was cast.

The door gave onto an enclosed expanse almost as dark as the stairwell. A slightly raised threshold. He goose-stepped through, careful not to disturb the crowbar arrangement. Drafts whistled, grazed his face. Air! He took a tenuous step, jumped back at a rush of startled wings. More bats. The contamination in this place must be phenomenal. He waited, hand on his chest, for his heart to settle.

He must be at the eastern end. From making the circuit outside, he knew that he had to cross to the south-west corner. The breeze meant unseen openings. He played his light around, grateful the batteries had held. The space seemed to be empty except for something huge, machinery probably, midway. But it wasn't really as dark as he'd first thought. He could make out slatted unglazed windows, reassuring indigo beyond.

Underfoot, the floors were linked steel plates, as on board ship. Slots and gaps where the heavy panels abutted. No discernible underpinning or superstructure, simply a drop, the possibility of plunging. In the recesses overhead, beam work and what might be gigantic fan blades, hard to tell. Ahead somewhere, the exit. He stepped skittishly forward. Almost there now.

♨ ♨ ♨

"GRAEME?" EDITH.

"Graeme, you out there?" He'd been out here forever. An hour, maybe two. It was getting light.

He stayed as he was. Heard her clanking across the metallic floor. Then inching out onto the platform, easing down beside him. Now what?

For a few minutes she said nothing. From the riot of her breathing, she was too winded. Incomprehensible, her coming all this way after him.

"You couldn't go through with it," she gasped at last, "Thank God!"

He flinched. Glanced over wordlessly. She looked distraught and dishevelled from the climb. Her face papery.

She wrapped her arm around his shoulders.

He made to pull away. She resisted. Held him. He had no energy, no will to fight her.

"You saw my truck?"

He had seen it.

Past caring what happened, he had watched the serpentine progress of headlights around the complex. Thinking, his luck, it was probably the RCMP. Relief when the pickup was close enough to make out. Relief and irritation. Edith Schellenburg again. The woman was a mule.

"When my Arnie hightailed it, I got pretty low—" she was recovering her breath now. "After supper, the house used to feel like a funeral parlour.

"Didn't want to sit moping. And couldn't abide the talk in town. So often as not, I'd head out here. Give Brandy a good run. Give myself a pep talk."

Edith, here.

"You won't remember the dances they used to throw, way back." She jerked her head in the direction of the RV area, "But the gully there, that's still a regular lover's lane."

"I've heard," he whispered. Common knowledge at the high school. And he'd parked here himself over the years. Sat alone in his darkened car more nights—listening to the stereo. While he was supposed to be in Saskatoon seeing a woman, he'd drive the grid roads till he was choking on his own chalky wake, then hide out here until it was late enough to go home. Mosquitos, the spectre of carbon monoxide. And though the compound was pocked with secluded cul-de-sacs, the possibility that someone might spot him. The irony: his fear of being ruined if he was caught parking by himself. His father's fear that he'd ruin himself in the backseat with some girl.

Edith gave him a quick squeeze; his ribs hurt. "Tore halfway to Saskatoon just now before something turned me around. Your father—I suddenly remembered how he used to make a pest of himself out here. Worrying the mechanics about this, that or the other thing. Going over the planes rivet by rivet, like he knew the first thing about them anymore. Reliving the war. A weekend Billy Bishop. Thought: *who knows?* He might have taken you along when you were little."

He shrugged the memory off.

She banged the metal wall, jolting him. "But Lord love us, man, this *tower!* How you got up here in the pitch dark! It's taken ten years off my life." Why had she bothered?

"Those *stairs–*" she grimaced, "I was starting to hope you *had* broken your blasted neck!"

He toed the flashlight.

"Well—that says something, doesn't it? That you bothered with a light?"

Maybe. He was still here.

Or maybe not. He despised himself for it.

"This is some lookout you've got." She sighed.

He scanned the folding hills, corded fields, the reddish lake and string of wetlands off to the east. Burnt tracts and coulees obscured by ground fog contrasted with the ochres, greens and rusts, the wavering stands of aspen. The view, emerging earlier, had undone him.

"How'd you come by keys?"

He made an effort. "One of the Winslow boys. I'm not much for heights."

"The Lord be praised." She leaned out to gauge the drop, then drew back, sobered. "Wasn't just that, though. Stopping you."

He shifted away from her. Felt his eyes smart again.

"Care to fill me in?"

Tell her. Try explaining to himself first. Two botched exits in one night.

"Fear of God, was it?"

God only knew. He was a believer, for the most part.

But he'd been planning to plead his state of mind, argue for some special deal or dispensation. Vaguely planning.

He studied his knuckles. They looked like chicken bones, chicken bones under wax.

Brinkmanship. All a game of brinkmanship with himself. And maybe with Peter in absentia.

"Something else, then."

Something. When the moment came, he found himself unready. Simply that. Unready. If he'd mounted the railing, slipped his legs over and let himself slide, that would have been it. Exit Graeme Thayer. Sum total. Some life.

So he hadn't. Without a thought in his head, he had huddled on the cantilevered platform and waited. Unable to proceed. Unable to picture his way back down. Fitting. His friendship with Peter had been a high-wire act for years. Exquisite pain being with him, unbearable without.

Edith spoke again, gently, "Leave it lie, then. No point hounding yourself." Hounding himself? He'd known hounds she couldn't imagine.

"What you said. Earlier, at the house, about your friend. I won't tell a living soul."

His friend. He gazed southeast toward Sedayko, west to where stubbled grainfields carpeted the uplands around Piebald and Steevers. Farms. Families. Edith's living souls. Normal people living normal lives.

"Some might find that kind of thing... disgusting," she said carefully.

He felt his ears burn. Turned to read her face.

"But I don't. Not disgusting." She was flushed. "Different, maybe. Seen it in my brother-in-law's cattle. Though the thought of you—of two men—"

"Not two. *One*," he whispered. "Peter has no idea."

"No idea? You mean to say you've managed to—" She

gave him a searching look. Sighed and nodded. "Well. I guess if there'd been anything that way between you, he'd never have had you stand up with him, Saturday."

Or camped with him those three summers, aeons ago, canoeing and fishing the indigo lakes out of La Ronge.

Or shared his extravagant poems.

Or kidded him about being unable to snag a wife when even a Lyle Lovett was landing a Julia Roberts. *Get a move on. The bait's not getting any fresher, Graeme.*

Or—any of it. God, the minutiae of deception.

"And they'd have put the pair of you out of the high school on a platter. They don't miss much," Edith concluded.

No they didn't, usually. The vigilance had worn him ragged. With jobs hard to come by, he'd moved back to teach at his old regional collegiate. Sedayko, small town hazards: he should have been married long since. But beyond that, local notions were hazy. He produced a decent five o'clock shadow and didn't lisp, he shuttled to Saskatoon periodically to take women out, women he wasn't about to show around town. He must be okay. His name was coinage, too. As a straightlaced-Baptist Thayer, immunity from speculation, up to a point. Immunity, period. He'd been as circumspect in private as in public.

"Did your father suspect?"

He started. "I hope not!"

"That's a pity. Keeping this to yourself all these years."

Pity? If he'd been alive, his father would have lined up with the rest of them to sign the petition posted in Calvary Baptist's vestibule last year. Lobbying for legalized persecution, human rights exemptions. His father's church, his father's people. Graeme's own church, till then.

"If you were like this—" His voice caught. *This. Like this.* Euphemisms. Was he thirty or thirteen?

He was thirty. A thirty year old unmarried high school teacher in rural Saskatchewan. Unmarried male high school teacher. Not some West Coast lawyer or filmmaker, casually *out*. Not some activist from Toronto talking about spousal rights on the CBC news magazine. Their world was light years away. He gazed toward Sedayko, invisible beyond the edge of the variegated tapestry. Light years.

"I thought I'd die before I'd tell." He startled himself, volunteering this. "Die if anyone found out."

"Seems like *not* telling nearly did you in."

There was some feeble consolation in having told even Edith Schellenburg. This one human being. Without a sinkhole appearing to swallow him. The sky falling.

"Climbing up here after you—" She hesitated. "A thought hit me like flash hail. You're the same person as before. Still Graeme Thayer, son of Scott and Tessie, not a blessed thing about you changed. So..." she touched his hand tentatively, "how can I start looking slantways? Thinking ugly names?"

He sagged. Let this surge over him.

Ugly names. *Queer, Sodomite, deviate. Faggot. Etcetera.* Scott and Tessie's son. His father's sense of benediction, of divine anointing, might have dissolved in the wake of those names. At least, that's what he'd feared. That his father's faith would be unequal to the fact of a deviant son. That his father's love, his fierce and exacting love, would fall short. *Old R. Thundering Scott.* That the truth might unleash an avenging angel.

Yet here was this woman, a neighbour, barely known to him. Would his own father have refused to lift him from the black tarmac?

Abraham with Isaac. But no ram blundering into the bushes. No miraculous deliverance or contravening Voice. What then?

Morbid melodrama again. An unfair question, posed posthumously. He blinked, swallowed hard. Unfair and pointless.

Meanwhile, Edith. "Thank you," he said at last.

"Never mind." She gripped his hand. *"I'm just glad."* Her voice was husky. "But don't make a habit of it. Poor old Brandy–" she shook her head.

She rubbed her calves and ankles, stamped her feet. "Get my circulation going." His feet were asleep, wedged against the upright bars. He moved them. Electricity.

Edith stood cautiously. "I've about had the biscuit here. You ready?"

Sweat. "I don't know."

"Lord, man! You lay yourself out like a corpse in the middle of the road, scaring me halfway to Beulahland. Then you bolt–between chasing that crazed dog and trying to follow you, I just about have a coronary. If you think I'm going back down those stairs alone–"

He shrugged weakly.

"Besides, the world doesn't begin and end in Sedayko, Saskatchewan. Move on, if need be." She sounded exasperated, "Or stay put and get help. Mercy, anything beats this."

The air wafted cool through his sweater, recalling the feel of pavement through the glossy evening wear. He shivered and hugged himself. Took stock again.

He was wasted, felt more dead than alive. But he didn't want to die. Had never really wanted to be dead. What he'd wanted was to stop living as he'd been living. Half real, half figment. Unloved, unlovable, where it counted most. At the critical moment, against all odds, he had grounded himself.

Had been grounded.

Whichever.

She rested her hand on his shoulder, a small warmth. "I took care of the lights for you. So nobody'd wonder about the house blazing away like a jack-o-lantern.

"And if anybody cares enough to notice my pickup gone, half the town has me stepping out with Jake Petersen on the sly." She reached for the door. "Now, let's hope we don't come to a bad end together in that stairwell."

He pulled himself up, suddenly woozy, and clutched the rail. The balcony was little more than a catwalk supported by struts against the tower. A breezy catwalk. Standing, he could see the ruined concrete flats of the old airfield. And on every side, sky and the muted colours of autumn in wheat and wetland. He watched a jet trail, far to the south, follow a silver needle through a clearing in the cloud bank.

NIGHTS AT THE LUCKY MOON

At first, the city seemed poised, taut with promise. It was there in the salt-petroleum-and-sulphur-tanged air of the harbour, the steadfast movement of grimed ships out to sea. In the strings of lights on the water by day, the bridges by night. Even, she sensed, in the now distinct, now vague mantle of mountains and clouds to the east and the north.

This conviction infected her swiftly, relentlessly, like a disease. Needing something to hope for, she decided that there must be an unspoken knowing here. The very essence of vitality. The waiters shared it in steaming espresso and tangled plates of shrimp and oriental vegetables. It was passed in sunset congeniality between joggers on the beaches. The Haida totems hummed with it.

Her own knowledge was incomplete. She had dead-headed in out of instinct. All would be revealed to her when she had accepted Vancouver with more than the jabbered curiosity of the Pentaxed one-week tourists. She decided to stay, sold her car.

And studied people. She watched passers-by from the backdrop of canvas sails at pristine Canada Place, on the bleached oak or marble pews of the sumptuous shopping temples. Sat for hours in precarious wire chairs on Gastown patios. In summer playgrounds, she squinted at children through a hail of glistening water-bullets. Their extravagant energy eluded her. She began to lose focus.

She left the Y and took a housekeeping room. As her money ran out, she sat at the scarred arborite tables of diners, breathing the grease of two-dollar breakfast specials, trying to think what she should do. She'd counted on revitalization or intervention by now. Instead, she walked endlessly, rode the Skytrain to the very centre of the city, the Seabus across the Inlet. And back, daily laps. Coming up empty.

Then, in the urine-stinking corner of a bus shelter during a downpour, a possibility appeared. Someone had taped a badly-worded notice to the wall. The garbled message led her to a Chinese confectionery called The Lucky Moon, about a mile from her room.

"You girl, you look for work maybe? Something do?"

"I don't know. I might be." The effort of forming words.

"Not know, you say? Why you come here for, you have something already do? Tell me that."

Belatedly, she tried to take in the store. It was eclectic, eccentric, packed. Him, she was hardly taking in at all, as if no connection between them were possible. Her voice carried on without her.

"I saw your notice. I need money to pay for my room."

"You got a husband? Some little kid maybe?"

She winced, shook that notion off. And found herself cornered.

"So. Then you come work for me, see. You be here every night. No boyfriends. No little kids. You work like I say and no problem. I don't want problem, you nice girl, you don't want problem. See, you come nights at the

Lucky Moon. Is a very nice store, very nice. You see."

She shrugged and took the job.

It was some time before it occurred to her that she'd blundered. Vitality? Each evening now she would wake from a profound sleep, put an elastic band in her hair, and pass through the streets against the current. She came back in the mornings half dazed and ashamed through the energetically made-up office corps who dominated the sidewalks at that hour. She was unarmed, marginalized, had neither the latest paperbacks nor hemlines. And was no longer visiting.

Back in her room she fried two eggs, usually, and ham slices. Eating on the board-topped radiator, swinging her puffy feet over the ruined hardwood, she would inventory the small events of the night past. Flurry at ten forty-five of husbands sent for breakfast milk. Teenagers, recklessly making out under the street lights come in at last for soft drinks. Loungers in from the donut shop for brands the cigarette machines didn't carry. Longer, empty stretches with the newspaper spread on the counter, the lights too fluorescent for the carefully suppressed hair-trigger nerves she suffered alone with a cash register at three AM. The final ragged hours of traffic again, the smell of ammonia sharp on counter and hands, before Mr. Wu appeared.

Mr. Wu was a puzzle. He had dedicated one sixth of his tiny confectionery to Chinese dishes, lacquer ware and remedies nobody wanted. Tiger Oil, Ginseng, and inscrutable boxes crowded ultramarine patterned fish plates and brush-painted tea things. The immutable section. The rest mimicked a Seven-Eleven. Disposable calories, overexposed brands, relentless turnover.

At first, answering his scrambled ad, looking around his cluttered store, she'd thought Mr. Wu pathetic. Now, she wondered. His son practised dentistry in Seattle; his daughter and grandchildren were somewhere in the city, estranged. Why was that?

"Not my business, this daughter. She have too much do, too much house, too many little kids, maybe. No time for own father. And my son—too many teeth. Best thing, forget about them."

His life had calcified around the confectionery; he pretended hers should do likewise. When he had a bad day, felt his age most acutely, he sulked or simpered, as though things might have been different if she'd arrived before his knees and back began to give way. As though binding her to the Lucky Moon might change things yet.

"You, girl. You very smart. You work for three years, four, you learn do everything right. Then we see. Maybe an old man can rest his bones. I think so. You very nice girl, some day you look after everything. I think so."

He was dissembling. She could read the contempt in his eyes. She'd washed up like flotsam, and he had opportunistically snagged her. He knew less about her than she knew about him.

When there was nothing left on her plate, mornings, she would go to bed and rest heavily, relying on the soiled ochre atmosphere from the blanket she'd hung over the window to wean herself from the world. She had passed from watching to dreaming.

In her dreams she could find her way back into her real life and carry on as though she had never fled to Vancouver.

She was very small. She felt the rasp of blond grass underfoot, picked her way carefully around cacti in her smuggled Sunday shoes. She was heading down out of the heat into the shadowed coulee.

She was budding, growing tall, but her father was

telling her she couldn't drive the pick-up until more tree than sapling. Now she was jauntily tossing the keys into the air before her first solo excursion to town, so that the nickel caught the sunlight. With her head thrown back in jubilation, her hair dusted her waist. All of her ripe as August wheat.

Then she was grown. Under her jacket she hugged a wonderful pottery plate, colours dancing across milky glaze like borealis. A surprise for Guy. She was turning the key, entering the apartment so quietly that he wouldn't hear her slip the treasure into the pine rack. He sat swathed in the music of Haydn just around the corner, she could smell his raspberry tea, his suede coat over the end of the chesterfield.

Until the alarm rooted her out.

In the store, it occurred to her almost nightly to quit. There were any number of ballpoint-ringed want ads she might answer. If not these, others. She read the death notices: with this turnover there would be new vacancies tomorrow, next week. Next month. For now, she had no phone number to leave. And her days were for dreaming.

WEEKS PASSED. She was sleeping twelve hours, fourteen, well into evening now. And groggy half the night, too, at the store.

Then this impertinent interruption. She woke one day abruptly, resentfully, hours early. Her dream had been the garbled rerun of a tennis match in which she wasn't even a player. She'd stood off to the side of the court draped in a gaudy chintz duster, trapping balls with her feet and rolling them awkwardly to another woman. That woman was dazzling in whites. Made things happen in the little knot of officials, took on opponent after opponent, crowded the net. Afraid Guy might be watching, she almost danced to keep up. But her legs and feet became elephantine. Her dress seemed bulky. She was swollen and sluggish, stupid. In her own dream. It humiliated and woke her.

Guy. She lay still, breathed slowly, wanted a better outcome. Placing the pillow over her head, she listened to the interminable ticking of the clock. Hours till she was needed at the store. She slowed her breathing further. Tried to imagine herself underwater, her hair and limbs flaccid. She lay limp and loose in the tepid water. Loose and limp.

Nothing worked. So mid-afternoon she got up, took down the musty blanket—she hadn't moved it for weeks—and unlatched the window.

It was one of those afternoons when the air is slightly cool and the light even cooler. Silver as mercury with remote clouds and not much sun. The city looked wonderful. Held her at the glass. For once she wasn't half drugged with sleep. She could get dressed and go down.

Moved by the obscure promise of the window, she bathed. Braided her hair back wet and clean, and went to the wardrobe. On an impulse she chose a jacket in which she used to be happy, opulently patterned corduroy in black and rose with a single theatrical button at the waist. Embellished it with a rosy scarf that felt Isadoran, a silk shirt and black velvet pants. She balanced on the edge of the bed to catch herself in the mirror over the sink. Fine.

Today she'd have no reason to look away from people. She hadn't worked her eyes or her hands into a red heaviness. Her silhouette was slender, not squat as in the dream. She stepped down, smoothed her jacket, even stopped to straighten the bedspread, before she locked the door and amazed herself going out into the late-day calm.

She put several blocks between herself and the tired rooming house, then slowed. The street was so different with neither morning rush hour nor evening lights that she felt she'd intruded into private quarters. Standing in front of a bookstore, she became aware that she'd been living as a virtual illiterate here. Why was that? She moved on. Passed shops which advertised health food and vitamins, boutiques, and more booksellers before turning out into the broader avenue where buses ran. Here too, the reflection of the sky off windows was cool as pewter. Her fingers and cheeks felt equally cool.

For the first time, a surge of the energy which had persuaded her to stay. She was completely anonymous here. No one could chart her life, forward or back. She could become anything; might have been anyone. Today, that seemed a state of grace. Worth celebrating. She made up her mind to go on to a café she'd often noticed in passing.

L'Habitant was a marvel after the jaundiced air of her room. Stuccoed walls with vivid hangings, the colour picked up in geraniums and handwoven Québécois place mats. Sturdy pine tables and pressback chairs. The atmosphere was redolent.

She decided to treat herself to a savoury cassoulet. Then, hating to leave, she ordered maple sugar pie and coffee. The dessert was perfect, a rich sliver drizzled with cream. She began to feel drowsy. She'd go to the rest room to splash her face, then, short-changed of sleep for her stint at The Lucky Moon, brace herself with more coffee.

A man had materialized in her place. She stood, stumped. Concede the table and call it an afternoon? Her scarf was folded over the chair back and she had another coffee coming. She had no place to go. Couldn't face her room, felt like being around people for once.

She said tentatively, "Excuse me? This is my table."

"That so?" He looked up lazily. He was big, ruddy and robust in the comfortable way of men from her girlhood.

"Yes. I'd just stepped out to the—"

He looked her over. Half-smiled.

"Plenty of room, have a seat." He nodded toward the empty chair.

"No. Really, I don't want to—"

"Suit yourself."

Astonishing herself, she whisked her scarf from the chair and sat down. Her. Across from this stranger. He'd gone back to scanning the menu. She fussed with her scarf, then worked at looking composed. He wasn't overly neat. Or handsome. But all right. Slate blue eyes, rusty hair a shade too long—she liked longish hair.

When the waitress served him coffee without asking and put a newspaper at his elbow, she felt safe with him.

A sluice opened.

As if he had just dropped in and not yet seen it, she began by telling him her impressions of the city. "There's something—it just glistens. And the way the mountains cradle the city, the city cradles the sea, and the sea—." She was boring him. "But I'm from the prairies."

He undid his jacket. It was woolen, a red and black checked lumber jacket. A logger, maybe.

"Were you born in BC?" she tried again. "Somewhere on the island?"

"Yeah. Cape Breton." He ordered refills and a sandwich.

She told him about Mr. Wu and the Lucky Moon. When he showed marginal interest, she embellished. Made Mr. Wu a medieval tyrant, the confectionery an anachronism. And when he rescued her scarf from the coffee and began to be busy with his sandwich, she suddenly wanted to tell him about before the city.

She found she could tell this, which she had never told anyone, in three sentences.

"I used to be married.

"My husband is in Saskatoon.

"He met someone."

Then she wanted to say more. And because he nodded and listened calmly, because he ignored the secretaries starting to drop in after work, she told him from the beginning. As though he knew her husband and could judge between them. Judge between her and the girl.

"She wasn't particularly bright, even."

"That so?"

"I read too much. Even my mother used to tell me that. No man wants a woman with her nose in a book all the time."

She picked up her spoon and turned it over to see her face cameoed. Set it down. The surface was too abraded.

"I went kind of crazy, after he told me. I would stare and stare at myself. In mirrors, windows, anything. Trying to see what I really looked like. Whether I was maybe peculiar or repulsive in some way. It doesn't work, though. You can never be sure you're seeing yourself as you really are."

He managed through a mouthful of french bread and ham, "Look fine to me."

"It's okay. I'm back to normal now, almost. For a while there.... I stopped eating. Got my hair cut in one of those—like feathers—it was awful, it's just about grown out." It was fine and fair; she still French braided or tied it back to hide the ragged ends. She felt the neatly plaited seam, turned her head to show him. "See?"

He looked, shrugged.

"Guy told me my head looked like a clipped bird's. So I went on a clothes binge. Almost bankrupted myself—"

He gestured to the waitress with his cup. The woman came right over to pour. Her hands were freckled, slightly reddened, reassuring. When she'd moved on, he asked,

"So what'd he make of all this carrying on? Up and threw you out, did he?"

"No. He wasn't coming home most nights anyway." She traced the rim of the mug with her finger. As a girl she'd coaxed soap film across mason jar rings this way, to be caught by the wind into bubbles.

"He used to tease me about not taking the initiative. Not making decisions for myself." She used to have a mind of her own, though. Before Guy. She'd even married in the face of her parents' doubts. She drank some of the fresh coffee, her hands unsteady.

"But he thought everyone in Saskatchewan was like that. No imagination. He said they kept their heads down disking and never looked up until they'd ploughed right through to the end of their lives—and there they were still out in the middle of the field and never been off their own quarter. He was always making cracks."

The man shook his head. "Where was it this fellah come from himself, then?"

"From Quebec—the Eastern Townships.

"Ah…" He looked around the café and nodded. "How was it you met up with him?"

"At the university. We'd have been married eight years in August."

"But when you found out he'd took up with this other, you sent him on up the road, did you?"

"Uh uh." She looked down at her fingers, braided tightly around her mug, his large hands, resting on either side of his plate. Guy's hands had been fine. All of him, finely boned. "I should have. I put up with it for seven months. He finally moved to Saskatoon with her in April." Maybe he'd be teaching up there next semester. Was it July? What was she *doing* here?

"I sat by the telephone for three weeks." Finished her

grading, then sat there like a dummy, hoping he'd change his mind. "Then I left. Unplugged the phone, turned the TV off, stuffed a couple things in a bag and left. Without telling anyone." The superintendent, her Department Head—not even her family. She'd left a note, though, to stop anyone imagining things. Wrote that Guy had jumped ship, she might as well do likewise.

She cleared her throat and studied her spoon again. "My dad must be worried sick, me running off like that, leaving everything. But I had to."

"That's when you come out to the coast, I take it." He signalled for his bill and began to dig for change.

She reached for her purse, unsure of the protocol. "Yes. I headed west on the Trans-Canada, drove right through the Rockies and ended up here. I should write them—" Getting up awkwardly, readjusting her scarf. "But out here, nobody knows me. I can live—The Lucky Moon, if anyone back there knew I was—"

He was fastening his jacket. Interrupted her brusquely, "Just forget it. It's nobody's business, that. You'll make up to your people when you've a mind to."

He had no objections to her paying both tabs.

Out on the sidewalk again, she felt depleted. The city was no longer fresh. A nondescript dog relieved itself against a bicycle while its track-suited master tried to hustle it along. The after-work crowds, the traffic and the competing pungency of restaurants made the atmosphere seem flustered. She sighed and turned half-heartedly back toward the café.

He had come out behind her. He was taller than he'd seemed, maybe a little older. The jeans and rough jacket didn't do as well in rush hour as they had in the homespun interior. His face—his whole posture—seemed as self-preoccupied and surly as the street. She felt a little thrill.

She'd had coffee with this unknown man. Had told him about Guy.

"You'll be off, then, will you?" he asked with indifference or nonchalance, she wasn't sure which.

She indicated that she was heading south. He nodded. She vacillated, hesitant to break the brief connection. The phrase *bow out gracefully* came into her head. To stall, she asked brightly, "Do you work nearby?" She pictured a warehouse. A factory of some kind. *Cape Breton*—maybe a fish plant.

His arm tightened over the newspaper. His face seemed equally closed. "Mostly."

So he didn't want to talk about his work, to talk further at all. He had said next to nothing throughout, she realized now. Disconcerted by her own boldness in sitting down with a stranger, she hadn't offered her name. She'd expected him to initiate introductions. He hadn't. Odd, in retrospect. Was he shy? Or worse: married?

That possibility galvanized her. "Well, I've got to get ready for work. Who knows what fortune awaits me tonight at The Lucky Moon!" Tossing her scarf over her shoulder, she stepped toward the intersection, trying to look jaunty. Feeling ridiculous.

He stopped her. "Wait. Where did you say the place was, exactly?"

"The Lucky Moon?" She flushed, caught by surprise, and tried to read his eyes. Battleship blue. He gazed past her, giving nothing away. Did he plan to look her up there? Should she encourage him somehow? She shrugged, told him how to locate the confectionery and left.

It was well into the long bright night at the store before she put the afternoon out of her mind. Why had she told him so much? Might she hear from him? Did she want to? Had she acted forwardly? Foolishly? She had been with no man since—or even before—her husband. She'd ceased to exist, in any explicitly feminine way, the morning Guy told her about the girl. Informed that he'd been juxtaposing and judging between them for weeks, going from her bed to this nineteen year old's *boudoir,* she had experienced the death of her womanhood retroactively. Brutally, past resuscitation, she'd thought. She had set up camp with blankets in the living room those weeks of waiting. The bedroom a crypt.

She pushed a display of smoked almonds aside and opened her paper to the classified section. Pulled the stool closer to the counter and planted her elbows and wrists carefully. She still wore her white silk shirt. The festive blazer and scarf hung from a hook out back in the stock room.

Then it was unexpectedly morning. Someone—Mr. Wu—was waking her up. The confectionery seemed as bright and blurred as a recovery room. Her legs and left side were asleep. She stretched painfully, squinting against the glare.

"Sleeping!!" He was enraged. "You!! Who's in here while you sleeping? You tell me that?" He swept the air with his fist to flush out unseen intruders.

Having missed her real sleep yesterday, she felt anaesthetized. Too sluggish for the moment to answer Mr. Wu. How round and smooth his face was. She imagined it would feel like a soapstone carving, only warm. More yielding. He was short and thick as an Inuit sculpture, too. But so exercised at the moment. How had this bitter little man come to take over her life? What if she'd never entered his store?

He jabbed at her. "You don't know? I not think so. You don't say anything. You don't do things. I just pay you for sleeping so somebody come in and rob."

She was waking up fast.

"So? You don't think about that, girl? No, you not care about an old man, his back—" The real issue was coming now. His eyes were obsidian. He hissed, "Tsss. You got a boyfriend now, you sleeping, you don't even do the shelves?"

The shelves. She'd promised to face up the shelves for him. He'd been busy yesterday, with two big deliveries coming in. The cartons must be obstructing the narrow back room still. The grocery aisle in need of reinforcements. Mr. Wu resented the space left by every can of soup, every box of Kleenex sold. It had become his life's work to fight the erosion on the shelves of the Lucky Moon. Her own indifference embittered him.

She had reasons beyond indolence, reasons only a woman would understand. Mr. Wu's banking was erratic. The early evening traffic was too heavy for her to risk leaving the loaded cash register; the late, too thin. Anything could happen in the interval between customers. Deep into the night she felt safe only by the telephone. Knew that if she waded out into the empty silence of the store, busied herself with boxes, someone would come in and be crouching behind the counter. Waiting for her and the till key. Quickly, cleverly, in a twinkling the thief would come.

Sometimes she could sense him there already, her nerves and mind straining ahead, her ears already tuned to the car door closed too quietly and the long pause before the doorway went dark with no shuffling of shoes to announce business. Some man was even now reading the paper, as she did, circling ads he'd never answer. Soon he would run out of money, cigarettes and patience. At the appointed hour, wearing black leather or balaclava, he would come.

She shook off the runaway vision. "I'm sorry. I'll do the shelves before I go."

There was no atonement with Mr. Wu. "It's not good. Too late. You go home. Sleep! You just sleep girl, while I working!"

She picked up the unfinished *Sun*, wondering whether she should do the counter at least. Mr. Wu imagined a direct connection between its condition and his customers' craving for Export A's or Nutty Club Frozen Drumsticks.

"So! You don't leave me the newspaper today?" His belligerent tone arrested her. She must have instigated some new and significant provocation.

In a flash she grasped it. She left the paper behind in the mornings. Always. Although he hounded her about everything else, Mr. Wu had not once commented on the inked up advertisements for waitresses, short order cooks, administrative assistants or teachers. Surely he'd noticed them. He'd said nothing because they pulled her back every evening, back through the streets to this counter. The want ads never answered tied her to his tiny domain as surely as though she had handed Mr. Wu her passport at a tight border crossing.

She moved to retrieve her handbag without relinquishing her paper. "I'll finish reading it at home today." She'd always made a point of paying him for a *Sun* before he left in the evening.

His lips relaxed too deliberately. He stood measuring her with his eyes. Then finally acceded, with an intricately casual turning up of his palm, "The paper is not important." He turned away with feigned ease and began to replenish the cigarettes. It was unsettling to see his poised back as she crossed to the door. Altogether, unsettling.

She went home and slept.

THE SKY THAT EVENING WAS OVERCAST, pregnant with rain. She'd be lucky to beat the downpour. She wasn't dressed for it, planning to retrieve the corduroy jacket forgotten in the morning's stand-off with Mr. Wu. In a press of people waiting for a green light, a woman's umbrella snagged her thin sweater. When they'd worked it free, she crossed and found herself in front of the café. Had that only been yesterday? She rushed on. She'd overslept. Had had to forgo her noodles and peanut butter sandwich. If she was late tonight, Mr. Wu would be implacable. He had even invaded her dreams today, appearing in a sepia-tinted street sequence before a bookstore.

He'd wrestled with her over a bag she was carrying. His upper body had seemed as massively muscular as a sea lion's. His arms slippery as flippers, but prehensile. She herself was no more substantial than in waking life—Mr. Wu had wrested the bag from her easily. But out from the brown paper bag, into the mud-brown dream, books had tumbled. Magenta, melon, periwinkle and persimmon. Brilliantly coloured. Bountiful. The unexpected colour had enraged Mr. Wu further. And energized her. She turned on him. Chased him up the boulevard and out of her dream.

She'd been let down on waking to find herself back in her dishevelled room. It was sallow from the re-blanketed window. The air seemed thick still with the morning's fried margarine and eggs—she'd overheated and neglected to rinse the iron skillet. From the hallway came after-supper noises, the smell of sausages and cabbage. She'd had to force herself from bed.

Now, hurrying to make her shift, appease Mr. Wu, she wondered whether she would pass the rest of her life trying to please him. She pictured his skin growing tighter over his cheekbones, his moods more brittle as his body became blubbery and inflexible with age.

The rules had changed. She realized that as soon as she stepped over the threshold.

The confectionery was a war zone. Potato chips and candies were still jumbled from the after-school blitz, milk cooler and bread shelf half empty. In the grocery aisle, the moving stock had been left decimated. Behind the register, the wall of cigarettes was ragged, columns listing and uneven. The film boxes had collapsed. Because the precarious stacks tended to shudder and slip, Mr. Wu was forever cautioning her about maneuvering in the scant metre between counter and window. What had possessed him today?

She spotted him in the petrified section. Armed with Windex and chamois, apparently dusting the porcelain and lacquer ware. A boxed miniature landscape of nacre and cork-like bonsai was now visible through the grimy glass which had encased it. Similarly preserved ornate eggs had also been rescued from obscurity.

"Mr. Wu?"

Without speaking, with a movement of his head slight and sharp as though a trip-wire were being tugged, he disappeared into the tiny back room. He came out wearing his mandarin jacket. It was the one thing that remained stoically oriental about his dress. Of navy quilted satin, ivory toggled, with elbows loose and worn to a gloss, it reminded her of an aged tuxedo. Relic of a receding world, dignifying. Ignoring her eloquently, he brushed past to the door.

"Mr. Wu, no instructions tonight? Nothing special to be done?" She was a hypocrite for asking.

"You do what you want." In the infinitesimal lifting of his bowed shoulders he semaphored a reproach: sleep, read the paper, rob. Squander an old man's lifetime of work.

He left without his umbrella. The rain wouldn't hold

off much longer. She could imagine how it would soak through the old padding and chill him as he stumped bitterly home. From the address he'd given her once, she knew he had terrain to cross. His house was as distant as her room, but due west through an even gloomier district. A customer had volunteered that years back Mr. Wu lost a store with an apartment overhead. A venerable store—in Chinatown, where his remedies and relics had been wanted. His wife must have been alive then, she supposed. To help him. Both upstairs and down.

Chastened, she attacked the cooler and aisles right away, even though it meant locking and unlocking the till, shuttling back and forth for customers. Her strategy was to be working at the front, close to the counter, when things got too quiet.

The midnight rush was long over, her paper still unopened. Having more or less rehabilitated the Lucky Moon, she was beat. She knelt on the floor in front of the counter, folding the last of the chocolate bar boxes.

There was a movement outside the door. The briefest shadow. She listened. No sound. She reached for another box.

Quiver of shadow again. Definitely. She went rigid, her heart skidding the breath out of her, head racing through the possibilities like sheet lightning.

The nucleus of a plan came. Not to look panicked, she should set the boxes down casually. She should get up as usual, move to the end of the counter. If there was someone out there, she'd be moving toward the telephone. If it was nothing, she could be getting a garbage bag for the boxes.

Say she made the phone. Who would she call? Not 911. Not yet. But she knew only one other phone number in this city. It was on a strip of adhesive, taped to the receiver itself. She'd never dialled it. It belonged to Mr. Wu.

The thought was debilitating. Call him? Tell him there was a darkness at the door? That she was frightened? He'd hang up and go back to bed. If he answered at all.

The darkness came again at the door, this time lingering. She wouldn't look over there, she would get up now and begin. She straightened slowly. Her hands full of flattened boxes, she edged sideways along the front of the counter. She gained the end and moved to reposition herself within reach of the phone. The door crashed open. He had come.

"You can stop there." The voice—she had to look.

Her thoughts collided. "You," she whispered stupidly.

"Myself." There was no leather jacket, just the red plaid.

Nothing came to her. She stood waiting.

He jammed the door, came across the front. She could see now that there was a gun. The room flickered, blurred and became bright again. She must be dreaming, she was such a dreamer. But this prickling under her arms and scalp.

As he advanced, she smelled alcohol. Rye. She could picture herself slumped unnaturally across the counter, Mr. Wu furious, berating her as though he had found her sleeping again.

He confronted her. His arm, the gun arm, jerked as on a string. He indicated the cash register. The keys were in her pocket.

Her voice surfaced, surprised her. Small and high, but whole. "You've been drinking."

He indicated the register a second time, his expression remote as the gun. "Best get on with it."

Again, her voice was on automatic pilot, no connection to her. "You don't mean that. There must be another way." Pleading, "Surely."

Blood flooded dark into his face. "Get moving."

He'd followed her eyes. "Leave that phone. This here's loaded!"

It hadn't occurred to her that the weapon might be empty. A hot wave of hope almost disabled her. This man had listened to her yesterday. Shared a table, ate with her. Would he kill her? "But—I told you things. I never—"

Chasing each other across his face now, what thoughts? She could smell the rain on his jacket. Wet wool and rye.

"Listen," she told him. "My pay. He owes me a week's pay." A high white whining in her head. She was talking to a man with a gun. "Two hundred dollars. Take it—I'll give it to you."

He hadn't moved, was watching her.

"You don't have to do this. You'll find work. Go home. Back to the island.

"You're a good man. I felt that. Don't make yourself a—"

She saw a flicker in his eyes, the hand. The alcohol in him was hesitating, confusing. It was time to unlock the till.

"Watch, I'm going to get the money now." She maneuvered towards it with meticulous care. Her arms, coursing with tension, held up for inspection. Her eyes leaving his only for a second, a fraction of a second, to be sure of her footing. She could be making a documentary. Choreographing: crossing to the money. Every shiver suppressed. The motive for each movement explicit, explicable. Out of respect for the gun.

"I'm getting you that money now. Two hundred dollars. My own money. No one has to know a thing about it."

He gave no sign as she showed him the key and unlocked the drawer. She proceeded. The ping as she hit the cash-tendered button startled in the suspended silence of the store. He froze. Watched her. She grimaced and eased the promised bills out gingerly, trying to conceal the stash that remained. She looked up. This was the moment when he might go for the cash—or the trigger. Afraid to shut the drawer, aggravate him, she held it close against the register with her hip. Hands trembling, she held out the money. Kept holding it.

His eyes went quickly to the door. Then to the telephone. He was sweating as much as she. Was he worried about getting clear? She had to finish this. Almost inaudibly, she told him, "Mr. Wu is an old man. Just a tired old man trying to make a living." She set the money down softly on the spotless counter. "Here. This is yours now."

He looked furtive, confused, undecided. What did she know about him? About any man? All at once dead exhausted, past caring, she sagged. The high electricity in her head flagged and failed her. She whispered, "I'm too tired," and closed her eyes. "Thank you for not shooting me."

With her eyes hooded, she concentrated on him as he'd been at the café. Casual. Calm. Not unfriendly. She pictured Guy. What he'd think about this, if she didn't— if things didn't—fragments of a childhood prayer came back. The timbre of her father's baritone. Something about sleep. Her soul to keep.

She heard movement again. Waited. Time had become irrelevant. She'd been led through deep water to the brink of a continental shelf, blindfolded. Had been left to take one sightless step more. She held her breath— felt the cold swish of the open door. And he was gone.

She gasped soundlessly. Groped for, then sank to the

stool. For several stunned minutes sat emptied of thought. When her heart had begun to reassert sequence, and she was certain he wouldn't return, she opened her eyes.

She'd survived.

Really.

She continued to sit there immobilized.

Mr. Wu. Come up with a plan. Something preemptive.

She got to her feet slowly but with resolve. First she counted out from the till the one hundred and sixty dollars that remained of her two weeks' pay. This took great concentration. In spite of her hands, still shaky, she managed to zip the bills into her purse. She left a raggedly pencilled receipt for her pay among the twenties. And locked the cash drawer.

Next she reached for the telephone. She lifted the receiver and taped the register key underneath, where Mr. Wu would be certain to find it. She followed the connection from the phone to its mouth. Yanked the cord loose. Saving the classifieds section, she discarded the evening's untouched gazette. The want ads and phone wire became swaddling. She gift-wrapped the telephone with care. Set it in a new position of prominence on the bleached counter. She used a marker to red-letter a message to Mr. Wu—to Vancouver—on a five-pound bag. Propped it against the ash-coloured package: "HELP WANTED." With any luck, Mr. Wu would be the one to find it. The night was almost spent.

She picked up the candy cartons, tamped them with her foot into the belated garbage bag. She rechecked the aisles. The confectionery had never looked better. From the back room she took the rose and black jacket she had left behind aeons ago, only yesterday. Wrapped her throat with silk against the chill. Sorry that she had to keep a key to barricade the store behind her, she lingered for a moment in the bright doorway of the Lucky Moon. Never again.

She got two blocks before stopping. Where was she headed? She had no idea: simply away. But letting herself be swept along again—finding herself cast up somewhere else—was that what she'd survived for? She wrapped her arms around herself, looked over her shoulder. Nothing astir yet. The donut shop would be open back there, though. She could use the pay phone in the entrance. She hesitated. Slowly turned around.

He answered on the third ring.

"Mr. Wu?"

"You!" the word had a shrill edge. "Why you calling for?"

She swallowed. "Something happened. I tried—" she choked.

"What? Okay, you tell me now."

She shuddered, picturing his agitation. Thought about hanging up. She had left the note.

"So something happen, you say." Less hostility. "You need a doctor?"

"No." She wiped her eyes. Ran her thumbnail along the metal coils of the cord. "No, I'm fine. But this man came in."

"To rob."

"I'm sorry."

"So you give him my money?" His voice wavered.

"No. I—"

"Best thing, don't make problem. Never make problem. Why you don't give this man the money?"

"I talked to him and he—left."

"Left? You don't see him someplace now?"

"No. He's gone."

"You smart girl. What you say to him? Best thing, don't say anything."   .

"It doesn't matter." She coughed. "Look, I took my pay—"

"Tomorrow, I pay you."

"No, Mr Wu, I won't be—," she hesitated. "I won't be coming back."

"Why? You have someplace go now?" He clicked his tongue, "Ah—you read the newspaper."

She saw his back again, stiff with censure. "Yes."

After a pregnant pause, "But everything really okay?"

She was startled. No argument? "Really."

"See—*Lucky Moon.*"

"Yes, lucky." She had to get off the line. "Listen, I've left the key at the Donut Castle."

"You just wait. I come right away quick."

"No, I'm going. Look, I'm sorry about your phone—I was upset." She leaned her forehead against the cool glass for a moment. "And Mr. Wu? I hope you find somebody." She broke the connection.

There. Mr. Wu's empire remained intact—and so, after all, did she. She fastened the single button that held her jacket, and made her way shakily out into the rain.

GLASS MARBLES

ulio kicked four alleys onto the manhole cover, grinding them between the sole of his sneaker and the embossed bronze plate. As three girls burst past him in a race for the corner, he forced the marbles through the opening and into the sewer. There—two crystal root beers, a silver speckled and a steelie, gone. So what? They cost nothing. He had not spent even one single loonie on marbles, yet which of the boys could say he had more of them than Julio? He had everything—creamies and crystals of all colours, plainies, pearlies, speckleds, misties, bloodsuckers, and too many cat's eyes for counting.

"Hey, Julio!!"

Annoyed, he looked up at the no-hands Black Jack MTB rider—it was Chuck, waggling his bike back and forth again and making noises like he was a big man on a real bike, a Harley, maybe. Ever since he got from somewhere that leather jacket and that black and silver mountain bike. Big deal. Julio pretended to be busy with bottle caps in the gutter until Chuck rode off. Then, because the girls had been running, he headed towards the schoolyard.

He was feeling mean. This morning he had tried, for

the one thousandth time, to make his mother understand that he was old enough to have a friend in after school. He was in grade seven! Walking home every day he saw the other boys run into each others' houses as if it were nothing, and come out again with Pepsis or Pizza Pops and ball gloves. In the classroom on Fridays there was always talk of Super Nintendo and sleep overs. Yet not once had any boy been to the house of Julio. Or he, to theirs.

Because whenever he asked her, his mother said no.

"Julio," she'd said again today, "Can I help it that I am working every day until my feet are too fat for my shoes, then standing on the subway, the streetcar and the bus until eight o'clock? You think that I like to do this? You think this is what I am living for? No. It is only for you that I do it."

"Yes, yes. But why must this mean I can have no one over?" he'd asked, crushing his toast. Although she had eaten while he slept, his mother sat with him at the table, putting on hand cream and lipstick.

"Please—what kind of mother would let children play alone, where no eyes can see them? Tell me that." She had raised her chin as though someone was waiting to insult her. She made her eyes like those of a cat, to see his thoughts. "Maybe you are a good boy, Julio, but what of the other boys—I know nothing of them or their families! And Mr. and Mrs. Johnston—have you thought even once about how it would be for them, with strangers in the house?"

Getting up then to brush her skirt, she had told him to wait until the week of her holidays. "Julio, think of it, then your friends can come—as many as you like. And I will make pastries with chocolate and cream for them—pastries lighter even than those at the bakery shop owned by the Greeks! This way is better. Until we see which are boys to be trusted."

Pastries! Her holidays—that would be August! Was he to sit alone all *summer* too, because his mother was working? It was crazy—for what had they moved to this neighbourhood? Because she thought it would be safer! When they left the other, she'd promised him that soon he'd make friends, fine friends. Better than before. But it was just the same here. She was afraid of everyone.

Julio passed the house of the dog he called Mighty Puff because it was so tiny and fierce. It wouldn't rush out on its chain until lunch hour.

How many times had his mother warned him about the trouble that might come because in this country she had no family, no history, and now, not even a husband? "In Lima or Buenos Aires, a boy's aunts and uncles can see that he stays out of trouble—a boy's father. But tell me, in Toronto, who is there, Julio? No one!" she would cry. "With my own eyes have I seen boys grown too hard in their bodies and faces, forgetting they have mothers and living only for the drugs. Near my factory, behind the warehouses, young men are all the time moving things from the trunk of one car to that of another. Quickly moving things. For what are they doing that—for what?"

Julio couldn't say.

"And every day in front of the Mount Olympus restaurant," she would continue, waving her arms, "These dangerous ones smoke cigarettes and look at their watches. All the time they walk and smoke and look at their watches and walk faster. Faster and faster—until they find reason to shout at each other. Then fighting begins. And it is terrible, this fighting! Terrible." Sometimes, remembering, she would shut her eyes against the fighting, crossing herself and covering her mouth with her hand. If Julio tried then to stop her tears, they'd forget to be angry with each other.

This morning had not finished so. Her face had grown darker.

"How many times have I seen this? And when the sirens come, all the people are telling each other, 'Good, it is the police at last!' Good? No! Only stupid ones, Julio, would say such a thing! Only niños, who know nothing of the world. In Toronto people don't even know how to be afraid of the police! Believe me—from my country, from your father's country—I know what men in uniforms are. Never," she had grabbed Julio and pulled him to her fiercely, "do I want to see my son with his arm twisted up behind him so, taken away by the uniformed ones. Never! Better you should put a sword in your mother's heart with your own hands, than let the police take you!"

For once, he had refused to become like a child for his mother. He had not cried that never would he become one of those hard young men. Instead, as though he were already like a stone, he stood stiffly against her. But trembling with anger. Never could he answer her fears! Never. Behind each thing that frightened her were a hundred others: sickness might find them. Or an accident, a fire. Mr. Jablonski might sell the blouse factory and move to America; this year many businesses in the streets near Spadina had soap on their windows. Since already a thing unheard of in her family had happened to them—his father had disappeared—who knew what might follow?

When she'd held him long enough to believe that he would live through the day, his mother had smiled and kissed him. Then, for the one thousandth time, she made him promise, "So? Tell me, now, Julio, my mosquito. Tell your mama who would give her eyes for you—until I come home, you will not go away from the house. And no one comes in."

Pulling away from her hug, wiping her lipstick, which was like butter, from his cheek, Julio had promised. "Yes, yes, yes." But this time, he hadn't stopped his tongue. "Always I have to give you this stupid promise. And why? Because you're a crazy woman with many fears and only one son. It pleases you to shame me."

His heart jumped, remembering. Until today, he had never spoken to his mother so. His words frightened him.

She'd sucked in her breath as though his hand held a knife. He had wished to take the words back, but rushed instead into the bathroom. There, ignoring her calls, he lifted his pajama top and stood before the mirror looking at the new hairs under his arms. They were black and curly as those hidden by his pajama bottoms. *Mosquito!* Did she still think he was a baby? He felt the edges of his hot face, then above his lip, for roughness. She was wrong!

He had come out only when he heard the apartment door close behind her. Then, he'd felt weak and sorry. From the clock on the stove, he saw that he had made her run for her bus. There were many women waiting for a chance to cut blouses for Mr. Jablonski, women who had worked behind the soaped-up windows. Those who made garments in Toronto, his mother said, could never afford to be late. Not one morning.

He spat now and kicked at the hedge of the McPhails, a hedge so thick and viciously spiked a ball could be lost in it. He caught himself about to kick it again—no, his sneakers were not so thick. For a hardball thrown crookedly, he had once scarred his left arm to the elbow in these same bushes. Tossing the ball in the air as he walked home from school, he'd been startled by a "Here! Toss it here!" from his classmate's lawn, and threw without thinking. Remembering, he stopped and looked at the house. It was the best house on the street, a fine looking house. So high and wide, painted whiter than a swan and greener than his darkest green crystal boulder. What must it be like for Ian McPhail to live in such a house? With such a mother?

Mrs. McPhail had called Julio up to the veranda that day of the lost baseball and wrapped his arm in a wet towel with ice, to take the sting out, she told him. He'd been unable to talk, even to tell her his name. "Ian, who is your brave friend?" she asked, turning her head so that Julio could take care of his tears. And later, as he was leaving, she said, "Next time that hedge swallows your ball, ring the doorbell and I'll give you a broom to beat it out with. Now, come back to play with Ian sometime, won't you?" The sweetness of her voice, the surprise of her prettiness, had made him warm and confused. Of course, he hadn't gone back—Ian McPhail hadn't asked him. Because Ian had never been to Julio's house.

He rounded the corner, stopped and turned to look again. What if Ian did come home with him—today? Surely it wouldn't be such a bad thing to break his promise to his mother one time. Only this once. The thought made his heart beat like the wings of a sparrow chased by a cat. He had asked and asked, but never would she give him permission for a friend. Would it be so wrong if he hid this from her? Because the bus didn't bring her home until the boys from his class were inside their houses eating dinner, his mother saw only the younger kids who played on the street even after the lights came on—the kids whose houses were also empty after school. If Julio brought someone from his class home for an hour, she'd never hear of it. And if she didn't find out, what trouble could there be? No trouble. He swung his leather bookbag into the air and down again. Maybe he would do this thing. Maybe he would.

When lunch time came at last, Julio did not join the others who ate in the classroom by the library. He went quietly down the stairs to the lowest part of the school, where the kindergartens and boiler rooms were. The whole long hallway was empty. Good. He walked past every door but the last, to the Boys' Room. Until the bell filled the school up again, no one would come in here. So he used these toilets, where it was cool and quiet. Sometimes he even brought his sandwich and banana or melon slice.

He sat and unwrapped that marble which he carried in a handkerchief in the pocket of his shirt, where it couldn't fall out or be lost. It was a silver speckled. He had others which looked like it, but this had been his very first. It was like his mother's Christmas ball, a globe of clearest glass. Inside, glitter hung like snow.

He lifted the alley to his eye. He leaned back carefully on the hard seat until the marble caught the light over the door. Then, even though its brightness was painful, he squinted and stared into the tiny globe. He wanted to remember.

Once, years ago, he had knelt to stare at a million minnows frozen deep in the ice of a creek. There were clouded walls and transparent rooms of glass, right underneath him. In the rooms, slivers of silver that turned out to be tiny fish, making him cry out. Never in his whole life had he seen anything so wonderful. His father was near—Julio shouted for him to come and see, too. Papa came at once, sliding and almost falling. But not to see the little fish. Instead, he pulled Julio up with anger, saying he hadn't brought his son to Riverdale for this.

"Get up and look at the skaters," he cried, "These ladies of Canada are like swans in bladed boots!!"

Julio didn't know what swans were, but he wished Papa would look down for one moment at the silver fish, which were like magic coins in a fountain.

"Get up!! Is my son a dog, to be lying on his belly so, licking the ice?"

Julio had not been licking the ice, just pressing his face close to see the minnows, but he stood and said nothing. Shivering at the edge of the pond, he watched the skaters in their colourful clothes. It was true that they moved across the ice in a moment, forwards or backwards, without stumbling. And never, in South America, had Papa seen this. Julio had heard him say so earlier—had heard many words between his father and his mother about watching the skating.

She'd been afraid, shaking her head and crying that Julio would surely catch cold, or fall through the creek and be lost. Papa had called her a crazy woman, who would ruin his son. This one time, he'd shouted, he was going to take the boy along—his boy! Truly, Julio thought, although his feet were so cold that he began to feel sorry for the minnows caught swimming, it was good of Papa to want him. And to promise him hot chestnuts and milk coffee afterwards.

That whole day was captured in the speckled marble. Reluctantly, he rewrapped and put it away. After sitting for a few more minutes, thinking, he stood, rubbing where the seat had pressed into the back of his legs. Mama had been wrong, he hadn't fallen through the creek. And now, she knew nothing of his life at school. As she had known nothing of Papa's life, of what it meant to be a man. She knew only what it meant to be a woman, and afraid.

By afternoon recess, standing to cool himself in the hallway, he had made up his mind. He was going to ask

Ian McPhail, and Chuck, of the black and silver mountain bike, who had called out to him. These two walked away from him less often than the other boys in the schoolyard or gymnasium. They had let him join their library group and would throw him the ball in soccer or flag football. He had come to know a few things about them from passing their houses every day—besides the time he had sat on the veranda and met the beautiful mother of Ian. They were boys his mother might choose if she could see them. But if he was going to ask them, he must go now—before the bell called everyone back into class. So he shuddered, drank strong-tasting water from the fountain, then went out into the noisy playground. His legs felt as they had on the first day of school.

He found the two boys apart from the others, crouched in the shaded corner made by the wall of the new gym. He nodded, squatted near them, and waited. The bricks felt cool against his back, calming him. Ian was showing Chuck some of his baseball cards—he had doubles of Roberto Alomar and José Canseco, and was wanting most of all Devon White, John Olerud, Juan Guzman or Joe Carter. Waving away flies which had gathered near a sticky root beer can, Julio asked him shyly, "So Ian, you have found John Olerud or Devo or Juan?"

Ian stared at Julio, surprised. He answered at last, "Chuck got Joe Carter last week, but he won't trade him even for Canseco. Can you believe that?" Ian's eyes were like the palest turquoise blue marbles, like swimming pool water in sunlight. Julio was suddenly shy of looking into them. His own eyes, his mother's, were almost black.

Chuck shook his head, wiped at the sweat with the back of his hand. He smelled like grape gum. He snapped it at Ian and said, "Why should I? You got another Canseco, but my Carter isn't even a double! Just gimme your extra Alomar like I said, and Joe's yours. Fair trade."

"As if! You know what that card will be worth if Robbie keeps playing like he did last year—he was just smoking!" Ian knew nothing topped Alomar.

Chuck knew, too. "Yeah, but what do you need *two* Alomars for?"

"One for my set, one for an investment."

"Do what you want. No deal." Chuck stuck his traders back into a pocket and zipped it. His face was redder than usual, he wore the leather jacket even when it was a day for sweating, like today. Julio had only his cotton shirt and was baking.

Ian tried one more time. "Come on—José Canseco!! Julio, tell him, is it a bad deal?"

Julio thought that Ian was not being fair, since he did have two Roberto Alomars. If he were Chuck, he'd keep the Carter. But because he, Julio, did not have cards, it was not a matter for him. He said simply, "It is not for me to say."

Ian shrugged and gave up. "Okay, but I still say Chuck's being dumb."

"And you're bein' a big jerk!"

"Give it a rest, Chuckie." Ian jabbed at him.

"Why don'tcha."

Julio was glad that Chuck found nothing more to say. If they fought, he could not ask them what he had come to ask. He decided to wait a few minutes still, watching across the field as classmates chased a soccer ball without energy in the heat. Playing on crusher dust, they raised clouds fine as pastry flour from a sifter. Most days, he would have joined them. His father had been a great lover of soccer as a boy in Argentina. Quick on his feet, able to dance in and out of the bunched-up players, Julio imagined, remembering the one time he had seen Papa with a soccer ball.

The bell would be ringing soon. His stomach tight-ened, he dug at a half-buried bottle cap with the toe of his shoe. Sprite—no contest liner to check out. Now! he told himself, or it will be too late. Watching Ian's face, he took a breath and asked carefully, "What do you think about maybe coming after school to my house? You and Chuck?"

"Your place?"

"Just for a little while, I mean."

Ian shrugged, and stared at Julio as though he might be fooling them. "I don't know," he finally said, "Sure. Why not? Chuck, you doing anything?"

Chuck's lips were sticking out as they did when some-one gave the answer he had not been able to think of, in class. He watched Ian, not Julio. "Hnhh. I was gonna ask you to practise ball if you don't have violin. But we can always take our gloves to Julio's and play after—long's my mom says it's okay."

"Violin's tomorrow. But I have to check too."

As they headed across the yard to line up, Julio, his heart beating hard hard, his head bursting, said quickly, "I hope it will be—I hope your mothers will not think—"

"No sweat." Chuck left them to shove his way in near the front of the line, so he'd have time to get a drink. He was one of the biggest boys, hard for even the grade eights to knock down.

At three-thirty Julio put his math books into his bag and buckled it. Tonight would be a good time to show his mother the science test he had been carrying for three days—he had been second in the class, with a grade of 37 out of 40. He saved his best marks, math and science, for nights when his mother came from the steps of the bus later than usual because of trouble at work. Then he could make her smile and say, "But you are the grandson of a professor of law, after all! If only they could see this in Lima!" Showing her the test tonight would help him feel better about lying.

As he left the schoolyard with Ian and Chuck, he hoped someone noticed that he, Julio, had two friends with him. Chuck cruised ahead on his mountain bike, but Ian walked beside him. Ian had been leaving his bike at home this week because of a fall on the crushed gravel. The nurse had taken tweezers to his knee, then poured on germ killer which made him scream like a crazy man, he told the class afterwards. His knee was still bandaged.

At the McPhail's, Julio waited out front with Chuck while Ian went in to ask. He felt shivery with excitement. What would Mrs. McPhail say? Would she remember him? It might be that tomorrow Ian would take him inside.

"Think he's ever gonna let me have that card?" Chuck was popping wheelies, bringing the front wheel down on the curb and bouncing backward into the street. He did this even though it had bent the front forks on his last bike. Julio kicked a piece of reflector glass from his path.

"Who can say? Maybe Alomar will be starting to slump at the plate soon. Then maybe, I think." Julio glanced nervously at the McPhail's large front window. No Ian yet. He felt the small lump made by the marble in his shirt.

"Yeah." Chuck nodded, pulling the bike up to the curb again. "But Robbie never goes cold for long. Probably find my own card soon, anyway. I'm getting five packs a week. Then Ian the Bee-an can keep his stupid trader."

Ian the Bee-an? Julio thought it amazing that two boys who left the schoolyard always together, who played at recesses and had sleep-overs, talked to each other like

Chuck and Ian. He would never, if he had such friends.

Ian was back, jumping from the veranda and wincing—his sore knee. "Let's go."

Chuck rode ahead half a block to his house, one with a high fence, a barking dog, and a Chicago Bulls basketball hoop. He threw his bike down by the garage, ran inside and was out again with his glove and a baseball by the time Ian and Julio caught up. "Gotta be home by five thirty. We're going out for pizza."

"Pizza Hut and nuh-thing but?" Ian sang.

"Where else?"

"Lucky duck!"

The two of them walked behind Julio, arguing about the Blue Jays' chances of beating Bob Welch in their next game with Oakland. After a few minutes Chuck exclaimed, "You sure got far enough to walk, Julio! Why don't you get a bike?" He had left his where it fell in his driveway, and they had gone four blocks further already.

"I have one."

"You do? Never seen you ride it!"

"Yes, because my legs have grown too much last year and the bike is not a very big one. So I am waiting for another. My mother, she says the summer is a good time to buy one. Anyway, it is not so far. Two more blocks only."

What he told them was true, his mother had shown him the loonies she was putting away for the new bike. In the summer, she promised, many people sold the things they did not want anymore. Boys of Julio's age grew quickly, and one would be finished with his bike and looking for one bigger still. At a garage sale they would find the bicycle just as Julio described it, a silver and black mountain bike with eighteen gears and a water bottle with holder. Like Chuck's. Although maybe his would not have centre-pull brakes, Julio thought, because he had heard Chuck say those made the price double. He was not even sure what centre-pull brakes were. He did not know either why a bike had need of so many gears. Someone would have to explain to him about using them.

They turned the last corner. Ian and Chuck were discussing the Blue Jays' shortstops, past and present. Tony Fernandez, they both thought, was the best ever. Julio listened, proud that these fine boys were his friends.

The windows were open! He stopped, sick—the old ones must be home! Why had he thought the Johnstons might go out this afternoon, when every single day they were at home? If she saw boys go upstairs with him, surely Mrs. Johnston would find something to say to his mother. On Sunday—rent day—when they drank tea together, the old lady always had stories from the newspaper about young hoodlums. And next Sunday?

He swung his bag angrily, drew a deep breath. It was done. But for now, so that the visit would not be ruined, he must keep Chuck and Ian from guessing that anything was not as it should be. He made himself smile.

"See, it wasn't so far! We are here." He started quickly up the walk, leaving the boys to follow him. The side door was unlocked, as he had guessed from the windows. Steamy smells and sounds came from the basement—good! Mrs. Johnston must be washing clothes. She might hear nothing. And on such a hot day, Mr. Johnston might be in the garage, where it was coolest, or resting. Julio's heart lifted.

He led his friends up the first set of plastic-matted stairs, holding his breath when they reached the shining wood floor of the hallway. So far, no trouble. As he opened the door to the final flight, though, Chuck caught his shoulder.

"Wait!! Isn't this your place yet? Whose is all this stuff, then?"

He winced at the loudness of Chuck's voice, and turned. There was the dining table polished so that the flowers and vase and hanging crystal lights could be seen in it as in a lake, the piano not one person played although he would play songs on it every day if it were his, and beyond it the living room where above the fireplace and on each table were china statues—not like those in church, but tiny ladies in hats and gowns. There were also, just over his shoulder, two bedrooms filled with other fine things which could not possibly belong to him or his mother.

"*Ours?*" He flushed and shook his head, whispering, "No, no. These belong to the old ones—Mr. and Mrs. Johnston. We are only two, my mother and I, we stay upstairs. Just keep going." Chuck did, with Ian following, in a hurry.

Julio climbed the stairs behind them with heavy feet, feeling all at once that there might be shame in living in the house of Mr. and Mrs. Johnston. Except for Fridays, when the whining of their floor polisher followed him upstairs after school and all the house smelled of paste wax, which made his nose run, they'd never bothered him. And Sundays, when they read to his mother from *The Toronto Star.*

Ian and Chuck had been stopped by the locked door at the top. Chuck asked impatiently, "You got the key?"

"Of course. Always I am the first one home. My mother, she is working." He bent to the doorknob, the shoelace pinching his neck a bit, and found himself clumsy with the lock, which he had opened one thousand times without trouble. There! The door catching on the coconut mat brought more heat to his face, but he said nothing about his friends' shoes as they pushed past him.

He didn't even remove his own. Today had been dry, and yesterday too. His mother would never guess that he had been careless of her rule.

"So this is where you live?? Some place!!"

Julio watched Chuck drop his glove to the floor and look around. He followed with his own eyes, anxious, trying to see what Chuck might be seeing. The apartment was in every way as it had been when he locked the door this morning. His mother's hand cream sat where she had left it on the table.

"Smells good. Like chili." Chuck, sniffing, had made his way across the room. "Good thing you're not basketball material!" He ran his hand up from where the wall bent towards the ceiling, as though this were something not to be expected.

Julio remembered now that he himself had stood wondering about the shape of the room, on the day his mother took him to see if they might live here. The old man, Mr. Johnston, had noticed him looking and said that many attics had such walls and ceilings, the slope made them special. He had winked at Julio and said with a laugh, "Who knows, maybe the little man will be a poet, eh?" Then he'd found a candy—he called it a *humbug*—in his pocket. He gave it to Julio, who didn't speak because he did not want to leave their other apartment for this one, where his father would never find them. The candy was very good.

Chuck had moved on. "Where's the TV??"

"We don't have one."

"What! No TV? Honest? Man! I'd go nuts—wouldn't you, Ian?"

"For sure." With his back to them, Ian was half listening.

"It is not so bad," Julio lied, "Except I would like to

see *Star Trek the Next Generation* sometimes, with Mr. Data. And the Blue Jays and *Deep Space Nine.*" Always in the lunch room, kids talked about their TV shows.

"Maybe you could try watching at somebody's place sometime." Chuck lifted the edge of the blanket hung across the middle of the room, found the single cot behind it. "This where you sleep, Julio? Out here in the *living room?*" And passing to the other end, finding only a bathroom beyond the kitchen, "Where's the rest? Is this *it?* Where's your mom's room?"

"My mother? Oh, after work she has many things to do besides sleeping. She has always ironing, and sewing, and food to cook—many things. When she gets tired— poof!—she sleeps here, on the couch."

"As if!" Chuck went to the sofa and sat down, hard. "It's a rock! Your mother sleeps on *this?* Really? Every night?"

"Yes, really." Julio shrugged and turned away. The couch was of cut velvet, dark as a plum and uncomfortable even for sitting. His mother's real bed, a fine one from Buenos Aires, hadn't come with them from the old apartment, and the sloping walls and single room were but one reason for that. She had not slept in it since the night his father went out and forgot to come home.

Julio watched Ian, now, crouched in front of the big trunk in which she had brought her bridal gifts from South America. That trunk, Julio knew, was locked. Fingering the line of studs on the dark chair that stood beside it, Ian whistled and said, "These things are so old!! Where did you get them—it's like stuff at the museum—I never knew you could actually *buy* furniture like this."

"Oh, I keep telling my mother every day we should buy new, why must she bring these old things all the way from Peru?" Julio shrugged and made a face. "She doesn't listen. I think no one told her they make furniture in Canada and here every single family buys it new. This she had from her parents. And they, from theirs. When I am a man I will let her keep it and have all new."

He saw Ian and Chuck look across the room at each other and smile in the way others in the class had, on his first day. He had guessed then that it was because of his clothes, like those worn by schoolboys in Peru. There had been trouble in his last school, too, about the way he dressed. Was his furniture—the chairs and trunk of wood and leather so darkened with age that there was no difference in colour between them—so strange, too? He wished very much to see what filled the wide, verandaed house of the McPhail's.

Now Ian had picked up a silver framed photograph. As Julio waited without breathing, Ian of the hair so bright and pale it seemed always in the wind to be like dandelion fluff, silently studied it. Something new came into his face. He held out the picture and asked, "Hey, who's the gypsy?"

Julio did not move.

Recognizing meanness in his friend's voice, Chuck dropped the lid of the smaller trunk in which Julio's winter clothes were folded, and crowded Ian. "Let me see."

He took the picture and frowned. Then Chuck, Chuck of the heavy pink legs who looked always slow and out of breath on the soccer field, said to Julio, "Does kinda look like one of those gypsy ladies at the Ex! The getup. Couldn't she do something about the moustache? Or those eyebrows, at least!" He handed it back to Ian.

Ian asked softly, "Julio? It's not your mom, is it?" He held the photo, squinting, waiting for the answer. Chuck was watching Julio now, too.

Julio blinked, sick. These two would never be more

than boys from his class. He should have known this from Ian's eyes, lighter than the sky, and Chuck's as green and muddy as the Don river. He should have.

His mother left for work at six-thirty, while almost all the neighbourhood was sleeping. Mr. Jablonski's factory was two hours away, in the very centre of the city. Ian and Chuck could not know that at dusk, Julio squatted alone by the bus stop in front of Cadet Cleaner's, practising marbles while he waited for her. And they could not see him walking back with her. They were at home with their own families, watching *Star Trek* or baseball or hockey. On Saturdays, his mother didn't take him to the big Dominion Store or the IGA near his school, where the other boys' mothers bought fruit rollups and juice boxes for their lunches. Instead, they rode on a bus until the houses were smaller, with no space between them, and the streets full of noise. Then they pulled the bundle buggy along the Danforth, filling it with packages, with meat and fruit from Cossimo's and del' Ambrosia's and New Spartica Meats, from many small stores whose owners had become known to them. It was impossible to imagine these boys in any of the places his mother went. So how could they know her?

How would they ever, unless he told them?

"Oh, that picture," he said finally, keeping his eyes, black as those of the woman Ian had called a gypsy, away from their bright ones, "It's such an old one, I almost forgot. The lady, she is no one. Only a cousin of my mother. In Peru." He took the photograph from Chuck's hands and shoved it aside face down to show that it was truly nothing to him.

Then, keeping his face turned so that the heat would go, he told them he'd get cookies. There was no pop in the fridge, his mother did not buy pop except to treat him while they were shopping, but he stirred sugar into iced tea. On such a hot day, his mother would believe him if he said he had finished it. Chuck said, "No kidding—the real thing!" when he saw tea bags and lemon slices in the jug. But he didn't drink much. "We always get Goodhost." Ian finished his glass and thanked Julio for the tea and the hazelnut crescents.

Soon there was nothing left to interest them. Julio had shown them his many glass marbles—Chuck had taken some out of the bottles to hold up to the window, and looked as though he wanted to keep them, especially a crystal boulder the colour of iced tea—his collection of Tintin books, some Argentinean coins from a grandfather he'd never met, and his *1988 Guinness Book of Records*.

Chuck dropped the *Guinness Book* onto Julio's bed and got up. "Cool. Like to borrow this some time. Guess we oughta get going if we're gonna play ball, Ian." Then, over his shoulder as though he had just thought of it, "Julio, you coming?"

"I have questions to finish for math tomorrow. You will have to throw the baseball without me."

"Sure, whatever."

The boys collected their gloves and Julio led them back down the narrow stairs. A cupboard door closed in Mrs. Johnston's kitchen as they passed. Something was sizzling. The hallway smelled of fish and dill.

Outside, they stood awkwardly near the umbrella tree until Ian said, "If you want to come, Julio, we can always take turns catching."

"Yeah, we're workin' on this great sinking slider Ian's dad showed us. But let's get going—can't be late for pizza," Chuck added. "You with us?"

Julio shook his head, "Not today. Maybe tomorrow or next week."

Ian tossed the ball back to Chuck and started off. "Well, see you, then. Come on Chuckwagon, let's get rolling!" Chuck charged after him, yelling about the name. And the visit of Julio's two friends from school was over.

He went back upstairs without a sound, glad that neither Mr. nor Mrs. Johnston appeared. At the top of the stairs, he bent to untie his laces, which every night his mother had to remind him about. This time, he set his running shoes neatly in the middle of her coco mat. The door had been left open a bit. He pushed it and stopped uncertainly just inside.

The apartment, changed by the visit, looked like that of strangers. He had thought of it always as three rooms—living room, kitchen, and his bedroom. It was only one large room. The space between where he and his mother ate and where they sat in the evening was no more than a break in the furniture, he saw now. The woolen wall facing the couch was just a blanket. No wonder Ian and Chuck had stared, touched, turned every single thing over in their hands. No wonder. But even worse, he remembered with a flush of sudden shame, had been that business of the photograph.

Hesitantly, he picked it up and took it across to the museum chair beside the trunk. The portrait had been taken on his fourth birthday. Another from that same day had been put away in the bridal trunk, because his father's arms were around her and his chin rested on the top of her head as she sat. Little Julio stood in front of them holding a toy sailboat. Here, his mother sat alone.

He traced the leaves on the beautiful frame, not so bright as they would be after the silver cleaning at the end of the month. He breathed on the glass and wiped it. Making his eyes like those of a cat, he stared. He must find the thing in this picture which had made his friends change suddenly, become mean. Because whatever it was, he might never be invited now to play in the green and white house with the terrible hedge; he might never say to Chuck or Ian, "Maybe you would like to come over to my house, during the week of my mother's holidays—she has promised to make pastries with chocolate."

In the picture, his mother looked like a fine lady. She was smiling with all her face, as she never smiled now. She did not seem so tired or heavy with worry. At the top of her head, her hair had been gathered up and twisted in some special way with a comb. She wore her best earrings, those from her grandmother, like fans of gold with rubies. Her breasts were high as those of the school librarian, Miss Geisbrecht, who made the boys whisper. The shawl over her dress was a fine one of black with gold thread, unfolded from the trunk only on special holidays.

Always, looking at this picture, he'd believed that his mother had surely been a beauty. This morning, if he'd looked, he would have thought that. Now he saw that it was true about the hair on her face. He frowned. That thing Chuck had said. Julio had never been to the famous Ex with its wonderful rides, knew nothing of these gypsies. What did they look like? Dark like his mother? Dressed as she had for the picture?

He touched his wiry hair and thought about Mrs. McPhail. Her hair was as light as Ian's, and her eyes as clear, turquoise-blue. Also, she was tiny. When she came from her house to fix his arm, he'd thought she couldn't possibly be Ian's mother, she was not much bigger than a girl. But what of Chuck's mother? Chuck was the biggest boy in the class. Surely the mother of such a son could not be small or light or beautiful, like Mrs. McPhail. Yet when Ian had said "Gypsy" with that hardness in his voice, Chuck had jumped up, and looking at the picture, understood.

Sighing, Julio set the photograph down on his mother's trunk. He felt as those boys must who got caught stealing chocolate bars in the variety store. Before cleaning the kitchen, he would sort his marbles. He kept them in bottles on the window sill over his bed. Chuck had put some back in the wrong containers.

The glass marbles were beautiful, better than baseball cards or comic books with dragons or leather haki saks. And even Ian had whistled when he saw how many Julio had. He had been saving them since before his father went away.

He held his arm in front of the jars of crystals and cat's eyes to see the tattoo they made—best when the sun was strong, like this afternoon. At the centre of each oval of colour was a spot of very bright, hot white skin. He liked to make the tattoos change by turning the jars and turning them again. Like the tails of peacocks. Today he tired of it quickly. Withdrawing his arm, he began to sort the alleys, rescuing several cat's eyes from the pearlie bottle, and digging out a black and cream Siamese and an amber crystal boulder buried by Chuck with the creamies. The amber felt sticky, so he slipped it into the pocket of his woolen shorts. He would wash it with the dishes.

Taking the lid from the speckled alleys next, he dug through them. This jar still smelled sweetly of pickles. He wanted a marble like that which he carried in his shirt. They were hard to see among all the colours.

Finding one at last, he polished it on his pillowcase, took a deep breath, and raised it to his eye. Yes. In this one, too, were the wonderful fish. And himself alone with his father, standing above the thousand rooms of ice. But instead of Papa's words to Mama that day, he heard his own words to her this morning. They seemed terrible. Had it happened, then, as Papa said: had he been ruined?

He dropped the silver speckled in with those of red, green, gold and blue, and lay back on his bed. The bed was soft and very warm in the sunlight. From downstairs now, came the faraway smell of dill and fish and baking. Sometimes, smelling the Johnston's dinner, Julio would pretend that it was he who had cooked such a meal, to surprise his mother. Not today. He turned his head so that the light fell across his left cheek like a bright bar.

Would his mother be forever afraid of the wrong things? This morning again, that talk about young men with drugs and cigarettes, about the uniformed ones who took them away. None of this could happen just because a boy had friends in with no eyes to watch them. Even he knew that. Had he not chosen Ian and Chuck, boys who would surely never fight in front of the Mount Olympus Restaurant? But instead, that moment when Ian held out her picture. And he, Julio, said, "The lady, she is no one." He turned the other half of his face into the sunlight. He had grown so hard that he'd forgotten, even without drugs, what it meant to have a mother.

Kicking at the blanket wall, he whispered, "Julio, be a man." Had he not won his marbles by risking flick shots at boulders so close that his fingers shook like fringes? Had he not learned to gather his alleys and quit playing at the right moment, no matter what the other kids said?

He sat up and reached for the nearest container. Once it had held slices of fruit floating in syrup, like the paper twists in cat's eyes. Now, it held crystals like jewels. He reopened it to pick out one blue as sky, clear as water. A gift for Ian. He would give Chuck the amber boulder. He pushed the blanket aside and went out to the kitchen.

After washing the sticky boulder and the iced tea glass-es, he took his key, the two marbles, and from outside the door, his sneakers. He still had time, if he hurried. For half an hour, anyway, he could catch the ball with them before Chuck went to eat pizza with his family.

On his new bicycle he would be there already, Julio thought, rounding the corner. *Gypsy?* That was only a stupid name which meant nothing. Like *Ian the Bee-an*, and *dumb jerk* and *Chuckwagon*. It was how every single boy at school talked to all the others. When they felt mean, they said things, then right away forgot them. They might forget this, if they came to know Julio and his mother. They never spoke so about the Blue Jays: about Roberto Alomar or Manuel Lee or Tony Fernandez or Joe Carter, whose eyes were as black as Julio's mother's, whose skin was even darker.

The picture was an old one, anyway. He couldn't remember when the fine shawl last came out of the trunk, when his mother had worn her hair so, on top of her head. The heat in Mr. Jablonski's factory had made her cut it. She wore coloured face cream sometimes, and powder, now, when she wasn't working. Maybe that was why he had never noticed the shadow above her lip.

He warmed the boys' marbles in his hand, the big amber boulder and the small sky-blue crystal. His heart was trying to make him a coward, beating so. Who could say that Ian and Chuck would never be his friends? They had come home with him, the first time he asked. They'd wanted him to throw and catch the baseball with them afterwards, to pitch like Juan Guzman. One day, Chuck might teach him about changing the gears on his bike and Ian might invite him into his house to play Nintendo.

One day—maybe not for many weeks—Julio might invite them both to his house on a Saturday. His mother would carry back from shopping bottles of pop and a box which must be kept from tipping. A box of white, with a picture of the Acropolis in blue, on the lid. As the boys ate the wonderful pastries, she would want to know something of their families. And the son of Mrs. McPhail, who had been like an angel to Julio, would surely say nothing to shame her.

ORIGAMI

halia leaned over the water—it was green and metallic-looking as grimed statuary—and launched her messenger. A vivid paper crane. "*For Hiroshima and Nagasaki,*" she had penned in tiny lampblack italics before folding the delicate paper, "*Nagasaki and Hiroshima. For the children. For mothers. For fathers. For indelible split-second shadows on pavement, and for the people who became immaterial by inches, perceptibly fading. For the men who conspired in shadow to make that obliterating light. That in the wisdom of God and in His mercy, even this their darkness—nuclear irradiation—become light, liberating light. Bringing life to afflicted children, which once brought death.*"

His mercy? On her knees beside a quiet Rideau bywater, she covered her eyes with the back of her hand, as hands and arms must have been thrown up to screen the eyes of women and children from that horrific Japanese sun.

KURT STOPPED SHORT OF THE PLYWOOD and plastic-draped tunnel, listlessly summoned an elevator. There was relative quiet in the hallway, the workers had quit for the day.

The hospital seemed to be perpetually under construction, another fund-raising drive, another ultra-wing. Did the oncologists ever envy the labourers—incorruptible mortar for flesh, building by blueprint, the outcome assured? He envied them.

The smell of fresh lumber stirred something. When he was young his father had built a home for his mother and furnished it. That was a thing European men did then. In this country they found room to use the grace they carried in their hands and backs, space for the salvage they found on the job site. Kurt's father, though, didn't build his house from salvage. It must be whole in all its parts, he said. The timbers must know that they were cut and planed for this one purpose, to support this one roof, to house this single family. The beams and floorboards must be fellows of the woods surrounding, must be of the place where the foundation was laid. There, where the saplings had taken root and the trees matured and expanded toward the sun, they would stand and prosper. And the house ribbed and undergirded so would stand and prosper, both without and within.

Ambushed by memory, he leaned his forehead against the enamelled wall and let himself see it. His father's house had been set into a scalloped hill, seeming to crown, but really halfway up the escarpment. It was tucked into a fold where he could stand in front and command the long slope to the cobalt lake and the wooded heights beyond with one sweep of his eyes—then turn and find his home buttressed by rock and trees that seemed to climb to the sky. His wisdom held. From rough fieldstone and fine hardwoods and butter-soft pine, from the remembered hours and tools of his lost boyhood, Kurt's father crafted not only a home, but also a boyhood to be cherished by his sons, who cemented and sanded alongside him.

In the existential inventory he'd begun to compile, Kurt might have to include this as a double negative. Might. For what had he accomplished in kind? His life was a carousel of hotel rooms. And his daughter's childhood, now, was a thought to be flinched from. A painful bruise.

An elevator was arriving. He straightened, got in and moved to the back, easing his fatigue against the carpeted wall.

"Main," he nodded to the woman poised at the control panel. His attention snagged on this woman. She was maybe fifty, no-nonsense hair and figure. The bouquet of heart-shaped balloons she held belied her pragmatic dress and bearing. Also, it was unusual to see a visitor carry gift shop items back down from the wards. He watched her size up the company, man the controls like a self-appointed commissionaire. For some reason, she irked him. Deputized by the occasion of minor spousal surgery, he guessed, one of those visitors who liked to manage things, cranking the beds, carrying carafes to the utility rooms for ice water, directing smokers to the airless duct-work gardens which passed for courtyards, posing as martyred regulars. More interested in the guessed-at lives of wardmates than in the familiar complaints of their own convalescents. A blight. On 6E, thankfully, they were scarce: a child's illness was eclipsing.

He stepped off into the lobby, cut across the corridor to a tiny lavatory to dunk his head under the tap. The shock of cold water did him some good. But God, he was getting jaundiced—perversely ascribing things to a stranger on the elevator, arguing earlier with a jittery student nurse, avoiding Thalia last night by stopping for a late supper in the Arrivals Lounge. He squinted at his gaunt reflection. He *looked* jaundiced. Coffee would work wonders, though, always did: if only someone could come up with a non-toxic chemo that quick. They were treating his daughter with nuclear medicine. *Nuclear.* He fought off a picture of Anna, convulsed, shivering with sweat or thrashing with fever. Wisps of hair like spun glass, almost colourless, on her waxen head. *Medicine.* Reached blindly for the door.

Twenty minutes later, beside a virulent bank of cafeteria greenery, he sat nursing a second cup. He'd been wrestling with his balance sheet. It was getting dicey.

Thalia, he'd never deserve. Definitely debits. But how many? The unlooked-for gift of her in the vacated apartment of a college roommate he called occasionally when he was in Vancouver. What if he had not decided to burst in on Greg with a rented car and Mariners' tickets? What if he'd stopped to phone first and found Greg's number obsolete? What if Thalia had not, distracted by stir-fry oil just at fragrance point, buzzed him into the building unidentified? *No Thalia.* He rubbed the back of his neck.

Eight years she had given him, and counting. How to weigh those in the great scheme of things? Say ten points owing, at least, for her. A hundred, really, a thousand, but then he'd never be able to jigger things to come out right. He felt a needling sliver of guilt. Took a hasty swallow of coffee, rocked the saucer by setting the cup down askew. He righted and mopped at it with a wadded serviette. Face it, closer to a hundred thousand for Thalia, if he brought his infidelities into this.

He shook his head, shook them off, reflexively. Better to deal with that subject elsewhere. There were sets and subsets, limitless categories, when it came to reckoning a life. Right now he was weighing his marriage, strictly his marriage. He had never let the women, any of them, touch his devotion to Thalia, or cast so much as a shadow across their home. A point of honour with him. They were no more than hotel lounge lonely hearts, business travellers like himself. Meant as little as his habit of relieving himself in the shower when fastidious Thalia was menstruating. And without fail, he practised safe sex. Fail-safe sex.

The sliver again. Almost cardiac, jolting him. *A hundred, then, a good hundred debits for Thalia and double jeopardy for the women.* Because she'd never see it his way, if she knew. Never. There were, sometimes, small awkwardnesses between them, and moments where, his hand cupping her breast, face buried in her hair, he sensed he might be playing loose and fast with their lives, and hated himself. The needle found its mark, the question insinuated itself again: *Was this catastrophe, his daughter lying upstairs deathly ill, his fault?*

A fine sweat, everywhere, two-stepping heart. He rubbed his brow. Lately, he would hear his father's bracing Nordic voice reading meditations at dinner: "Shall The Ancient of Days change? Or the Father of Justice be unjust? The sun would bury its face in the sea then and come no more to fire men's dreams in daylight. The rind of the moon, a silvery herring slipping from His hands, would be lost, if God erred. No man would rise to cast a net, no man would weigh anchor to seek his daily bread on the waters. Because darkness would be again over the face of the deep, from that very day, if the Eternal One erred." He would shiver, a boy again, unnerved by all-seeing Jehovah, too afraid to slip the oily herring from his flatbread into the slackened collar of his brother's shirt, in protest, as the prayers began.

Now, cosmic counterpoise, this theory of his own. But—God or no God—if the universe in its machinations somehow gave every man his due, it still might be that he,

Kurt, had brought this down on them. On Thalia, on Anna. By ingratitude, thoughtlessness. His myriad minor deceptions. Sickened at the thought, he balled his fist. Slammed it into his thigh. Strike *him*. Not the innocent.

꒳ ꒳ ꒳

STILL KNEELING, THALIA EDGED BACK A LITTLE from the crumbling bank.

Yes, His mercy.

Her cupped hand lit on her breast three times, feather light, as though it were glass, her ribs a glass cage over her heart which, were it a bird, would have fled, would have taken flight long since. At the hospital her hopes had evaporated, like spirits from a lamp. Her heart fluttering. The lamp guttering. Low.

Here, by the stagnant bywater, in the act of releasing the paper bird, she was rekindling. As she had earlier, where the river descended in brief fury toward the cataract, and beside the appeased water downstream, too, and leaning over the docile piped-in shallows of the canal. Releasing. Rekindling.

The scrub and grass prickled through the knees of her flimsy pants. She rose stiffly, gathered her hair into a loose chignon, then let it fall back to her shoulders. She'd taken the time to have it trimmed and conditioned for the first time in weeks, had even put on her Thai silk outfit, for Kurt. She'd been letting herself go recently, living in leggings and T-shirts, hairclips. Unwise, with a husband as winsome as Kurt.

She checked her watch. It was almost seven, he'd be starting to look for her at the hospital soon. She was doing the Pullman shift. This round, desperately sick, Anna needed her overnight. With Kurt away for the past week, she'd bivouacked in the bedside armchair or visitors' lounge, stealing home for a few hours mid-morning. So this day off had been a godsend.

She climbed the slope, her sandals slipping a little, and stopped for a moment to listen to the restless willows. Feeling the quiver of breeze through her silk, she turned toward the narrow channel again. It looked even more polluted from up here, opaque as the dung-coloured Ganges. No matter. The water may have become world-weary, soiled, but it still responded to the movement of air, still carried the weight of a paper crane, of her fragile prayers.

Small rituals. She'd grasped early on that they were going to be crucial. She inhaled slowly, distinguishing scents. Creek, summer grasses, bitter and sweet weeds, the charged smell of unreleased rain. She'd sit on Anna's sterile bed and try to describe them. As every day, she brought tokens of the world, to remind her, tokens to buy a moment's relief from the fallout of her cobalt therapy. Yesterday she'd carried up a trio of caterpillars, black velvet and Tabasco, in a grass-lined jelly jar. She'd been lucky enough to spot them as she retrieved the mail during her dash home. In her handbag today were twigs, pebbles, willow fronds imperfectly braided into a bangle, an oily-looking feather, a ripe apricot which would feel soothing in her palm, and a tissue-wrapped origami crane made especially for Anna.

Inside her bird, no prayers, no mention of nuclear holocaust or stricken children. Instead, Thalia had pencilled faintly, "Anna ♡ Mommy ♡ Daddy ♡ Anna ♡ Mommy ♡ Daddy ♡ Anna..." Over and over on the white lining, covering it, in three scripts. Their names linked so, because when Anna floated away from them in her fever, Thalia felt as though their love was the only thread tethering her. Pencilled, because Anna's crane was of the most precious paper of all, copper tinted foil embossed in an opulent scallop-shell pattern; she loved sea shells and anything shiny. Thalia had had to make every fold perfect the first time to avoid scarring the delicate surface, the little bird trembling in her hands as it emerged.

She closed her eyes and began to whisper her incantation once more into the early evening sky. "For Hiroshima and Nagasaki, Nagasaki and Hiroshima—" Years ago, before Kurt or Anna, she'd gone to see a show of Japanese survivor art and poetry. The images, even in watercolour or wavery pencil on paper, were indelible. Implacable as fallout. She'd had nightmares about them then, and again when Anna began treatments. But lately, she'd wondered, radiation therapy—atomic swords into ploughshares—wouldn't it please God to heal even one child with a force so malign? If she were God, looking down at all those wan faces...she shivered.

"Mercy. Please God—mercy."

She could do no more here. Following the loose ribbon of gravel to the turnaround where she'd left her car, she watched for an unusually glittery stone, a bright penny, some little thing which might delight or distract.

❧ ❧ ❧

THE IDEA OF THE TALLY had come to Kurt during a dismal forecast and strategy meeting. Like something glimpsed between sleep and waking, beguilingly lucid and simple. A metaphysical ledger sheet. No hocus pocus. If he scrupulously reconciled his personal debits and credits—debits for undeserved grace notes in his life, and credits for undue hardships or merit unrewarded—he should break even. And because nothing, absolutely nothing could counterbalance the pain of watching his daughter die, Anna must live. *Must.*

In the actual tallying, though, both the lucidity and simplicity eluded him. What seemed an asset in one light was proving a liability in another. His personal virtues and heartaches, under scrutiny, became almost too insubstantial to warrant enumerating.

His watch chirped, prompting him. He pushed himself to his feet, cleared his coffee things and navigated between tables towards the exit. He dreaded going back up there. Felt, every time, like an infantryman trucked in for a second tour in the Maginot trenches. How did Thalia do it, day after day, night after night? He had his work, at least, some vestige of normal life. She had dropped everything unrelated to Anna.

The elevator stank of noxious perfume, stopped at every floor. By the sixth, he felt gassed.

Lots of visitors on the ward now, he'd stayed downstairs longer than he'd meant. He paused at the station. Anna's favourite nurse, Gwen, a cute strawberry blonde, was doing paperwork.

"Has my wife come in yet?"

She looked up, recognized him, tucked her hair behind her ear. "Haven't seen her myself, but I've been busy charting."

"Anna's kept down her supper?" She'd tried applesauce and toast at noon, lost it, and retreated to ginger ale, a bit of consommé and Jello at supper.

"The ginger ale worked like a charm."

"Great!" It was fantastic news. Anna had apparently vomited so much earlier this week that she'd ruptured her esophagus and started to throw up blood. Not a lot, but enough to terrify her—and her mother. Thalia had put in a panicky call to Kurt in Montreal.

The nurse nodded. "She was still sleeping when I took a peek at her ten minutes ago. So let's hope she's over the worst of the nausea. But Dr. Newcombe will be by tomorrow morning, in any case, to have a word with you about the treatments."

The hallway dimmed, dipped for a moment. He grasped the edge of the desk, suddenly nauseated himself. "They're not having second thoughts about radiation?"

She capped her pen, looked away. "I couldn't say. He'll do whatever he thinks best."

His throat tightened. Chemotherapy had been ruled out months back.

"He's good, Dr. Newcombe." Her voice was soft. "Best there is."

He nodded mutely. Told himself to go, walk down the hall to his daughter's room as though nothing had changed. Which it hadn't, possibly.

But he leaned over the counter instead to ask her— Gwen—stupidly, "Do you think people bring this on themselves? Deserve it, somehow?"

"What, cancer?"

"Anything. Tragedy. Disaster."

She looked tired. "When you work here, when you've seen some of those little ones flown over from Chernobyl—if you see the news, for pity's sake—" she shook her head, "questions like that—"

"Yes, you're right. Tunnel vision. Sorry." He felt like a drunk who'd blurted something asinine. The whole idea of weighing things out— "I'd better get a move on."

Mercifully, Anna was still sleeping. Curled on her good side with her IV arm flung back, her other arm wedged under her head—she could almost be winding up to throw a discus. Almost.

Her face looked wizened, translucent. Someone had made ink markings on her scalp around the tumour site. A nuclear target zone. A bright zipper arced back from her temple, followed the crest of her skull, then down, and curling back on itself, forward again, to end just below her ear. Surgery. God, having to let someone do that to her. When she was an infant, he'd been almost reverently careful of the soft spot on her head, calling Thalia in to shampoo a bit of cradle cap, because he feared the strength in his fingers. Now this.

Queasy again, he sank to the armchair. Looked at his hands. He'd forgotten what it felt like to physically care for his daughter. Forgotten. After bathing her, changing her, holding her against his chest to jostle out air bubbles, breathing the powder-sweet infant smell of her until he was inarticulate with love. After all that, in a few short years, he had let himself forget.

The tumour, if it kept growing, would teach him again.

Cancer. At first he'd been dazed, disbelieving. Cold fusion, energized into a state of malignant calm in which he wrote off their family doctor, the neurologist, radiologist and oncologist as lunatics. A rank of predatory lunatics goose-stepping into his life. Over his expectations, over his hazy pictures of his daughter growing, grown, everything.

The witless comfort of colleagues and golf partners, of Thalia's "holistic-health" friends: "You can beat this thing. Mind over matter. Just visualize Anna's red blood cells vacuuming up, *devouring* the cancer cells, like Pac-Man." Or, "Get your little girl on shark cartilage and mega vitamins and six months from now you won't know her..."

Go to hell, all of you, he'd wanted to shout, *There are no cancer cells to be eradicated! There's been a misjudg-*

ment, a laboratory mix-up, they've misdiagnosed her. He'd wanted to beat everyone back, physically, to stifle their twaddle as he and his father used to smother insidious embers too close to August scrub, protecting their home.

Thalia had been sure Anna had a tumour, then morbidly certain it was cancerous, even before the doctors confirmed it. Overnight, she who'd never owned a Bible before, who'd never been remotely conversant with mystery, became spiritual, navigating currents that had years back left him floundering. Floundering? Beached, on a shoal of doubt and despair.

The doctors had proved to be professional realists. And Thalia, sadly, prescient. In the surgical waiting room, she had prayed and recited *Psalms* like mantras, the low murmur keeping them both just this side of panic. He'd felt his own disbelief transmuted, somehow, for those eleven crucial hours. So that the sins of this imperfect father might not be visited upon the daughter. At least not then. Not in surgery. Anna had come through: with her sight, with full movement, with her life.

But also, Kurt understood when the euphoria of that reprieve faded, with an obstinate, tentacled remnant. A malignant remnant.

He reached out now, involuntarily, and touched Anna's arm. The skin felt too warm. But the shivering had stopped and the sheets were no longer darkened with sweat along the small bow of her body. Lest he wake her, he drew his hand away.

Five years ago, this same hand, these two hands on Thalia's belly. The baby's—Anna's—tentative knee or flailed foot, delightful, from the other side. Their self-conscious panting to indulge the Lamaze instructor. Designer breathing to help them ride accelerating crests of pain toward a memorable birth experience. He'd schooled her, giddy himself with Anna's advent.

Now Thalia was using that breathing again. On her own. He'd caught her.

Timed bouts with the possibility of Anna's death. *Her death*. For five minutes, no more, Thalia had told him. Three hundred seconds. She set her watch to make the pain finite. A manipulation of oxygen, finessing of the bellows, as though controlling breath could keep the white-hot tongue of pain from flaring into a firestorm, if they lost their little girl. *Thalia*.

He groaned. God, he loved her. His skin prickled. He had to stop cheating. Had to. The ledger sheet was irrelevant. A husband was faithful or faithless, his own doing. That was one thing. But shells fell from the sky here, and not there. That was another. And cells started to mutate, multiply. This time, his daughter's cells. Leave it at that, the nurse had been saying. Try to leave it at that.

He gazed at Anna. For all the ravages, she looked as eerily beautiful as the other spectral children who'd so spooked them at first. Her days ruined by torments and restrictions she didn't understand. Her nights alive with unnamed noises, visitations from monsters she'd never dreamt of at home. She submitted to everything, weakly, trusting in her parents', in the doctors' benevolence.

Anna's trust. Thalia's. God. Kurt rubbed the back of his neck. He could stop trying to undo what was done—and do better.

❧ ❧ ❧

IN THE PARKING LOT THALIA SAT in the car for a few minutes, steeling herself. Taking the entire day off, not even calling the nursing station, had been an excruciating stab at faith. But Kurt had insisted she rest, and she was grateful. Maybe the precariousness of Anna's condition had got through to Kurt, too, sitting with her, having to care for her. Sometimes he seemed almost oblivious. Not indifferent, but oblivious. Although she'd described how drastic Anna's reaction to the radiation had been this time, he planned to fly out again Monday, first thing.

She hated his going. Now, more than ever. He'd always travelled; she'd met him through a west coast trip. But these past few years, he'd missed whole stages of Anna, and marred them for Thalia too, by his absence, by her need to run for the video camera, to take things in almost vicariously herself.

She ached for him when he was away. Just ached. And often, after a trip, she sensed distance like a diaphanous wall still between them. She'd catch herself calling a friend first with news which was rightly Kurt's, or undressing half turned away from him, made fragile by her neediness. She would feel him pull away momentarily, hesitate, when he first came back into her. His flesh at once hot and familiar, and strange.

She met her eyes in the rearview mirror. It was unwise to buy trouble. The sense of estrangement was probably nothing more than exhaustion and the strain of Anna's illness. Of having to cope with so many of the side-effects, so many minor crises on her own.

Well, she'd probably kept them waiting. She reached for her purse and the bag of Danish pastry she'd bought for Kurt. Got out and locked the car. Gazing up at the sixth floor windows, breathed a prayer.

She had the coppery crane, their names inscribed in an unbroken chain. When she first saw her daughter's disfigured head again, Kurt's dismal eyes, she must remember the other birds adrift on the waters, carrying her plea for mercy.

And hope, whether Anna was still bent over the kidney basin in her father's hands or not, she must hope and breathe, counting, for all three of them.

※ ※ ※

KURT MET HER IN THE CORRIDOR, with a convulsive, almost tearful embrace. She pulled away, alarmed. "She's worse?"

"No." And surely it must be all right, she could see nothing disastrous in Kurt's face as he told her, "No, she's sleeping."

"But how *is* she?" Her voice was tremulous.

"She's beautiful. Like her mother." Thalia was, Kurt thought, just beautiful. She'd worn the sky blue tunic and pants he'd bought her in Bangkok. Her hair, so silvery blond he called it the colour of moonlight, glistened, newly shaped. He tried to pull her to him again. "Honey—"

She stiffened, wild to get to Anna. "But has she kept anything down yet?"

He touched her hair and let her go. "Supper. Ginger ale, peach Jello and consommé. She's been asleep ever since."

"Thank God!" Between them now, Anna. Still pale, motionless, dreaming. And still mercifully free of pain.

Thalia's eyes brimmed. "I won't wake her."

She stood transfixed, just watching Anna sleep.

And Kurt stood, watching Thalia. Weak with love, stung by remorse. He should tell her everything. She deserved the truth. The chance to forsake or forgive him. But no. However it ate at him, he would have to remain her debtor. She didn't deserve the pain.

She lifted her eyes at last and whispered, "She looks so much better."

"Maybe she's out for the night. Why don't you come home and get a good night's rest yourself?" It wasn't just that he needed to hold her. She needed to sleep. Her eyes were almost bruised with exhaustion.

"Shh," she bent to listen to the rhythm of Anna's breath. "I don't think I'd better."

"Let's have a coffee and check back. If she's still—"

"Will you just let me sit with her for a few minutes? I haven't seen her all day."

"Sorry," he whispered. "I wasn't trying to aggravate you."

She handed him the bakery bag and sank into the arm-chair.

He faked a grimace, held the bag away from him. "More caterpillars?"

"They were fresh out. Danishes. Why don't you go down ahead? You must be beat. I'll be along in a bit."

"I'd rather wait and go together." He lifted the extra chair over and set it carefully beside her. Sat, resting his hand on her thigh.

Her eyes on Anna. His heart turned over. How to shield her? Tomorrow morning, Dr. Newcombe. What if they decided to terminate the treatments, after all this? What then? He held his head in his hands.

"Honey?" A catch in her voice.

"Just jet lag."

❧ ❧ ❧

WAITING FOR THE ELEVATOR, he pinched the silk at her hip gently. "I wish you'd come home with me tonight."

She leaned her head against his shoulder for a moment with a sigh, making him shudder. But straightened quickly and said, "Kurt, she's been—if she should wake up sick again and—"

"They can always call us."

"Could we talk about this later? After coffee?"

"Sure."

The smell of sawdust again. He indicated the cordoned-off construction area, "They've made terrific progress."

She nodded. "The noise has been nerve-wracking all week."

"At this rate, they'll be admitting people by the end of the month."

Her voice was wistful, "If only there were a chronic shortage of patients, instead of beds and nurses."

They rode down in silence. She found a table while he got the coffee.

As he broke a packet of sugar into her cup, he made up his mind, "I'm going to arrange for some time off."

"When?"

"Next week." He was improvising. "I'll need two more days to finish up in Montreal. Then I can probably manage...three or four weeks, say." He had the time coming. Always had time coming.

"Weeks!"

"To start on the house."

"What?" She was incredulous.

"Get someone in to do the kitchen and bathroom. But I'd like to tackle the den myself."

They'd bought a well-worn, three-storey Victorian a year and a half ago, planning to strip it to the bones and start over. Kurt could do most of the carpentry himself. He'd envisioned the splendid transformation of the house, room by room, under his hands. The pantry making a den, the hardwood floors, doors and mouldings coming into their own, the baroque kitchen sky-and-sunlit. If she was too young to help, Anna could at least watch her father work.

Within weeks of their move, though, Kurt had been called overseas. Three months lapsed before the firm replaced the man who'd had a coronary in Saudi. Then, just when he and Thalia had agreed on finishes and fixtures, Anna collapsed at Playskool. Their plans, and their lives, had been put on hold.

Thalia was staring at him now as though he'd decided to drill for oil in the back yard. She took a sip of coffee, then asked cautiously, "Do you think it's wise? Now, I mean. I thought you were ready to look at bungalows. Condominiums."

He felt himself flush. A month back, fed up with the vindictive plumbing and the run-down look of the place, he'd suggested they settle for something in a new subdivision. Something low maintenance.

"*Especially* now," he told her. Assuming Anna went the course, she'd be in hospital for the better part of a month. "If we hire contractors, we could still manage even if Dr. Newcombe discharges Anna early. She's only just—"

"Why would he send her home early?"

A blunder. He said vaguely, "Contingencies."

"But if she takes a turn for the worse. The added disruption—"

He covered her hand with his. "When she does come home, there's no reason she shouldn't have a great playhouse. Maybe something built *around* the maple." He'd promised to build a tree house out back; they'd chosen the property, in part, for its mature trees. But that was before. Anna wore a helmet now, to play. Even indoors. They'd had to pack away her training bike and cut down the makeshift swing.

Thalia's lips quivered. "I made her a paper crane. Origami. People bring them—thousands every year—to

Hiroshima. To the Peace Park. They float paper lanterns, too, on the anniversary of the bombing. I made a special bird for Anna, then I set the rest afloat."

* * *

HE REMEMBERED SOMETHING from the news, a night shot of candles in waxed cartons, drifting past a bridge. Luminariums. But why—

"I wrote a prayer inside, for the radiation. All those children. Our Anna...."

He squeezed her hand, nodded slowly. "But where could you set them afloat?"

"The Ottawa River, the Rideau, the canal.... Half a dozen places."

"Sitting with Anna today—" his voice caught. "I've been missing out. I'm going to try harder, Thali. Help you with her more." The care his own father had taken, building a family. The care it would take for him to rebuild, with Thalia and Anna, if she was restored to them. With Thalia alone, if they lost her.

Maybe all you could hope to do was cling to each other, wait for the fallout to subside. Then salvage what you could and start over. How you did this, the materials you used, the almost forgotten grace you called on, might make some sense of what had happened. Some sense.

Or maybe, like Thalia, you could wrestle with the angel. Launch luminariums for the living before it was too late. Hope against hope for a blessing.

MYRRH AND ALOES

1949, Toronto, The German Club on Sherbourne Street. A dance. The whole crowd: the neighbourhood guys, Notre Dame girls, her sister Thérèse, even her brothers. They'd lost Yves in a Lancaster over Holland in 1944, so the boys were still edgy about the opulent nightclub run by the "German-Canadian Friendship League," but they were celebrating Johnny's successful audition with the Boston Symphony Orchestra. Boisterous champagne toasts.

Although Johnny wouldn't move to the States to join the Symphony till next fall, Marie felt abandoned already. She'd outdone herself tonight—white chiffon, orchids and rhinestones, with her jet black hair—and all her fiancé could talk about was making principal cellist. Hardly a word about how she looked, how he'd miss her. He'd be on his own there for at least the first year, maybe two, while she was needed at home. Since Papa's heart attack, she'd given up her piano studies to become a steno. Both Ovide and Roland were in college, and Thérèse didn't make enough at Eaton's to keep the household afloat; Marie had to work, had to stay behind.

Her Johnny in Boston. Boston, Massachussetts. She

couldn't imagine it. Had never been to Buffalo or the American Falls, let alone Massachussetts. What if some American debutante turned his head? Or a pretty violinist, flautist, from the orchestra? He was good looking, tall and sandy blond. Old Rosedale family, Upper Canada College, he'd be a good catch. She wasn't thrilled about playing the dutiful wallflower back home in the interim, either.

She touched her hair, smoothed the stiffly-beaded bodice of her gown. Took a sip of her champagne. Cold air like ice-box vapour across the back of her shoulders: she turned to see who had come in. Shivered.

A soldier, alone and deadly gorgeous. Dress uniform, an arresting physique. Hair cropped but wavy, dark chestnut. A way of moving. She stared. Then, caught, turned cooly away and ignored him.

He materialized at her elbow the moment the band waltzed into the next number. "Hope you have on your glass slippers, princess." Smooth. A hot flush of pleasure. She'd be lucky to drag Johnny up for half a dozen dances all evening. A bit of harmless competition might do him good, tonight of all nights.

"I don't believe we've met," she said, pushing her evening bag across the table toward Thérèse, and getting slowly to her feet. Her dress, décolletage was spectacular. She wanted him to notice.

An electrifying smile. "Lieutenant Michael Boudreau. In town overnight on leave. On my way overseas on special assignment—don't ask where." More wattage. "Might not get an armful like you again for quite a while."

Brash. She liked that. "Marie Doucette."

"Marie." He gave it the French inflection and nodded.

She rested her hand on Johnny's shoulder. The ring hand. "You don't mind if I dance, Johnny?"

"I'll be right here." She was piqued. Recounting the details of his try-out, measure by measure, he barely glanced up to see who was partnering her.

The waltz was a Strauss. Lieutenant Boudreau floated them into it like Fred and Ginger.

"This Johnny—you known him long?"

"Two and a half years." At nineteen, forever and a day. He'd been her first real boyfriend.

"You must have a platoon of beaus."

"Just Johnny."

"A knockout like you?"

Surely he'd noticed her diamond. "We're engaged to be married."

"You don't say." He tightened his hold on her, whirled her almost fiercely. Then relaxed and eased up. He didn't speak again until they swept by the bandstand. "So when's the big day? Wedding bells."

When indeed? "We haven't decided yet," she admitted, "Next spring, next summer, maybe."

"Cold feet?"

"No."

"You don't look under age."

"My fiancé's a musician. Plays the cello. He's just got a terrific offer from an orchestra in Boston. We—"

"And he's leaving a dish like you on the shelf? What kind of fool would go off and—"

"Don't get fresh."

"Sorry. But I'd go AWOL before I'd—" he whistled, shook his head.

She closed her eyes and gave herself over to the music. Sweeping, high-stepping, swirling. Pure Vienna. The Lieutenant, for all his brashness, waltzed like a dream. Johnny—she couldn't resist comparing them—danced as though he had a steel rod through his knees.

Her partner didn't move away when the song was over. "Another whirl?" His colour was high, voice husky, eyes a blue Elizabeth Taylor would envy. "Since I ship out tomorrow?"

When she turned to check, Johnny was still regaling her brothers.

"I don't know," she hedged, flustered, "one of the other girls might like—"

Wrapping his arm around her shoulders, he interrupted bluntly, "You're the angel. Worth a dozen of these—" dismissing the room with a majestic wave. "I know all I need to know about them."

Her scalp prickled. "Come again?" He caught her up in a fox-trot.

Quick, quick time. Quick, quick turns. Expertly in and out of the crush of dancers. In and out, in and out. So deft. Light on his feet. Gorgeous. Quick, quick *heart*. But she'd never lay eyes on this soldier again. Never see him.

When the music died they were at the far side of the floor. He drew her into shadow, not releasing her hand. She caught her breath, tried to get her bearings. He was too close.

"Does this fiancé of yours appreciate what he's getting?" His eyes smoldered, inky blue. "Because *I* do. My God, Marie, you could be a geisha. All porcelain and ebony."

Her knees suddenly water, her head, all of her. She took a step back.

"Don't. *Please.*"

"Call me Michael. Say it."

"Michael."

A current arcing between them, running right through her. She trembled. She could tug her hand free or move away from him into the footlights that ringed the dance floor. Could signal Johnny or one of her brothers to claim her. But this man's—Michael's—eyes, his body, the way he held and looked at her. As though she belonged to him. Had bewitched him. She faltered, hesitated; the band was launching into a jazzy rhumba.

The fleeting heat of his cheek, his hip brushing hers, swivelling away, pressing in close. Syncopation. Prickly-heat from the torrid tempo, tatoo of heels. Bravado. Overseas, he had said. Overseas, tomorrow.

When the rhumba finished with a rococo flourish, she dabbed at the moisture on her temples and without a glance across the room, let him whisk her unresisting into another waltz.

A slow waltz, this time. The musicians surpassed themselves. Mutes on the horns, percussion brushed like Spanish moss in a breeze: the nightclub became a gossamer Southern night, moonlight and magnolias. She felt deliciously indolent. She had swept her hair up into a soft French roll for the evening. Michael rested his face against it as they drifted to a stop at last, and whispered, "Your hair is fragrant as incense. Myrrh and aloes."

"Myrrh and aloes?"

"*Song of Songs.*" He pressed her hand, murmured, "*My beloved is like a garden...my sister, my bride, like a garden of lilies, fragrant with myrrh and with aloes, with all the chief spices.*"

She stood transfixed. Poetry.

"King Solomon to his dusky bride. You haven't read it?"

She shook her head.

"I'd recite it to you, Marie. Every night. I'd write you poems. Play Schubert and Debussy."

"You play the *piano?*"

"With a passion. By ear, though. So I'm no Johnny."

The name broke the spell. She stiffened, made herself look over her shoulder to where he must be sitting. Couldn't spot him. "I'm forgetting myself," she told Michael. "I've got to go. My fiancé will be wondering."

She edged away and left him. Moved across the dance floor like a convalescent, taking the long way back, drifting past the outside tables toward the entrance. When she paused there to cool herself, a stranger with the smooth brow and manner of Bing Crosby approached and tried to speak for the next dance. Still dazed, she shrugged and moved on without a word.

No sign of Thérèse at their table. But Johnny, her brothers, the rest of the gang. She smiled and steeled herself for questions; she must have been gone half an hour. They all seemed oblivious, though, listening to Ovide hold forth about college high jinks. Good. She tweaked Johnny's ear. He kissed her cheek and pulled her chair out. Not a word about her dereliction. Not so much as a look askance. Resting one hand on her forearm for a moment, he filled her glass, kissed her again and turned back to her brother. Nice to be missed. She told herself to count her blessings and sank back in her chair.

The sparkling wine was icy and sweet. Began to revive her spirits. She traced the veins on the back of her hand, a capital M. For *Marie,* she used to tell her sister. For *moongazer,* for *mischief,* Thérèse always retorted. Mischief? For *Michael,* then. Poetry, and the piano too, of all things. Probably more flash than finesse, but still. She smiled, • wriggled her feet in her flimsy evening sandals. Some dancer, he had been. The spot just over her breastbone where his button had pressed into her was still tender. She massaged it lightly.

Thérèse was back. Reaching across the table for her bag, Marie met her sister's eyes. Caught. She'd never been able to slip anything past her, she was worse than a flock of Carmelites. Probably watching her with the soldier the whole time. Too bad. Now, arch signals toward the Powder Room. Marie withdrew the velvet purse and ignored her. Twisted in her chair a little. She'd freshen up right at the table. She was in no mood for a sermon. She took another sip of champagne, drew her compact from the bag, ran her fingers over the elaborate case (gold-filled, a gift from Johnny's mother) and snapped it open. No mood at all.

A jolt as she tilted the mirror. Michael Boudreau! Reflected in the tiny glass, somewhere close, eyes afire, watching her. She shuddered and straightened in her chair, moving the compact. His face disappeared.

Where? Surreptitiously, turning her head ever so slightly, and again. There, over her shoulder. By himself, from what she could see. He blew a kiss. The wolf!

She felt impish. Began to rouge her lips. Slowly. Then carefully tissued them.

"Shouldn't you be doing that in the Ladies Room?" Thérèse. Had she spotted him, too?

"I'm all right here."

Pointedly: "The light would be so much better."

"I can see."

She stroked on a second coat, raspberry-tinted red. Flicking her wrist, rhinestone bracelet flashing, manoeuvering the compact to make Michael's face vanish and reappear, vanish and reappear in the silvery surface, man in the mirror, in the moon. She powdered her nose and forehead, watching him drink her in. Touched the nape of her neck, remembering how he'd said *porcelain*. And her skin was carnelian.

Johnny's sleeve brushed her forearm. She started guiltily and lowered the compact. Closed and put it away;

enough monkey business. Checked to be sure she hadn't dusted face powder onto her new gown. She'd just managed to get it for tonight, had made the last layaway payment yesterday. Opalescent peonies on the fitted bodice, spaghetti straps, chiffon layered over a tulle underskirt. It was stunning on her, even Thérèse said so. And she had the figure to fill it. A wolf-whistle figure.

She sighed audibly.

"You tired, sweetheart?" Johnny leaned toward her, all concern.

"No, just restless."

"Next waltz, then. I promise."

She nodded. He waltzed impeccably, Johnny. One-two-three, one-two-three. You could set a metronome. Whereas Michael Boudreau.... She tapped her feet under the table, fiddled with her ring. Her sister's amber eyes on her, searching. Thérèse, the little mother. Marie nestled closer to her fiancé and turned to watch the band. See, behaving herself.

The evening wore on. Past midnight. The band was playing something moody by Gershwin, the party winding down. Marie had managed to get Johnny up twice, then danced with her brothers, with a couple of De LaSalle boys. The dashing Lieutenant, she guessed, had left to make curfew. Finishing her shrimp cocktail, she cooled her forehead with ice chips from the silver dish. Then her wrists, the crook of her elbows and discreetly, the backs of her silk-stockinged knees.

After several slow numbers, a lively box step. She prevailed on Johnny, Thérèse grabbed Roland. The floor was jammed. As they jostled a table at the far end, someone leapt to his feet and tried to cut in. Michael Boudreau. Marie started, thrilled. He was still here!

Johnny held her, though, and said, "What do you say

my fiancée and I finish this one first? Then if she'd like—"

"Certainly." Electricity in his eyes.

"Marie?" She nodded mutely.

She was breathless, shaky all through the box step. As Johnny steered her back through the mob to find Michael, her heart began to beat like a trip-hammer.

"Johnny Meijer." He offered his hand.

"Michael Boudreau."

"Stationed at Downsview?"

"On my way through. I ship out tomorrow."

"Best of luck to you." Johnny kissed her lightly and handed her over.

After Johnny's slenderness, Michael Boudreau felt dangerously muscled. But familiar, disconcertingly so.

They danced without speaking for a few minutes. A subdued and bluesy ballad. He still moved like a dream. Moved her like one.

"Want my two cents worth?"

"Hmm?"

"Ditch that guy. He's a stiff. You'd be wasted on him."

"I beg your pardon?" She broke step.

"My God, you're an angel and he doesn't even see it. I've been watching all evening."

She tried to free herself, pulse jumping in her throat and breast.

"No offense." He was easily stronger than Johnny. "But you can hardly blame a fellow for being smitten." The mirrored ball revolved lazily overhead, throwing a galaxy of starlight over the room, across his face.

She was burning. "It's time I got back to my fiancé."

He moved his hand on her back, a caress, making her shudder. The song died on a soft tenor riff. He whispered, "Too late. Midnight's been and gone, Princess."

Weakly, "Will you let me go now?"

"A moment." He buried his face in her hair, breathed deeply and released her.

She broke away and looked around her. No sign of Johnny. The gala atmosphere had taken on a hard edge. The dancers seemed to be heading for the tables, while the musicians had words about whether to break. For all the haze of tobacco smoke, the women's gowns looked garish to her, as though someone had inadvertently switched on the overhead lights. The buzz and hum of voices. Her head swam. As she moved to follow the surge toward the edge of the dance floor, someone grasped her elbow.

Michael again. Leaning in alarmingly close, murmuring, "Come on Marie, sweet Marie, won't you marry marry me?" She laughed nervously and tried to keep going.

He spun her roughly to face him, wrenching her arm. *What?* "Don't think I'm kidding." His breath was coming fast, eyes overlit. "Don't ever think that I'm kidding. I am a serious man, Marie."

She gasped, stepped back. He looked like a serious man. Then, in a moment, his face crumpled. "God, I'm sorry, I didn't mean to—" He was disarmingly concerned, examining her arm where he'd gripped it. "Forgive me."

"It's all right."

"I'm not myself."

"Since when?"

"Since you. Tell me where Mr. Meijer croons his moonlight sonatas."

"Pardon?"

"Your address."

"I couldn't."

"Please. No *Belle Dame Sans Mercy*. Not now. I'm shipping out, I'd like to be able to drop you a postcard. A poem or two. But I won't bother you, honestly." She'd be crazy. But overseas. Tomorrow. What were the chances he'd even remember?

She told him. Then walked away through spangles of light like sequins scattered over the deserted floor, like iridescent netting moving over the filmy cloud of her skirt, across her stricken face. He was utterly unlike anyone she'd ever known.

Later, at home, winding her hair into curling rags, she held a soft skein to her face to catch the fragrance. *Myrrh and aloes.* What a strange—strangely lovely—thing to say. She twisted the strand around her hand, let it fall loose again. *Noir Francais,* Maman called the colour, a true black. Ebony, Michael Boudreau had said, like a geisha's.

"I don't care what you say, that soldier didn't look like a man to trifle with." Thérèse had been lecturing her on and off since they got home. She was in bed now, waiting for Marie to put out the lamp and crawl in. "And neither is Johnny. Boston or no Boston."

"I wasn't *trifling,*" Marie said, exasperated. "Anyway, I told you, he's posted overseas somewhere. Leaves tomorrow."

"Good thing, too. He gave me the heebie-jeebies, the way he watched you."

"Gave me shivers. Nice ones." She knotted the last strip of cotton and reached for the lamp. "And he plays the piano, too."

"You'd better say your rosary, Marie-Eve!"

"Say your own."

FIVE MONTHS LATER, the first letter came. By then, Johnny's dispatches from Massachussets were arriving regular as the Wednesday ragman. This letter came on a Friday.

Just home from Eaton's, Thérèse brought an envelope

in from the letter box. "Smells good in here."

"Pound cake." Marie was in the kitchen. There hadn't been enough typing to keep her all afternoon, so she'd offered to fix dinner while Maman took some weight off her varicose veins. She was grinding stewing beef for meat loaf. The gristle crunched as she cranked the handle, the moist minced meat crackled on the waxed paper as it landed. She fed the last of the cubed beef into the funnel. Ground it, then wiped her hands on her apron, rubbing where the wooden knob of the handle had imprinted itself. "What's that you've got?"

Her sister waved the envelope. "For you. From Korea!"

"*Korea?* Who on earth do I know in Korea?"

"I don't recognize the name." Thérèse undid her sweater clip and hung her cardigan over the back of a chair. "Want me to finish up for you?"

"No. I won't be a minute." Marie loosened the clamp which fixed the grinder to the counter and set the gadget into the sink, careful not to chip the enamel; Maman was always harping about that. Her fingers felt lardy, smelled of the onion and pickles she'd diced earlier. She scrubbed with scalding water and Ivory soap, then a paste of baking soda. When she'd dried her hands well, she reached for the envelope. Her sister was scrutinizing it now under the light.

"Don't snoop." Marie snatched it from her.

"*Snoop?*" They'd read each other's diaries for years. Marie shared most of Johnny's letters with the family around the dinner table. As Papa used to read Yves', until they stopped coming.

She studied the postmark and return address, puzzled. "Boudreau? Lt. Michael Boudreau?" Then it came back. The German Club. She was dumbstruck.

Thérèse was scandalized. "You gave that guy our

address? Honest to goodness, Marie, I don't know what gets into you."

"I never thought I'd hear from him. That he'd even remember. Not in a million years." She slit the envelope with a clean paring knife. Unfolded a thin sheet of stationery and sucked in her breath. Felt herself blush scarlet.

"Don't stand there like a dope. Read it."

She shook her head vehemently. "It's not—."

"Marie!"

She couldn't possibly. It opened:

M.A.R.I.E. My **M**use, **A**phrodite, **R**avisher, **I**nspiration, most **E**xquisite among women.

"What's the matter?"

"It's *crazy.*"

"Let me see."

Reluctantly, Marie lay the sheet on the tablecloth. They read:

> My Marie, sweet Marie: I am haunted. Waking or sleeping, alone or in company I see you, hold you, breathe you. You must know we were destined to meet, must have felt it, too. You are my Cleopatra, who beggars all description. You are a garden of spices, a grove of delights, a goddess who leaves me reverent and humbled. My own angel.
>
> DO YOU UNDERSTAND? I am reverent before you, sweetest Marie, I am undone by the scent of myrrh in your midnight hair, by the trace of aloes. Sacramental balm, an ageless perfume, a sweet, sacred scent. I am undone. Do your hands tremble as you read this, does the paper tremble, as it does in thise pleading hands? I am a candle in the wind. YOU HOLD MY FATE. Forsake all oth-

ers or I flicker out. Don't go to Boston. I will have myself shot if you marry Johnny Cello. SHOT. Believe me. I AM NOT A MAN TO JEST.

But Marie. First, WRITE TO ME. Tell me there is hope. You haven't married him yet? That would be DEATH. But I tell myself you can't have, because you are mine. And will be. Must be.

I'm reading Nabokov. A genius. But wait till they read my books. Now that I've found my Muse. You, dear.

Now, my lips in your hair. My breath on your alabaster cheek.

YOURS FORVEVR.
Michael Boudreau

P.S. Korea is hell on earth. Don't torment me. I will wait eight weeks. Beyond that, all is lost.

They sat speechless. At length Thérèse said, "He must be touched!"

Marie lowered her eyes. *I am undone.* "A hopeless romantic, anyway."

"A romantic *lunatic.*"

"Well, he is in Korea. There's a war. Heaven knows what's going on."

"Sure. Deranged by midnight sentry duty..." Thérèse bent over to read it again. "What's this about your hair, for Pete's sake?"

Marie's cheeks burned. *Myrrh and aloes.* She shook her head, shrugged. "How should I know? Something he's read, I imagine." The timer sounded. "There's the cake done. I have to get dinner in the oven."

As Thérèse checked the cake and set it on a rack to cool, Marie hurried to mix the meat loaf, breaking an egg into a bowl, whipping it with a fork and adding the diced onion and pickle and breadcrumbs. *Does the paper tremble?*

Across the street, she could see a few leaves beginning to turn on the Trimble's maple. Their sumachs were already scarlet, the whole city would be ablaze soon. Late September. She'd have to borrow a bicycle to ride down Pottery Road into the Don Valley. Last year, she'd pedalled through the leafy splendour with Johnny. Motored up to breathtaking Haliburton with the whole gang and a three-wicker-basket feast. She'd been studying at the Conservatory then, too, her life full of music. And Papa had been well. She sighed.

A pinch of dry mustard and of thyme, a generous sprinkling of salt and celery seed, minced parsley and chives. *You are a garden of spices.* Holding her breath and averting her head so she wouldn't sneeze, she ground black pepper in fresh. Then dumped the meat on top and worked in the seasonings by hand. Her eyes watered. "Get me out a bread pan, please? I forgot." She held up her gummy hands.

Thérèse set the pan on the counter, then stood watching her. "So what are you going to do about this nut?"

"Do?" Marie whacked the bowl to free the meat mixture. Tamped it solidly into the loaf pan and spooned a little water on top so it wouldn't overbrown.

"You have to make your feelings plain. Or get Johnny to write to him."

"I can't tell Johnny! He has enough on his mind." Mastering new pieces with performances looming, Mrs. Meijer unwell here in Toronto. "I'll write myself, after dinner."

But later, standing before the window in her dusky bedroom, Marie found herself curiously unsettled. She gazed through the flimsy curtains at the "umbrella tree," an "elephant tree" when they were small, for its extravagant leaves. How many tea parties she and Thérèse had held under it, dressed up in their Easter bonnets and gloves, sipping lemonade from thimble-sized cups on a worn pink blanket. Maman used to let them have one of the good china bread-and-butter plates for their sugared biscuits, they were so dainty and careful. Practising to be grown-up ladies. Well-mannered, well-loved wives. She'd have all that, now, with Johnny.

So why that jolt of jubilation right through her, when she'd first recognized the name on the envelope this afternoon, when she'd read the Lieutenant's feverish words? Re-read them half a dozen times, alone. *I will have myself shot.* What kind of girl was she? She shivered, rubbed her forehead with the heel of her hand. Then rested her elbow on the sill, the scratchy curtain bunching up like a bridal veil.

"Marie?" Thérèse. "Mind if we put on your *Rhapsody In Blue?*" A gift from Johnny.

"Of course not." Since when had her sister asked? Any excuse to check up on her, to remind her of Johnny.

No need. She had just missed her ring, a marquise-cut solitaire chosen, Johnny said, to grace her generous pianist's hands. Ironically, at the Conservatory she'd always had to take it off. Her teacher insisting she rest a ruler across her knuckles to practise correct hand position. She must have forgotten the ring on the saucer where she'd set it while she made meatloaf. She'd get it when she went down to say her goodnights.

The room looked gloomy now, light almost gone. She crossed to the vanity, switched on the milk glass lamp. Her reflection in the mirror. She studied it for a moment: face pale as porcelain against her hair. Eyes unreadable.

Never mind. She'd better get writing.

Later still, in the dark, trouble sleeping. Everything—the intimate crackle of feathers in her pillow, the murmur of voices in her parents' room, her sister's breathing—seemed bent on keeping her awake. Her legs felt weighted down; she rolled back the hated serge and flannel quilt. Browns and blues, heavy and ugly. Maman had pieced it together from old service trousers and jackets and who knew what all. If only she could sleep. *Waking or sleeping, alone or in company.* She hugged herself and said another decade of the rosary. Pressed the small of her back; the mattress listed toward Thérèse. When they were girls, they had scratched simple words on each other's backs and tried to guess them. Squinting, she tried to make out the small rectangle of white she had left on the dressing table. Too dark. But it was there, propped upright against the lamp, a sealed letter to Michael Boudreau. Her words sounded so pale and wooden, after his. Should she mail or rewrite it?

She and Johnny hadn't parted well. She'd been blue about his going, he'd been enthused about opening the season in Boston. That stung. Even with the key to a practise studio, and too many evenings free, she rarely made it down to play the piano anymore. She'd lost heart for it. She would never perform Tchaikovsky or Rachmaninov at Massey Hall, not now. But she might someday get to hear Johnny perform at Carnegie Hall. Might. He was *good.* She'd been promising. There was a difference. More and more, no matter how she fought it, she caught herself feeling wistful. At nineteen, life should be unbounded. Hers wasn't, anymore. Not with Johnny. She shifted her pillow again, trying to get comfortable enough to drift off.

Next morning she slid both envelopes into the bureau under her sweaters and prepared to deceive her sister and fiancé. Only for a few days, she told herself, no longer.

Days stretched into weeks. She sidestepped Thérèse's questions and began to lock her diary. Lifted the soft cloak of sweaters to finger Michael's letters at odd moments. The stack grew to three, four, six. Extravagant poetry and promises. She'd never read anything like them.

At Christmas she told Johnny, before her sister could. He blamed himself, making it all the more painful. Tried to give her the ring as a memento. She felt terrible. But afterwards, she could look Papa in the eye again. Ovide, Roland. Not Thérèse, not yet. Thérèse had read Michael Boudreau's first letter, had pronounced him a lunatic.

APRIL, MICHAEL TOOK A BULLET IN HIS ARM. A superficial wound, he wrote, left arm. Marie was distraught. And Thérèse—newly smitten herself and maybe remembering Yves—was sweet and genuinely sorry. She fixed a dinner tray for Marie with irises from the back garden.

Five weeks later Marie was rushing down to Union Station in a new lavender outfit with Maman's cultured pearls, trying to look the part of a soldier's hometown girl.

He'd arrived early. Was waiting for her just inside the terminal.

"Marie! You're a knockout!" He looked devastating himself. Nearly crushed her. Kissed and kissed her in front of everyone. She pulled away, unsteady on her feet. Touched her numb lips.

"Your arm—"

He flexed it, lifted her off her feet and set her down. "I could jitterbug."

The threat of tears. "I lit candles for you. Said a Novena."

An odd expression, guarded voice: "I was never in

danger." He touched her cheek.

They went for breakfast on King Street, he hadn't eaten on the train. Shy with him, she traced their names—Michael and Marie, Marie and Mike—on the tabletop. He covered her hand with his. He'd been writing again, he said.

"To who?"

"Not letters, poetry." He looked vulnerable. Said hesitantly, "Someday, I am going to write a novel."

"A novel! About what?"

He touched his finger to her lips and leaned in close. "Shh. Do you want to kill it? A masterpiece, something unprecedented, that's all I can safely say. Any more and..." He made an eloquent gesture across his throat. She started.

"You believe I can do it, Marie?"

"Your letters—they're beautiful."

"Here you are, sir," the waitress. "Two eggs sunny side up with bacon and home fries. Side order of grilled tomatoes."

He ate intently, drawn into himself, as though she weren't there. He seemed to do everything intently. Trying not to stare, she sipped her coffee. He gulped part of his black, then emptied half the pitcher of cream into what remained in his cup, with six cubes of sugar. She winced, just watching him drink it.

"You promised to tell me about your family today." She had written him pages about hers. Knew nothing, so far, about his. She'd started to wonder whether he might be estranged from them.

He set his cup down and looked out at the street. Lit by the sunny window, his hair was burnished auburn, curlier than Thérèse's. But there was something in his eyes: sadness? anger? both? There was a difficult pause before he announced softly, "Father unknown. Mother best forgotten. And little Mikey lived happily ever after. With the Christian Brothers, for the most part."

She dropped the knife she was using to butter her toast. "Michael, I'm sorry, I had—"

"Years back. But *all that glisters is not gold*, Marie. That much I remember about Mama."

She was staggered. Maman, Papa. What could possibly?

"So there's just you, honey." He gripped her hand, "Now, what if I get us a room?"

"A *hotel room?*"

"Somewhere nice. The Royal York or King Eddie." He leaned across the table and stroked her wrist and palm. She flinched, stiffened. "Or we can wait a bit, if you'd rather."

"Michael," she whispered. Heat all up her arm, up the back of her neck, behind her knees. "*I can't.*"

"There's nothing to be afraid of."

"That's not it."

"What, then?" Again, something she couldn't read behind his eyes. Like the shadow of clouds over water.

"I'm Catholic. You are. I don't want this between us."

He pulled her head toward him abruptly and buried his face in her hair. Cried, "*Thank God!* You're the one, Marie." Gooseflesh. Her coffee cup overturned in the saucer. "I knew it the moment I laid eyes on you. My little Madonna, my angel. My sister, my bride."

She shook her head, speechless. Her heart hammering.

He was almost in tears. "I wouldn't lay a hand on you, darling. Honest to God. I was just making sure."

If she'd said yes—what in heaven's name if she had said yes? She felt weak. He was forever throwing her off balance. Was he trying to? Was it normal? She had next to no experience with men. Going from St. Joseph's to Notre Dame to Johnny, she'd only ever known Papa, Roland and Ovide—who didn't count—a few of the boys in the neighbourhood, and then Johnny. No one as complicated as Michael. She rubbed her arms to warm herself. Hadn't she been attracted to him in the first place because he was so brash, unpredictable—passionate? She'd have to keep her wits about her, that's all.

So. She reseated her cup, took a serviette to the bit of spilled coffee, smiled and suggested shakily, "Then—if it doesn't matter to you—why don't we go to Kew Beach? Today's perfect for the boardwalk, bright, not too much breeze. I'll wrap the rest of my toast for the seagulls."

"Sure."

As midnight approached, they were back in the cavernous station. The chill night air, chalkily lit platform, the noise and diesel fumes were making Marie slightly nauseated. She'd started to shiver. Mike—he'd asked her to call him Mike—was off to Ottawa, en route to points unknown. His train had begun to take on passengers. It was a matter of minutes at most.

Mike said quietly, "Say the word, and I'm AWOL."

She shook her head. "No. You can't. Take this, though." The St. Christopher's medal was worn, had been Yves'. "For safe passage."

He rested his cheek against her hair and groaned as the final boarding call sounded. Behind him, all along the coaches, night porters were pulling up the metal boxes for mounting. The train was hissing, shuddering in earnest. A mechanical screech from up ahead.

"Marie, say the word."

"My father would never forgive you: Yves. So go."

He did, at the last moment. But from the doorway of his Pullman, as the train lurched, he shouted: "Marie! My wound–." The coach began to pull away. "I took that bullet for you."

"*Pardon?*" The exhaust, clatter, roar of the engine, the conductor's call. She rushed alongside.

"*You!* So I could see you!"

"It's too loud!" She broke into a trot. Quick, quick steps. A cold sweat. She couldn't keep up. "What do you *mean?*" She ran out of platform. His face wavered and disappeared.

She stood, clammy and sick to her stomach. Sicker. She ran for the stairs, rushed down into the marble concourse. Hurried past more stairwells, platform signs, benches. Found the Ladies Room just in time, beyond the deserted shoe shine stands. Afterwards, she leaned, spent, against the wall of the cubicle. Was that love, what Mike had–? *If* he had. His scar didn't look much worse than a bad vaccination mark, she'd made him show her. A nick, he'd said. The bullet had barely grazed him. *Whose* bullet? Her head throbbed, base of her skull, behind her eye. Get herself home now. Get herself to bed.

She ran cold water over her wrists. Used a wadded handkerchief to cool her forehead and scrub at the cuff of her new suit. She tugged her slip, smoothed her skirt and left the lavatory. Up at street level, a seasoned redcap took her elbow, steered her to the cabstand out front and put her in a cab. Probably thinking she was tipsy.

MIKE WANGLED AN EXTENSION IN OTTAWA, pending a request for discharge. Was back on a weekend's leave within the month. He'd arranged to bunk at Downsview, but agreed to come home for dinner with Marie to meet the family.

In one of his letters he'd boasted that he had a way with presents. He proved it. He brought Dutch tobacco for Papa, a vial of water from Lourdes for Maman, and for Thérèse, a tiny box of lavender soapstone with a mother-of-pearl lily inlaid across the top like an olive branch. Uncanny. Good pens for Ovide and Roland, too. Nothing for Marie, he teased her at first. Because *he* was present enough. But then, from his rucksack, a watch—beautiful, silver filigree with diamonds. What had he done without to pay for it? Plenty, he told her, and pinched her waist.

Her parents loved him immediately. Seeing how his eyes swallowed her up, Papa grinned and told him, "Don't mind us. Give your girl a big kiss. We're all family." Thérèse's head came up then, wary again. She watched him, sidelong glances, the whole evening. While Marie watched her watching him, and wondered what Thérèse saw.

By the time Mike boarded the train for Ottawa on Sunday, they were engaged. The army had granted him discharge in August, and leave owed in July, to start university English studies on a service pension. He'd kept it from Marie until last thing, alone at the station. Because he wanted her to make up her own mind to marry him, he said. He was crazy about her, had been from the first moment. *"All beautiful you are, my darling; there is no flaw in you."* If she was his, would have him until death, plan a late July wedding.

"Are you *sure*, Marie?" Thérèse. Back home, Marie had wakened her with the news. "Think. How well do you really know him? Two visits—"

"I know all I need from his letters."

"That's not the same."

"We've made up our minds, Thérèse. What good will come of waiting?" They were both silent then. *Johnny.*

"You're giving up your music, then?"

"No. I can still start back at the Conservatory, as soon as we're settled." With Ovide working now, she'd planned to do that in the fall. "Mike understands what it means to me. More than Johnny ever did."

"How so?" Thérèse's voice softened. "Really, tell me."

Marie hesitated, "He's always wanted to write a book. A wonderful novel."

"Maybe he will, then," Thérèse's voice caught. "Maybe he will. I just hope he makes you happy."

SLOWLY, SLOWLY, IN WHITE SATIN AND TULLE, stephanotis fluttering from her shoulders and veil, Marie mounted the stone steps of St. John's. Behind her, the sky was bright and hazy. She'd never looked more beautiful, she knew it. She'd seen it in the mirror and in her mother's tearful eyes, her brothers' sudden shyness. Thérèse was elegant, too, in lilac crêpe. Her Maid of Honour.

Papa touched the cloud of lace and tulle around Marie's hair, gingerly, as they paused at the threshold. Through the oak door she caught a glimpse of the sanctuary, aflicker with candles, dappled with a confetti of coloured light thrown by the stained glass windows. There, at the marble communion rail, flanked by Roland, Michael. Gorgeous in dress uniform.

The music. Thérèse stepped ahead of her through the doorway. Marie shivered, gripped Papa's arm and genuflected. Time. The rustle of her gown as she moved forward.

꙳ ꙳ ꙳

1958, TORONTO, THE PROVINCIAL LUNATIC ASYLUM ON QUEEN STREET.

She had come down early, needing time to collect herself. It was sunny but windy, the flowering chestnuts fragrantly hectic, her hair and skirt wild. She wore a pretty floral frock instead of the lustreless clothes she usually chose to reassure him. Today, she'd dressed for herself.

She stood on the broad lawn watching the clouds scudding eastward over the lake. She couldn't see the water for the building, but it would be a riot of whitecaps and gulls, waves foaming up onto the scruffy beach. Not so long ago she'd been a carefree girl, swimming or picnicking at Kew Gardens and Sunnyside. Yesterday, watching Julie and Markie scavenge pock-marked shells and coloured lozenges of glass, she had wondered how that earlier Marie and herself could be connected.

She touched her sun-warmed hair, her fingertips finding the livid part on her scalp that was still painful to brush. Courage. One more hour and it would be over. She turned back toward the hospital. Feeling the jostle of her grandmother's beads in her pocket, she whispered a *Hail Mary* and followed the walk to the front entrance. Overshadowed by the building, she lifted her face for one last breath of breeze. *Jesus, Mary and Joseph, help me. St. Jude, St. Theresa, fly to my aid. Please.*

Then, for the last time, she climbed the stone steps to Mike. Slowly, solemnly, as though there were flowers fluttering from her shoulders again. Behind the heavy door, at the end of an awful corridor, he would be waiting for her. In sour, unwashed flannel.

He wasn't, though. He was late. This had never happened. Panicked, she paced the tiny visiting room. It reeked of paint, the glossy walls a nauseous pea soup green. She would like to look out. Impossible. The windows were filthy, tiny, set behind metal grilles so high on the walls that she would have to climb up on something. What on earth could be keeping him?

The hallway had been harrowing. As always, the stink. Urine, feces, something carbolic. And noise. *Squirrel-monkey ladies*—Julie's name for the wraithlike women who materialized to form a gauntlet of fingers clutching at visitors' hair and clothes, of gibberish and shouts. But today, something unexpected, too. Maybe it was the vivid dress or her stiletto heels on terrazzo. A woman had stepped in front of her—so close that Marie saw for the first time that her shock-blasted eyes were as amber as Thérèse's—and pressed her hand to Marie's cheek. The palm was trembly, papery, no more weighty than a butterfly. Then the woman whimpered. Tragically, eerily. As though she knew Marie would never pass through that corridor again. As though her hands recognized Marie's re-knit cheekbone. It had taken all Marie's nerve to step around her and hurry on through the corridor.

It took all her nerve every time. Dreaded *999 Queen Street*, a byword, a Toronto schoolyard taunt. But here she was, here Mike was. Paranoid Schizophrenia. She shivered. She could not let herself pity him, not for a second, today. Remember the past seven years, she told herself. That they wouldn't keep him forever. That one day, he'd get out. She rubbed her arms, suddenly cold. Turned to check. No sign of him.

He would have to be late, today of all days. How late? She couldn't judge. Had no timepiece, she'd sold it six months ago. To a pawnbroker with tobacco brown teeth whose address had turned up in Mike's clutter with a description of her precious watch, silver filigree and diamonds. So much for his heroic sacrifices to buy it. She'd torn up the pawn ticket afterwards and released the pieces out the trolley window like so much confetti. When she wanted the time, she could look for a clock.

There was no clock, here. And no magazine or newspaper or anything else that might distract her—or disturb a patient. Anyway, she felt too jumpy to sit, let alone read. She smoothed her dress again. Twisted around to check the seams on her stockings. Straight.

She dug out her compact, a relic from her glory days. Peered into the tiny mirror. She was pale, her lips almost white; she'd been afraid to risk lipstick. The wind had made a bit of a rat's nest of her hair. She took a comb to it, tugging gently, with one hand pressed protectively against her scalp. It had grown in thick as ever, glossy, black as lacquerware. *Geisha.* She grimaced. Those combs Mike had given her for their first anniversary. Mother of pearl, to wear with a red chiffon dress.

SHE'D CONSIDERED THEM A HOPEFUL SIGN, at the time. In less than a year, life with Mike had plummeted from exhilarating to perplexing to unsettling. He seemed crazy about her—poems on her vanity mirror, little gifts on her pillow—but increasingly moody. After three months of dancing, concerts, the movies, he'd begun to beg off everything and refuse to have people in. Even her family. He was studying and trying to write, so she didn't let it chafe, just went out without him. Until he started to grill her about what she was wearing, where she was going, who she'd seen. Then she began to stay in. There wasn't much money, anyway. Not enough for piano lessons.

There were other things. For all his talk about his magnificent novel—he kept her up at night rehearsing its wonders—he didn't seem to be writing a word. He went out to the library many evenings now, but no sign of notes or books when he came home; sometimes very late, smelling, she was almost certain, of drink. Then he started to sleep in and miss classes. When she finally asked, he roared, "Those professors read books the way kids smoke Turkish tobacco. Suck at it, scared witless, and blow it all out like mustard gas. Words, words, words. Not a whiff of meaning. They're bleeding the language out of me. *Bleeding* me." She didn't mention school again.

Sometimes he was quiet, not speaking for an entire day. Two days, three. What did he think about? She'd learned not to tease or coax conversation out of him. He didn't always bathe as often as he used to, either. He'd started to gain a bit of weight, eating whole loaves of bread, jars of mayonnaise or marmalade, half a week's groceries at one sitting. It was hard to plan meals. More upsetting, borderline crudeness in bed. Just borderline.

Still—minor things, all of them, she kept telling herself. Not worth mentioning to her mother or Thérèse, who was getting ready for her own wedding and a move to Saskatchewan. Papa's heart was giving him a bit of trouble again, too. Besides, it would be disloyal, unfair to Mike to complain. He'd had no family to speak of, no home. Marriage couldn't be easy for him. If she was patient, good to him, he'd come around.

And he did. Learning that he'd passed all his courses buoyed him up for weeks. He was *that* close, he said, to finding his way into his novel. Talkative, exuberant, he seemed almost himself again. He'd passed his first year, they were about to pass theirs—their anniversary. For days he teased her about what he might be buying her, badgering her to guess, telling her she'd have to open her gift the night before, so she could wear it to celebrate. Eau de cologne, she thought, refusing to speculate aloud. Or new lingerie.

He ambushed her instead with a whole new outfit. A stunning gown they couldn't afford, mother-of-pearl fan combs for her hair and a pair of evening shoes, red satin, strappy and old-fashioned. Inside one of the shoes, a slip of paper that read: "Feel like storming the German Club, angel?" Did she! She had bought him a book of poems recommended by the owner of a book shop on the Danforth. Leather bound, gilt-edged, a beautiful book. In bed that night, old tenderness between them. He read some of the poems aloud to her, called her his Muse. Talked to her again about his novel, how splendid it would be, how much better he would be once it was written. Afterwards, his lips on her eyelids, his warm breath in her hair.

By morning he'd disappeared. She was glad, she'd have her hands full in the kitchen. She'd planned a knockout dinner. Crown roast of pork with apple stuffing, roast potatoes, aspic. She'd already baked and stashed his favourite boysenberry pie and cloverleaf rolls. Just after noon, she decided to run out and splurge on wine and Italian candied almonds. She took her time walking home; the day was brilliant. Everything seemed to be brightening again; maybe their troubles were behind them. She cut snapdragons and wisteria from the tiny front garden. Set the table with their best dishes and linen, the pinwheel goblets and decanter from Thérèse.

When she'd done all she could ahead, she bathed. Treated herself generously to dusting powder and eau de toilette, manicured her nails. Teased and twisted her hair up loosely into the French roll she'd worn the night they met, set off this time with the new mother of pearl combs, not an orchid. She slipped into the gown, straining to latch the hook and eye fasteners up the back. Then twirled and gazed at herself in the mirror, impressed. The dress was spectacular, maybe a little risqué. Strapless bodice and filmy skirt in a gorgeous true scarlet, cut to set off her curves. She hadn't dressed up in months. She leaned closer to the vanity. Were those fine lines around the eyes and mouth? Maybe just tiredness. She dabbed on more foundation and face powder. There, she looked terrific. Raring to dance. She wriggled her feet into the sandals and bent to wrap and buckle the ankle straps.

He was late. She'd told him half past six.

Her lovely meal. She fussed with the oven temperature. Seven o'clock. Eight. The roast was drying out, potatoes shrivelling. She tried cooling and reheating to salvage them. The heat of the oven blasted her every time she bent over to check, she had to freshen her makeup and repin loose wisps of hair. Light the candles? She wanted Mike to get the full effect the moment he walked in. A sheen on the linen, sparkle on the china and crystal. She lit, then snuffed them four times.

By nine-thirty, her dress felt wilted, her complexion caky, and she had finally lacquered her hair. She'd wanted to avoid that; the smell of hair spray upset Mike. The new shoes were chafing, would probably blister her feet. She sat fiddling with the matchbox, on the verge of tears. Even if he showed up now, it would be too late to go out anywhere. And to top it all off, she had cramps.

The door. She turned.

"Wrap yourself up, Jezebel!" Mike. He yanked the tablecloth off and thrust it at her. She shrieked. Wasp sting—glass hitting her calf. Their goblets, dishes, water running into her lap. She couldn't move. Breathe.

His eyes were ice. "I see what you are now. Just like all the rest."

What on earth—

"Nothing but a whore!"

She gasped. Couldn't quite register.

Struggling to her feet, she backed against the counter,

clutching the tablecloth. "What's wrong with you, honey? Did something—"

"Shut your trap. Think I don't know where you've been in your scarlet dress, sweet Marie? In those tart's shoes?"

She stared stupidly down at the high heels. A trickle of blood on her hose. "But you picked—"

"Not so you could walk the streets! Not so you could make a fool of me!"

She shook her head, bewildered. "But I'm wearing them for you, Mike. For our anniversary."

"I saw you at the corner with my own two eyes."

Which corner? He must be drunk, he'd spotted some woman who looked like her and—

"I was going to read *Song of Songs* to you tonight: *Until the day breaks and the shadows flee, I will go to the mountain of myrrh and to the hill of incense.* Solomon. But I came across something in his Proverbs instead."

His eyes, the tone of his voice.

"*I have perfumed my bed with myrrh, aloes, and cinnamon. Come let us take our fill of love...for my husband is not at home; he has gone on a long journey.* Her *husband,* Marie. The wayward woman. Luring men at the street corner."

She was hot all over, hot and cold. "I've been right here, Mike. Right here fixing dinner. Getting ready. All day."

"Not all day. I followed you. You thought I'd gone."

When? "I only went out to buy wine for our dinner! It's in the icebox."

"Wine. Whoring. You took your own sweet time. If you could just see yourself!" He hit the side of her face, hard. She staggered, whimpered, covered her cheek with the back of her hand.

"Painted up like a harlot. Someone should put a stocking in that mouth." He grabbed at the hem of her skirt, flailed it up at her face, then yanked. A piece came away in his fist. Fluttered to the linoleum, a geranium petal. "Whose wife dresses like that? Nobody's. You planning a trip to Boston, maybe? To the symphony?"

"Don't!" She tried to edge away. Glass underfoot, water, the tablecloth. "You know you bought this for me."

"And why do you think I did that? Take a guess."

The timer rang. The meat again. She sobbed, "I don't *know.* Mike, stop this. I don't know what to say—I've got to get the roast—"

She took a step toward the range. He knocked her back against the cupboards. "Should have bought you a toy, maybe. A little toy top to keep you out of mischief. You, giving me that book to taunt me."

"Taunt you? Wh—" her voice failing her.

He shouted. *"You know I'm trying to write my own!"*

She shook her head, speechless.

"Think I read it? Well, think again. I know what you're up to. I know all right. I ripped it up. Threw it away, one page at a time. Walking home. Like Hansel and Gretel. One hundred and thirty seven pages, all along the sidewalk. Go read it yourself if you think they write better than me."

Shivering. Nausea, a wave of it. *Holy Mary, Mother of God—*

"You can shut that bloody timer off." He rubbed his head, staggered a little. "I got the message. It's anniversary time, Jezebel. Zero hour. Time to remind you of your vows."

"MERRY CHRISTMAS." MIKE. She jumped, almost screamed.

He was holding something wrapped in newspaper. This had never happened before.

"It's not—. Where's—?" There, in the corridor, a burly

orderly, new. He was supposed to come in. She gestured, tried to catch his eye.

"Sit down."

Please. "No, Mike, listen. I can't stand it anymore. I'm leaving."

But he was moving her towards a chair, his hand on her forearm. He must weigh three hundred and fifty pounds now. She started to shake. Hard.

She sat. Poised, on the torn edge of the chair. Cold, bus seat vinyl. He was staring. She regretted the pretty dress.

Now, before she panicked. "I mean it, Michael. I've applied for an annulment and if I don't get it, I'm going to divorce you."

She hadn't meant to say it like this. Everything was coming out too fast. Where was the orderly, she couldn't see—Mike was in front of her—someone was supposed to stay right with them the whole time. He would go up in smoke any second now.

He nodded, though. Touched a finger to her lips. "Shh. Shh. I know, I've kept you waiting, honey."

She stared.

Smoothing his pajamas with his left hand, holding the package in his right, huffing a little, he knelt at her feet. His hair looked freshly washed, chestnut auburn, wilder than ever. She'd never see him again. Never see him.

"Close your eyes," he told her.

"No, get up. *Please.*" The orderly. Halfway down the hall, towards the women's wing.

Softly, "I said shut your eyes, darling. I've made you a present."

She did, stupidly. Closed her eyes, held her breath. The rustle of newspaper, the weight of something in her lap. She opened her eyes.

Stared. It was just beautiful. A fruit bowl. Variegated

bands of wood curved above a pedestal. Rich, meticulously finished, smooth and perfect. She stared at Mike's hands. Tried to picture them working on the bowl, patient, respectful of the wood. The picture wouldn't come.

She began to cry softly. It was hard enough, hard enough.

He took the bowl from her lap, rewrapped it and placed it in her arms. Reverently, tenderly, as though it were a baby—or a book.

"Go home, you're tired. Come back next week."

"No. I won't be coming."

He was starting to look dreamy, drugged, moving off somewhere behind his eyes. He kissed her eyelids and hair. Murmured, *"All the chief spices."* She cringed.

"I can't come back, Mike. Or bring the children. Ever."

He knelt there. Didn't believe her. Never believed her.

"They do terrible things here, Marie." His voice was a whisper, "Terrible."

She got to her feet. It seemed incredible that his eyes should be so blue, still so blue. "This is beautiful Mike. You have a way." She cradled the empty fruit bowl and stepped around him. Headed towards the hall, the sound of her stiletto heels on terrazzo.

STORY TIME

is fist was a mess. Have to hold the pen like an ice pick, gouge out the words. Marie's fault. Whore. She'd provoked him.

Around him, ruins. That wretched chesterfield, gutted. Television set a ragged window, sleet-coloured glass everywhere. Jagged liquor bottles, sweet rotten smell, oozy boozy smell. Three mickeys? Four? Why hadn't she picked up yet? Sunshine already bleeding in through the venetian blinds.

He listened. Nothing. Whore, sleeping in like a drugged streetwalker. Where had she sent the kids, she was always sending them somewhere, he knew that trick. And what if he wanted to eat? What if he needed coffee? She knew he couldn't run the percolator. Black water jumping out at him like a bubbling swamp, hissing into the glass eye, trying to mark him. When he put the eye out, silt everywhere, scalding java ash. He knew what she was up to. She was trying to leech the words out of him.

But his brain was hot, *hot*. In there where the language bred was steaming, smoking with life. He could feel the novel swelling like a hissing perfect white chestnut against the inside of his skull. His skull was a scorched nutshell, it was thin, seared, a black eggshell, it was the thinnest human skull on record, they should measure it some time, they should keep track of these things. He knew because he could hear everything through it. Everything.

There was no voice Michael Boudreau couldn't hear. The air, the airwaves, radio voices that hadn't even hit the wireless yet, he heard them all while they were still streaming out from the broadcast centre, from New York or Chicago, from Los Angeles, it made no difference to him, he had this skull like the skin of a conga drum, a bongo passing night messages. And other voices, too, crooning, cursing, it made no difference. He heard them all. Soon, they would be hearing from him.

It was story time.

"Hear that, story time Marie, Marie, wherever you are! Got it in my sights, caught it in the cross hairs, Bingo! They've been whispering to me all night all day all my life and the time is *now*." Humming, whispering, jabbering all night, every single night of his life, whispering stories to him whispering names to him, whispering things to come and things gone, whispering about himself obliterated and the whispering going on, going on, just going on like a winnowing wind, like a wind harrowing the worn-out husk of the earth. Trying to scare the life out of him, trying to pop the kernel out of him, trying to smoke the language out of him, but wake up world, he was juiced up now and ready to write.

He was going to write this book. This sheerly beautiful, majestic book. This Antarctica of a novel rising out of the sea of words, rising from the current of voices, this thing of beauty from the very bottom of the world. That would silence them. That would cool his overheated brain. The steam from that would ascend forever before it melted.

He gripped the pen. Grimaced.

No paper.

Of course. Sun stripes on the hardwood. The *floor* was ruled for him.

He swept sticky glass aside with his foot. Squatted. Scratched his initials into the hardwood.

A good nib, a steely nib. Such a rat-a-tat current in it that his hands started hopping like eels, it was like writing with a jackhammer, he was chiselling on stone, tabula rasa, he was engraving something monumental, in the year of Our Lord nineteen hundred and fifty seven he was leaving markings for the archaeologists of the human soul.

No.

He wasn't etching, he was sculpting. It was marble, he was Michelangelo reborn, he was carving to get at the essence of life, going to the centre, the dead immovable absolute ground zero centre. He was going to fix, transfix movement itself, trap the flickering, whickering moment in alabaster white stone.

He was. He alone. That was the meaning of his name– Michael–Michelangelo–the meaning of this pen in these lacerated fists, these bleeding hands, that was the meaning of these bruises, these voices piercing his scalp like a crown of thorns, he was pummelling truth out, giving it form, and when the voices were carved in stone, they would be still at last. Still. Mute as a pillar of salt on the plains of Gomorrah. And no one would be able to alter what he had written. No one.

Because he would write it perfectly. No, he wouldn't write, he would *create*. His novel would breathe, palpably. Grace beating at its heart, threads of breath on the mid-

night air, the tiny hot wind in the ear of a rhumba partner, the stubborn frailty of gnat song. Like that, he would
write like that and silence them all.

The steam already building up, building up in his
skull, behind his eyes, a fine stream of images, charged
particles, word fragments, minute dust motes of speech,
he would trap them all on the page, on the magic lantern
screen, on this lit patch of flooring. Fix them forever, so
that the voices stopped.

Silence. It was about silence.

He cradled his head.

Silence his mother's sighs, silence his mother's
moans, silence his mother's gasps when they used to
pound themselves into her, those men, hammer their
sweaty shape into the soft face of her body, pound,
pound, pound themselves in.

Little Mikey heard them all right, heard everything
through his barricade of building blocks, through his
magical tops which he kept pumping and pumping by the
red wooden handles until they were whizzing and blur-
ring, swirling up and down, up and down, the colours
whizzing off as they screamed around their shanks. The
screw, the screw, the turn of the screw as he kept pumping and turning the crank and still he heard them right
through the walls, did they think he was deaf, some deaf
thing instead of a boy with the thinnest walls, the thinnest
human skull on record?

Oh, she knew about his skull, Mama, how it throbbed
and made him whimper at night. How it beat out the
noises, whispered the voices which came in and went out
with a rude rap on the door, a tap on the floor. She knew.

Sometimes she sent him three corners over to the IDA
Pharmacy for a soda and comic book. The IDA. Ida. I'da I'da
what, he used to ask in his head, while he hopscotched the

squares of sidewalk to the store. I'da, I'da what?

Mama always said: "Be sure to read your comic book cover to cover, Mikey, don't skip nothing, don't you skip nothing or don't bother comin' back. Don't you come back 'till you can tell me every word, I'm warnin' you. And I'll know if you're just figurin' it out from the pictures, Mikey, so you better read it all and take your own sweet time comin' home." That's what she said.

And he tried, he tried, he really did read every word, he did learn every picture and cover them up and not cheat and not cheat and whisper the words over and over and take his sweet time getting home, his own sweet time, jumping and counting the sidewalk squares again like blocks of chocolate, like Snakes and Ladders, like ice floes in Alaska, *I'da Ida what*. Even that night heaven's dam broke and the sky pelted down in rivers and transformers sparked wickedly overhead like boxcars coupling and crashing while he wanted to race for home with nothing but his comic book between his eggshell head and the noise of it, nothing but his comic book and the great crackling current searching the treetops, jumping off the fallen wires trying to get inside his skull.

And when he did get home, when he got around the last corner onto the last square, leapt shaking onto the verandah and sneaked in under the noisy-boy-eating gargoyles guarding the door and tip-toe tip-toe tip-toed up the stairs only when the red velvet hallway was clear so that the smells of gentlemen's cigars and of ladies came from behind well-closed doors, when he got to the last door at the top and rat-a-tat wait, rat-a-tat wait, got inside that door and knocked over his blocks, there was silence.

For the first time since the beginning of the world, since the beginning of his mother, since the beginning of the voices, there was silence. And she never spoke again.

Not with that stocking stuffed mouth. She never opened it and spoke again. Never opened the door, never opened her purse to give him a quarter dollar for the drugstore, never opened her perfume, never opened anything, anything, anything. She lay there not interested in opening anything again but her eyes. Which were opened so wide watching him she couldn't shut them. So terrible and wide he wanted to shut them for her. But couldn't. Couldn't.

Mama?? If I'da been here, if I'da been here I'da–Ida whaat?

Silence.

He told her the story then. Told her the book, every single little word, how Superman fixed Lex Luthor, how yesterday Captain America outwitted the Krauts, dripping onto her pretty rug from the rivers of rain, trying to talk loud with his disappearing voice, trying to talk loud while everything around him spun like coloured tops he wasn't even pumping. *Mama?* He held the comic book up, all the colours running, so she could see the pictures if she wanted to check, and every book since, he learned every word, every single little word, he took his own sweet time just in case someone asked him.

Then one day, a thought like lightening. He would write his own book.

Maybe she would stop looking like that in his head if he wrote a book for her, filled with words of his own. A story never written, a story never told, a story full of the voices and the melting squares of sidewalk and the boxcars shrieking that night and lightning cracking like a whip overhead like sometimes they used to crack the whip at her, those gentlemen, snap their belts. A story filled with all the sighs and silences, filled with all the pounding and pumping and pictures and words. Maybe then.

He could shut Marie's eyes. Her mouth. He'd done it. Hammering, yammering away at him, trying to kill the words, trying to kill the current, trying to kill the book which would change the history of the world, which would bring about universal silence, a perpetual rest from motion, clamouring till she'd almost killed all that, Marie had. A whore. Just like his mother. At the corner even now, must be. At some corner.

He wasn't sure at first, about Marie. Didn't recognize her, in her white gown and flowers, with the veil over her hair, her promises. Didn't know her. Then when he bought her the dress, red chiffon, all straps and shoulders, and the shoes like his mother used to wear, German whore's shoes, all straps and ankles, and the mother of pearl combs to see how black her hair really was, coiled up and lacquered like a geisha's, smelling the way he remembered from that house of gargoyles, then he was sure. Then it all started over. And went on and went on, never stopped, even when she had Julie and Markie. Whose kids were those? Who did she think she was—Mama?—sending them away and saying she was leaving. Who did she think *he* was—little Mikey? Not anymore.

So he drummed himself into her like the skin of a conga, shunted himself into her like a boxcar until there were no sighs no moans, her skin was white marble. He wanted her to lie still, to just lie there still so that he could learn about marble, for his work. When she shut her eyes at last, when she lay still, he lit the dusky room with the high bright glare of his words, filled the corners with the voices from New York and Chicago, from the City of Angels, the midnight whispering and jabbering, the jittering and skittering in his head.

He couldn't stand the silence, because he hadn't made it perfect yet. With his story. And his skull got so hot, so crackling hot that he opened the icebox, opened the bottles, opened the drawers, all her perfumes and cupboards and boxes and cans, opened the humming tireless all night warning signal of the television set with his precious fist. Then, finally, he slept.

Woke with pants soiled stiff. His feet cramped, his hips. A tingle down his legs into his toes as if a splinter of the glass had got inside him, a cinder of lava, a barbed shaft in his veins.

"*Marie??*" Nothing. At some street corner.

Didn't matter, he was ready. He had a nib of steel. *Time.*

He blew on his broken hands with the wind of the world, with the wind of his mighty words. And he began to pump, pump, pump, until the stream of colours and voices began to scream around the shank of his spinning, turn the screw spinning, until the hissing spitting steaming words hummed against his skull, sizzling and scorching, about to erupt like the crack of doom, like the very crack of doom from his pen. *Pump.*

"TAXI?"

n a cobblestoned café terrace, under blue Bistro umbrellas implausible in wind-bedevilled Regina, sat a collection of tables and table talkers.

Julie—sequestered in the corner, trying to rebound from her father's letter. Frizzled pastel hair, madras tent dress, spaniel eyes, pretty enough, slender. Still, splurging on hazelnut torte with cappuccino, then ordering Pirouline with mocha gelati, she'd be lucky to get into her costume tonight. After the letter, she'd be lucky to get into her role.

Several vacant tables—the umbrellas looked ingenuously askew, copper tubs of dahlias, zinnias and salvia rimmed the perimeter of the patio, the menu itself would have passed muster in any continental bistro, but it was a gritty, overcast workday post-noon hour. Foot traffic and buses had fled the neighbourhood.

And a pair of smokers—seated at the table next to Julie, two men she had mentally cast as potential players in a reprise of Maxim Gorky's *Lower Depths*.

The first was dead white and gaunt and jumpy enough to have made the waitress wince, recoil slightly, and wrap the edge of her apron around the handle of the glass mug he'd held out for a refill. Yet he had the exposed face, marbled blue eyes and fine flat hair of a child. As he fidgeted in his chair and shot quick looks around, Julie thought maybe he was only hungry, not ill. Maybe he was only jumpy, not wired. She was jumpy herself. His stirring four packets of sugar and three containers of cream shakily into this second cup of coffee was a sure sign of hit and miss meals—she'd picked that up performing in a psycho-drama about an urban mission. Besides, he was keeping an eye on his companion's leftover tomato and lettuce.

"Can you believe it? The same woman twice!" The second man was fat and increasingly agitated. He was waving his meaty arms, broadcasting the powerful stink of his stained T-shirt. His Roughriders cap was oily. Men of his size made Julie nervous, and she didn't like the look of his eyes, either. Too brilliantly hazed. Too like Mike's. She shivered a bit.

Michael Boudreau, her father, was a failed novelist and left-wing rabble rouser. He was also paranoid schizophrenic, a naturalized American and a sometime journalist. She'd tried to distance herself from him, even moving west when he resurfaced in her beloved Toronto three years back claiming the feds were after him south of the border. She hadn't quite got it straight whether it was something he'd written, or his involvement with rioting day labourers that precipitated his repatriation to Canada.

As Mike himself had told the story (to everyone within earshot) in a cramped pub in the old Woodbine racetrack district, he was still dodging delayed fallout from his activities during the Spanish Civil War—and from a clandestine rendezvous with Trotsky circa nineteen twenty-five. In his latest skirmish for the great cause, he claimed, he had been hit on the head with a brick. The scar was indisputable and fresh. Even in the tavern's murky, blood-red lighting, Julie could see that someone had tried to re-educate Mike. His audience, stableboys and linimented trackhands, was soggily impressed.

It would have been mean, undaughterly, to remind him that his year of birth was 1927. That his brief career as a militant overseas had been in Korea, in the wrong uniform and on the wrong side, given his sympathies. That his recent journalism linked him to a casual labour network targeted by union-busters far more likely than the FBI or CIA to use bricks. Or that he himself was not above taking a deadly swing at someone's head—or heart. Edgy, afraid to provoke him, Julie had elected to finish her tinny-tasting sangria and let it ride. Where her father was concerned, the fantastic was nothing new. He'd left home when she was five—had vaporized amidst a maelstrom of lights and sirens. Domestic, not international, that incident.

In his more coherent periods since, Michael Boudreau had worked for a tiny belligerent press in a burly American city; this Julie knew for a fact, because she'd kept a covert clipping file since her teens. Guerrilla fodder, she called the overheated writing. But fragmentary documentation of a sort, a collection of playbills from the dubious travelling road show which was her father's life. Her mother would have torched the lot, if she'd known. Julie had needed the clippings, though, and erratically related anecdotes, to construct and reconstruct her paternal history. The next best thing to knowing her father. What she'd come up with was a nebulous, colourful pastiche, checkered with contradictions and anachronisms. Suggestive gaps, where he had most likely been institutionalized.

That night in Ye Olde Horseshoe & Clover one thing

was clear. Dodging some kind of trouble in the U.S. of A., Julie's mercurial father was neither going back nor moving on from Toronto. He'd rented a couple of rooms over a Pape Street laundromat. He'd conceived of a block-buster Socialist novel. And figured her into his hazy plans for self-publishing. If it ever got written. Long-lost daughter cum business partner with Mike wasn't a part she cared to read for by then. Just meeting him for a drink had felt reckless. She'd pulled up stakes inside a week.

Vancouver, Winnipeg, Montreal, Edmonton and Regina, since. And a half-dozen less notable stopovers at least. In Toronto, she'd combined Gilbert and Sullivan or Tennessee Williams at an amateur regional theatre, with a pretty good community college drama position. (She'd started to write a bit, too, nothing serious.) Suburbia, but salaried. Post Toronto, she was still winging it. Rented rooms, a repertoire of roommates. The bust and boom, splurge and scrimp life of barely professional theatre. (And notebooks, now, full of stories and rough scripts.) On the surface, a life as unsettled and precarious as her father's. Maybe lonelier. Mike's doing or her own? She could never decide. Reminded herself whenever it dragged her down, that she had traded normalcy for security of a different order.

Now this letter. Addressed with disconcerting accuracy to the Regina YWCA woman's residence on McIntyre Street. To her bedsitter, two floors above the shelter for battered women. He knew her room number.

An outburst brought her back to the terrace. "How do you explain a thing like that? You tell me! How??" The beefy man slapped his temple with Mike-like fervour.

"Bad luck. Some kinda coincidence," the younger one said mildly.

That didn't help. Jack's outraged face was flooded,

almost bruised with colour. His eyes overlit. "Coincidence was it? The very same old lady! Both times?"

"What do I know, Jack," nudging the man's cigarette package cautiously toward him. "Here. Settle your nerves before the guy comes."

"Nerves?" Jack knocked the smokes away and worked himself up to hammering the table with his gavel of a fist. Lightweight, maybe fibreglass, the table wouldn't stand much abuse. A large Coke glass was in peril. Julie turned edgily toward the restaurant proper. Where was her ice cream? The waitress? Behind the reflected scene on the sliding glass doors, the café staff remained invisible. She resisted the urge to inch her chair unobtrusively toward the wall. Impossible on cobblestones.

"The old bat's out to finish me off, dragging me to court!"

"Yeah, well, court." The boy sighed. "I been in court myself."

"*You?* What for?" Jack subsided stupidly into his chair.

Julie looked over, grateful to the boy for defusing him.

He fidgeted with the cuff of his worn denim shirt. It was fully buttoned over a hooded greying sweatshirt. At least one layer too many for the muggy day, Julie thought. Even the dirty breeze was hot. "Nothing much. Can't remember." He shifted in his chair, glanced over his shoulder, licked his blistered lips, deciding. "Prob'ly some smokes."

"They hauled you in for stealing smokes? Tobacco? Lousy cigarettes?"

"I got off light. But the judge said a thing I can't never get out of my mind." He frowned, ran his fingers through his fine straight hair. It was as platinum blond as a Dutch toddler's and needed cutting. "He told me that my kind was nothing but fleas on the hide of a healthy dog."

"Fleas."

"Uh huh."

Jack was looking puzzled. The boy finished, "And when the rest who do their part in the world get sick of scratching—according to him—I'll be shook off into the gutter, dead. If the law don't come along first and vacuum me up." He shuddered. "Fleas on a dog. I can't get it out of my—"

"What you can't get out?" From the sidewalk.

Julie started. At first astounded glance, the man catapulting over the railing seemed to be Ike Turner. She stared.

To Jack, extending his hand, this newcomer sang out, "You lookin' steamed. Sorry, man. Me couldn't get away sooner. Who this be?" He was not Ike Turner after all. But a black man just as feral looking, in an opulently hued shirt, white linen trousers, sandals and heavy duty gold. Potent aftershave, something musky. Julie touched her uncouth hair, regretted the oversized dress. Mustardy earthtones, not her best colours, either.

"Nils. Nils Jensen. Buddy of mine," Jack said.

The boy confirmed this with a nervous nod.

"Dion." The new man held his hand up for a high five. Had a horseshoe of amethyst and diamonds on his ring knuckle.

His flamboyant arrival had drawn the waitress out at last, with Julie's mocha ice and a murmured apology. At the other table, Dion insisted on espressos and cheesecake with fresh raspberries for the trio. When he had watched the girl's backside disappear inside, he shook his head and exclaimed, "Mmmm mmnh. What me tell you? Dis place do know cheesecake!" She was maybe eighteen, wearing a zippered black jumpsuit. Born to wear jumpsuits.

Jack wiped his forehead and asked anxiously. "So—any news for me?"

Dion raised his eyebrows, pursed his lips and did a little noncommittal dance with his shoulders and head. Then he smiled, handed out cigarillos all around, and slapped Jack on the back. "Me playing wit you. It's like I say, Jacko. Name de day. My man in Toronto he be ready to set you up."

Toronto? Julie set her spoon down.

"What will I do for a unit? I got no car, now."

"He got a whole fleet his own cabs, man. So he say jus' come. Don't be t'inking about replacing dat car."

Cabs? Taxicabs? Julie's heart fluttered, sped. The dizzying news in her father's letter was that for some two years now he had been driving taxi in Toronto. Although the letter seemed lucid overall, she'd hoped the job was a fiction. Another of Mike's unrealized realities, like his novels.

"And he ready to set you up wit' new papers, too, he's sayin'."

"New papers?" Jack looked unconvinced.

"Nobody trace you. You be t'inking about the licence, not so? It be jus' fine. Your troubles won't follow you." Dion waved a finger at Jack.

"You won't believe who he got driving for him, dat Tonio. Man, he tell me he got head cases." He began to punctuate with his cigarillo. "Black Pant'ers from across de border. Communists. American G.I. acidheads. He say he got two twin brot'ers belong to some Islamic Ji-had—Tony don't give a damn. Why he care? He say one cabbie turn a fare jus' like any other. Me tell him all your trouble here. De whole story dat old she-devil. And he say he have room for you. He do have room."

Julie felt weak. Was she hearing this? Was there a whole cadre of subversives transporting the unsuspecting Metro public? She rubbed her arms and wriggled her suddenly icy feet.

In Toronto, she had owned a little taxi-yellow Carmen Ghia, stuttering and battered, held together by sheer resolution and duct tape. It took two complete hummings of Bizet's *Toreador* to get it moving in the morning. When she had read her father's bulletin an hour ago—that he'd sworn off his writing to go underground, "As *chauffeur* to the proletariat, obsequious *saboteur* to schedule-ridden bourgeois bureaucrats, as a metered Mercury"—she had heard the 401 thundering like the Niagara River above the Falls. Actually shook, her tremors real as those she and the Ghia had suffered negotiating the snakelike Gardiner Expressway, inch by inch, in rush hour, jammed between eighteen wheelers with shoddy airbrakes and Esso tankers with overdue payloads. Too vividly, she'd remembered the Don Valley Parkway. That helpless sinking, almost into tears, that accompanied the sound of sirens. One motorist's—one moment's—lapse undoing everything. Appointments, private urgencies, everything.

The tyranny of traffic. To Torontonians, she had once theorized glibly, the taste of exhaust fumes must be subliminally associated with rage and desperation. She didn't feel glib now. Her father working Metro as a cabbie was beyond the realm of possibility. Beyond.

During one highly volatile period, Mike had gunned a succession of automobiles into collisions with buildings, passing cars, even bridge abutments. Julie, her mother and brother hadn't been living with him then, but her mother's left leg had been crushed in a much earlier run at a lakefront sugar warehouse. Had had to be painfully reconstructed. She'd been pregnant at the time, had nearly lost Mark. Bone fragments and blood clots surfaced years later, like shrapnel. Cutting her down again, nearly killing her.

Very young, Julie had survived that crash herself, although the memories (shouts, a terrific rocketing, glass and heat) were too blurred to be differentiated from whispered family lore. Whenever relatives visited, there were veiled allusions to darker Mike episodes. To the dread 999 Queen Street, which she pictured somehow, in a startling flash of images (shrieks, women with terrible hands whispering at her in corridors, a warm puddle under her legs in a vinyl chair from fear of that hallway gauntlet). Throughout her childhood, Julie had secretly resisted both the stories and memories of her father's excesses. He wasn't crazy. He was missing and idealized.

Later, she had lost her innocence. During a rare meeting with Mike (at Yorkdale, Toronto's first indoor shopping mall, with an uncle in attendance on a nearby bench), fourteen-year-old Julie had given her father the chance to clear himself of the car accidents at least. He hadn't.

Instead, he had lit up. The automotive mayhem was real. But not unprovoked, he had explained passionately. His offensive was perfectly justified. The other motorists in each instance were McCarthyites. His actions had amounted to a kind of pre-emptive roller derby.

"Even in Canada you must have heard about those fascist yellow bloodhounds! Bastards have been on my tail for years. Decades!!" He'd got so he could pick out Senator Eugene and his goons anywhere, he said. "*Storm troopers!!*" It was either duck or immobilize them. "Remember this, baby. Drop and roll. Or *lunge!*"

As for that first time, when little Julie and her mother had been in the vehicle, that was unrelated. Her mother's fault, the whole thing. She had set him off. "But you know all this—you were there."

I was a toddler, and she was pregnant, Julie wanted to say.

But a moment later, his voice had gone pinched and his eyes queer. "They've been wearing me out, honey," he whispered tearfully, "just wearing me out." He had sagged against her and clutched her hand alarmingly. "Nobody gets it. *Damn Brownshirts*—you got to get them off my back. Will you do that for me? Will you?"

Something in her face must have alerted her uncle. The visit had wound up, fast. They had left her father beside the fountain, helplessly pounding the bench. Her uncle had said, rushing her past the stores, "Don't worry. I'll call somebody for him when we're out of here, Julie." In his car, as she curled up against the door and cried soundlessly, he told her, "Your mother tried to tell you. Now you know. Seeing you just sets him off." He had stopped at another plaza, though, and bought her a Beatles single—*Yesterday.* A good uncle.

She watched the waitress serve cheesecake and espresso now—two trips, giggles, a bit of clatter—to the next table. Shook her head at the girl's unspoken query in her direction. Too much caffeine on performance days was deadly.

A red Corvette revved and roared needlessly through the lights. Hot-shot. Nothing else was moving.

In time, most of her mother's stories about Mike had been corroborated.

At nineteen, Julie herself had been forced to play the gunpoint hostage. A pre-dawn phone call had startled her from light summer sleep. Her father. In town expressly to see her. He had her address, would swing by right after lunch. She was dazed. It had been five years since she'd even heard his voice. He'd missed her high school graduation, lead roles in school plays, everything.

He must have picked up her ambivalence through the wires. Or (she'd been cataloguing his virulent articles) her newfound wariness. He had radar for such things. Because by the time he came to get her in a borrowed station wagon (she'd counted on a taxi and driver), he was visibly agitated. He was also unkempt, seedy, almost unrecognizably obese. A shocking parody of the father she must have made over in memory. She had spent the morning desperately shopping for the perfect dress— grown up enough, demure enough—to impress him, all the while warning herself that she was setting herself up for another fall.

Mike had started right off trying to wheedle her mother's address out of her—a long standing non-negotiable between them. He'd driven her from Harvey's to Howard Johnson's to The Donut Castle to the Pump Room at The Beverly Hills Motor Hotel in Downsview, to—most unnerving—the vacant house of a "comrade" in Rouge Valley, well east of the city limits. By which time he was demanding that Julie move to the States with him.

He had plans for her. Forget her theatre studies. Time to begin her real education. The world was an orange, he told her. One big juicy orange. And she was living on the peel. Not her fault—the general ignorance was astounding. He was going to introduce her to some *real* people. People who were peeling it all back. Forget everything she'd been taught. Ground zero. Time to make her life count for something.

He managed to keep her away from telephones all day, unobtrusively at first, shadowing her to successive Ladies Rooms; then, after an offhand display of what looked like a real pistol, by dramatically yanking his friend's phone off the kitchen wall. The wrenching sound was like a neck snapping. Julie, dizzily taking in the dead refrigerators out back, the rancid cat food, sticky shag carpet and ruined furniture, told herself quickly that nothing had changed, the telephone had probably been disconnected anyhow, things were still manageable, definitely manageable. She'd pretend this was a run-through, nothing more. A white-knuckle run-through. She'd play the scene out, improvise, work at taking over the lead without upstaging him. Watch for her best exit. Miss no cues. Breathe, remember to breathe.

She brazened it out for eight harrowing hours and survived. Was released at last after Mike, exhausted, gave her a quivering performance of *Moonlight Sonata* on the derelict piano, recited plagiarized sonnets into the growing gloom, then collapsed weeping. "Peel it all back, Julie-Jewel," he whimpered helplessly, "peel it all back."

She had peeled his soiled jacket back, gently, to get at his keys. Telling him all the while, "I will, Mike. I promise. I won't forget."

Safely home in her well-lit basement suite, she had collapsed herself. But still didn't call the police. Couldn't. Fortunately, Mike had melted back over the border into obscurity. His next appearance had catapulted her out of Toronto permanently.

She'd kept part of her promise in spite of herself—she had never forgotten. At night sometimes, even out here, the stench of that isolated house woke her, and she sensed her father, both barrels crazy, across the room.

So how could he have maneuvered himself into the driver's seat of a passenger cab? Stayed there? Had he met up with this same Tonio *(Torontonio)?* No, it was absurd to mentally link them, just because she'd received the letter and overheard the table talk on the same day. That would verge on paranoia. She gazed across at the three men.

Dion had lost interest or been disappointed in the

dessert, after a few mouthfuls telling Nils to help himself. Which he did. Jack was lifting his tiny demitasse self-consciously, his fingers too thick. He gagged on the bitter coffee. Setting it down, he pressed Dion, "You're not kidding me? You told him what happened—about my smash-ups? With that same old lady?"

Smash-ups! Was it an epidemic? Julie must have gasped because Jack was suddenly glaring at her. She flushed and ducked her head. Pretended to melt the chocolate lining of her Pirouline in the quarter inch of beaded cappuccino left in her cup.

Dion slapped his thigh, saving her from Jack's scrutiny. "Relax! De man he jus' laugh! He say, jus' like this: *How often dat going to happen, how often? It got not'ing to do wit' me. Ain't know a t'ing about it. Here, a man leave his trouble back home. Who know his business?* That's what he say.

"You hearin' me, Jacko?" He wrote in the air now, his ring flashing. "Tonio sign de papers, he fix it so you see someone, you see the man, say what he want to hear—and de future yours!"

He took a long draw, exhaled luxuriously. The smoke curled up, white beside the glossy black of his hair. "He do keep his piece de action, Tonio. An' me tell you right out I keep a piece myself. But Tooo-ronto, man. Toronto! You going to be a rich man wit' all dat beautiful traffic." Julie flinched.

"And he even supplies the cabs?"

"It's what I'm just saying! He get dem on auction in Quebec. Me don't say they Cadillacs, man. It have some troubles. A accident, too many owners—some sort of t'ing like dat. Tonio don't care. He know how to fix dem so dey be running fine for him. Runnin' real sweet. It so happen he know somebody in Motor Vehicle Inspection.

Tony's de one who know somebody everywhere! My man, he going to set you up in no time at all. What you t'ink?"

Jack sagged. "I just don't know." He slapped the table weakly. "The guy at Legal Aid said maybe since they were messing with my pills—"

Dion snorted.

"Who's gonna believe I'd wreck my own cab, just to scare some old woman—how many fares you get in a week—a *week*—let alone a whole year. Out to get her—I never even recognized her! Just driving along minding my own business, she was going to Loggie's Shoes—and bam! Don't remember a thing." Jack shook his head. "Grand mal."

Epilepsy. Not schizophrenia.

"I got nobody out east. Nobody. And how long'll it take me to learn my way around?" He gestured toward the quiet intersection. "Gonna kill me, after this."

Julie followed his gaze. The streets here were narrow, straight and predictable. Three blocks from the city core at two thirty on a mid-week afternoon, there was no snarl of traffic, not one kamikaze bicycle courier, no sign of a police cruiser. Plenty of unused parking meters, even.

Dion reminded Jack softly, "Injurin' a nice ol' lady, though, you know how dat go over wit' a judge. Repeat offender, it so happen, too." He waved his smoke away. "Accident or not. You be runnin' outa options here, Jacko. Wit dem seizures, the victim sitting right there, how dey going to give you back de license?" He clicked his tongue.

Jack jumped. Shot his hand out to rap the wooden railing adjacent to the table. "Don't put the jinx—"

Young Nils broke in, "Maybe I could go with you."

As the others turned blankly toward him, a curious

look flushed like pink water over his gaunt face. His blue marble eyes became dazzled, hopeful. He licked his lips and continued, "I was thinkin', maybe this guy Tonio could help me out, too. You think he might?"

"I got not'ing to say against it." Dion's hand gracefully signed his indifference.

Jack, though, reacted. "You go? To Toronto? What would you do—you don't even drive!"

Dion raised his eyebrows, gazed at Nils speculatively. "My man Jacko here said it," he finally murmured. "It time you be t'inking about makin' yourself useful, boy."

Maybe reminded of the judge's remark, Nils seemed to draw into himself, to shrink. He ran his finger around and around the rim of his cup, unconsciously moving his upper body in unison. It struck Julie as something a child would do. "Something might come up," he said at last in an undertone.

Jack rubbed his temples and grimaced, "I got no choice." He shook his head wearily. "That woman's gonna be the death of me yet. You can't escape a thing like that. Twice. You tell me."

That woman. All at once Julie did not want to know the outcome. The complicated story behind it. She did not care to imagine Nils or Jacko in Toronto, jittery, overheated, trying to negotiate the teeming downtown corridors and jammed expressways. Trying to keep one buck, one jump, ahead of fast Tonio. Either might become another rush-hour collector lane tragedy, taking a family out with them. Or maybe, just maybe, they would both make it.

Out there somewhere was her father, Michael Boudreau. Mike, playing the ersatz cabbie in a life which continued to unfold like a scriptless solo entry in a cosmic Fringe Festival.

Perhaps he did not do so badly after all. He had survived intermittent, involuntary commitment. He had never given up on life. On his quixotic causes. His emotions and reason volatile as ether, he managed to costume himself for reality from a rag bag of illogic, impulse and ideology.

Sometimes he kept his lines straight. Sometimes he even remembered to take his medication. So who was she to begrudge him any role he might conjure for himself, even that of a border-line professional driver in a troupe like Tonio's? Or off-and-on father to a long-distance daughter. So long as she kept it long distance. So long as her mother was safe.

How much better was Julie doing herself? Really? People were always telling her to lighten up. To cut herself some slack. After all these years in theatre, she was still utterly incapable of improvisation. Paralysed. On stage, she had to remind herself to breathe. And after all these years of writing, she had never sent a story out, had never even had a director look over a script for her.

She sucked the rest of the melted ice cream up through the Pirouline straw. Let the chocolate and rolled wafer dissolve sweetly in her mouth. Sat for a few minutes more, appreciating the tubs of flowers. Someone must be lovingly maintaining that copper. And the blossoms, which remained vivid and fresh despite the sirocco-like air.

From her tapestry handbag she fished out a ten dollar bill and quarters for the waitress. She checked her watch. Just three hours till she had to be at the theatre for half-hour call. Before that, her wilted hair to be revived. She hesitated, took a deep breath, and shakily reopened her bag. Drew out cabfare.

She got up slowly, ducking to avoid the skewed umbrella. It was still game in the stiffening breeze. As she straightened, she felt paper through the thin cotton pocket of her skirt.

The world is an orange.

An hour ago, she had been planning a panicky exit from Regina. Mid-run.

She retrieved her father's letter from her pocket. Unfolded the messy coil-ring sheet. "Oyez!! Oyez!! Oyez!!" Mike had inked around the edges of the paper. "To a prairie lily, a thespian of rare talent, whose accomplishments have not gone unnoted even in humble cabbydom. Oyez!! Oyez!! Oyez!!"

RESURRECTIONS

he was shy with me now. I hardly knew myself. We walked. The sky was lapis, trees stripped to their pewter bones. I'd survived. Had crossed a vast frozen field. Beneath it, black water. Beyond, this possibility. An afternoon walk—*life*—keen and quick and vibrant. My mother finally understanding that I had crossed back to her from that far shore, was solidly here now, alive. After four harrowing years, the illness, for the moment, behind me.

As we chattered about small things, her hand found my arm, my scarf tail, my fingers, her touch light with reverence still. She had flown all this way, all the way from the east, to see me well again. There was wood smoke, sweet and distant, the sidewalk delicately glazed, and the Fabergé dome of the sky: everything conspiring with us in celebration. Even the air was thin and heady and splendid with cold. And I was here to breathe it.

Then this. These words slipped into the afternoon.

"I think he died."

"Who?"

"Your father."

Died? My father, died? Doors slamming shut in my

head, my heart. A severe calm. "How do you know?"
Twenty years at least, since their last contact. (How long
since mine? How old were my sons?)

"Mark went to that rooming house—they told him."

"The people there told Mark that he was dead?"

"That he was dying. That he'd been taken away to
some nursing home to die and never came back. They
threw out all his things. He didn't have much."

He had books. At least, one book. Every decade or so
he wrote my mother letters, as if they could beguile her
again. Shameless with plagiarism, bizarrely beautiful. She
gave the unopened letters to me, so I knew this about
him: my father owned, at the very least, a copy of
Shakespeare's *Sonnets*. But what did that matter? She was
telling me he was *gone*.

I gasped, slipped, caught myself. Became wary of the
sidewalk. Several moments passed, a lifetime, impossible
words. Finally these, possible: "Did Mark check it out?"
With my father (with my mother about my father) nothing was ever quite what it seemed. But this time, my
brother's word, too.

She looked to the street for help, her eyes running
away from mine. "I think so. I don't know much about
it, really. He asked around. The house, the racetrack.
Places he would go to eat. No one had seen him. Julie—
he never went back for his things."

So that was the end of it, for her. Like some of my own
doctors. How many times had they given me up for dead?
So that even now, their forecasts—*irreversible organ damage
if you recover at all*—overshadowed me. "When was this?"

She adjusted her gauzy scarf nervously. Pulled it forward over her hair and temples. "I don't remember exactly. Quite a while ago."

"Last month? This year?" An edge I hadn't meant.

It cut. Her voice was small. "Well, Mark checked again six months ago. Still no sign of him."

"*Still?*"

She stopped walking, hugged her coat to her like a blanket. Teal. Teal wool. Pretty with her blue-black hair. Her eyes met mine, skipped away. I was hurting her; he was hurting her. Again. She said, "The first time Mark went to the house—he hadn't seen him at the track for a while—that must have been three years ago now. He was a bit vague."

Vague? "Three *years?*"

She winced. Nodded.

It was not possible. They had been writing, calling me, she and Mark, all along. Withholding this? Somehow neglecting to mention it? "All this time, no one bothered to tell me? The man was my father!"

"Julie, don't. Shh." Now she was wrapping her arm around my shoulder, turning me away from the street, toward the wide front window of the house we were passing. "Look," she said. A tremor in her arm, her upper lip, the simple word.

I resisted. (Why should I let her distract me?) I looked. A cardinal, beautifully wrought in stained glass, fixed in a brass frame. In front of the dove grey house, berries of the same scarlet on a delicate tree.

"Isn't that lovely, honey?" It was an apology. And I saw in her averted face, suddenly, heard in her unsteady voice her fear of telling me. She'd been afraid for me. Because three years ago—I shivered, just remembering. I was out on that ice, then. Only the most translucent of hopes to support me. It had taken all this time, all my faith and strength, to cross back. Even after the healing started. And she understood about thin ice: my father had taught her.

Shamed, I wanted to touch her cheek, tawny and slackening now over her bones. There was no trace of him there, a small grace. He broke her jaw, once. Her nose. Her leg. And inconceivably *(but the sirens, the men in uniforms ruining our door)* he fractured her skull. That finally freed her: got him put away, dissolved her scruples about leaving.

"It is, Mom," I managed, "lovely," acknowledging the fragile, flame-red bird.

"You were always one for stained glass. Any kind of coloured glass—remember how you used to fill your pockets with it at the beach?" Wave-smoothed lozenges of Canada Dry green, or Alka-Seltzer blue, or Molson's Ale brown or inexplicable heavenly turquoise, from the sands at Toronto's Kew Beach.

"I remember."

The sky still vivid, the air bright, we resumed walking. She talked about small things. I tried to listen. But my heart had become quicksilver. Quivering.

A resurrection wasn't out of the question. Not with me. Not with my father.

MY FIRST COMMUNION DAY. I was dressed in white. I, Julie-Jewel, who fell down, who could find the one patch of ice in the school yard and slip on it, whose leotard knees were darned thick as felt Christmas stockings, always. I had a white chiffon dress and blossom-crowned veil, my mother's gift.

The Sisters' voices, the sanctuary shimmering. There were remotely beautiful *Kyries*, the uplifted hands of the priest, liquid herald of bells for communion. Fasting since midnight, I went forward in reverie, half expecting a dove to alight. At the marble rail, a deep cushion of velvet met my uncertain knees.

The priest advanced. Six communicants, five. I closed

217

my eyes. For several exquisite moments, I waited.

"Corpus Christi."

"Amen." Finally, the fragile, clinging taste of the papery wafer. The body of Christ. Beyond all imagining.

Afterwards, moving dreamlike past the altered faces of my classmates, through a shroud of incense, a haze of colour from the high stained glass and the dazzling banks of candles, onlookers, I seemed to be coming down the aisle forever. Then suddenly I was out into the startling daylight—and there he was. On the stone steps of the church. My father, back from the dead.

It dazed me.

"Caught you! How's my girl?"

"But...." I shook my head. "It's a miracle! You were dead....You died!"

He was squeezing me too tight, crushing me, my white dress. His whiskers scratched my neck.

"Die? Why would I die?" He was excited, half laughing.

"You were in that hospital."

He stopped laughing. "What hospital? What are you talking about, me in a hospital?"

He grabbed my face then. "Wait a minute. *Dead!* Who told you I was dead?"

"Ow!" I didn't want people to see him squishing my cheeks like that. I started to pull away.

"Tell me who."

"I *saw* you there. You remember—we came to visit you." He'd looked nasty, in peed-on pajamas, with his hair all wild. The squirrel-monkey-ladies in the hall scared me. I got a candy apple after, for not crying and upsetting him.

"You don't know what you're—"

"Me and Mommy. We even brought Markie once. Your head was sick."

My mother came up behind me and yanked my arm,

hard. Her hands felt like popsicles. "Julie! Get away from him."

She said over the top of my head, "What are you doing here?" She sounded mean.

What *was* he doing here? I looked around: First Communion Day. The boys looked like Christmas Play angels. The girls looked like princesses. They were spilling out of the church and bunching up on the steps. Everything was a confusion of sunlight, families, nuns from the school, and pigeons fussing back and forth to the eaves. Not at all the way we practised. My mom, my dad and I stood right in the middle of it, like those big huge stones in the Humber. Unless they wanted to step on us or bump into us, people had to keep going around.

"You had no business coming and ruining her day."

He wasn't ruining it! He was a miracle. He'd been raised up, just like Jesus. No, just like Jesus's friend Lazarus. Some people didn't want Lazarus back, either; they were worried about the smell if they opened the tomb after four days. But Jesus loved him and felt sorry for his family. So He raised him anyway. And everyone who saw believed in Jesus after that, so it must have turned out all right.

"Did you tell them I was dead?"

"They'd be better off if you were."

"You *said* that?" He spoke too loud. His face was getting redder; he didn't look nice anymore. It made me shiver.

My mom hugged me against her, just as tight as he had. I didn't like it. My veil was getting pulled and the bobby pins hurt. And she told a lie: "They've forgotten all about you, Mike. You'd better go."

"The hell I will! I come back and my little girl tells me—"

"Please, for once. Don't wreck this for Julie." Now she

shoved me a little, whispering to me to go find Markie, to hold onto him.

I didn't want to—I was going to miss the picture taking! My beautiful dress and veil, and that smelly Toni perm they had given me so my hair would stay curled. Father Larivière would be coming any minute with the camera. So I wriggled out of my mother's reach and stood closer to the other kids, up a few steps, in the middle.

Then I tried to smile at my dad so he wouldn't be mad at me for thinking he was dead.

It worked.

He said to my mom in his quiet, nice voice, "The thing is, sweet Marie, I've decided to give you another chance. I'm coming back."

I stopped breathing, leaned forward to watch.

She had her hand on her head, where he'd broken it. Like an egg, I'd heard Grandma and Uncle Roland say.

"Back?" She looked dizzy.

He gave a little bow. "Michael Boudreau, at your service."

"You've got to be—"

"I'm better now." He smiled and made his eyes crinkle. "That's all over with."

So he *had* gotten better! I knew it!

But my mom looked really scared now, like when she used to lock us in the bathroom and tell us not to come out no matter what.

"*Don't,*" she said. "Leave us alone for pity's sake. Julie! Get your brother."

I was too mixed up. And Father Larivière was coming down to the landing now, they were going to have to move, it was time for the picture. My dad wasn't moving, though. He just kept talking. Louder.

"Let me see you for an hour—the kiddies too. Look,

what's an hour? I've rounded up a car, we can grab some fish and chips, I'll drive you right back—" So he didn't know about the party.

"*Just go.*"

"Wait—" He turned and stared at all the people in front of the church, like he was just noticing them. Compared to them, he looked awfully sloppy. "What do you say I come by later—"

"I said no!"

Father Larivière started trying to organize us. The boys were at the top, against the church, jittery as in choir practice, fidgeting with each other's gowns. All the girls wanted to be in the front row; we had our fancy dresses and veils. I was one of the smallest. Father beckoned to me; I was supposed to stand lower, at the other side. My dad's side. When my mother saw where I was headed, she started waving at me to go back up into the church. Waving harder. She was pretty upset.

I shook my head no. Took my place. But what if my father got really mad and threw her down the stairs—what if he started kicking her head again? I felt like I was going to throw up.

That very second Uncle Ovide and Uncle Roland came out through the doorway with Markie. He was rubbing his eyes and nose, they must have been letting him light candles in the vestibule.

"Markie! *Quick!*" my mother shouted, then ran to grab him.

Uncle Roland spotted my father and started down the stairs two at a time. "Oviiide!" he yelled, "It's Boudreau!"

Uncle Ovide leapt after him. "You dare—"

"Don't fight him," I whispered, all shaky, "he's a miracle."

My father didn't hear me. He didn't even say goodbye. He passed by me, running all the way down the million

221

steps to the street, so fast I thought he would fall. The sidewalk pigeons scattered in an uproar.

My mom yelled, "Come anywhere near that house and I'll call the police. I mean it!" Her voice was like hearing the sirens again. Glass breaking. Everything got really quiet for a minute.

Then people started talking. Turning their heads to stare. My father had disappeared. Again.

Markie started to cry. So did I. I'd prayed so *hard* for him to get better. They'd seen him with their own eyes and they still didn't believe. They'd chased him away. And he hadn't even been talking crazy, not like before. What would happen to him now? Would he have to go back? *Where?* Go back where?

Father Larivière clapped his hands and called softly, "Attention, little ones. Let's rearrange ourselves before the photo. So everyone looks their best. *Comme ça*, now." He passed very close to me, closer than my dad had. Resting his hand lightly on my head as he went.

I FELT A LITTLE LIKE LAZARUS MYSELF. Four days, four years. Slipping away and coming back, slipping away and coming back, never sure how completely I'd be restored. My beleaguered children, preparing to let me go, spurred to hope again, then, disappointed, letting me go, until they had wearied of prayer and unreliable miracles and mothers. Their childhood forever tarnished by weariness and disbelief. My husband, tender or enraged in my crises, exuberant in my health, resentfully wary in the twilight between. The twilight forever looming.

Even now, when I was clearly back, ambivalence. A friend had rebuked me. My resurrection joy was too bright for the rest of them. Who preferred to see the world, their own lives, dimly, through a tarnished glass. Disbelief and world-weariness.

But Jesus raised him anyway. Raised me.

"Do you remember my First Communion, Mom? How you'd told us he was—"

"We had a big party for you after, with your cousins. You cried when you got chocolate icing on your dress—cried and cried—I remember that. And at first you didn't want to swallow anything, because of Jesus."

"But at the church. My father."

"You looked like angels, all of you." Her face was closed.

What right did I have to disturb her frail peace? Even my own life felt like a thin fabric, sometimes, stretched over the hole he had made.

A fabric torn again and again. Seven years after my First Communion, when I'd given him up for dead beyond even miracles, he had reappeared. Just as mercurially. And still his splintering sickness, my mother's abject fear, his vanishing again as though he'd never been. Then two, three, further resurrections, years apart. Each time, the phone call or letter from oblivion, the optimistic arrangements *(maybe this time),* the visit that turned volatile. I broke with him finally, forbade further contact when I was pregnant, to shield my children. I hadn't spoken to him since.

Now, if my mother could be believed—if my brother could—he was really gone. Lost irredeemably. I felt bruised. I would never, not for one moment, know the person my father might have been, unfragmented by schizophrenia. I had learned, in my years of illness, what it really meant to be lonely and isolated. To suffer and to cause suffering I was powerless to lift. Was *mental* illness so very different? One day, I might have made that phone call from oblivion myself. Might have. I had written him once, years back. When I was still single, living at the Y.

"It's unbelievable to see you out like this, honey. Well again." Tears in my mother's words, calling me back. The smell of exhaust from a passing pick-up truck.

I met her eyes. So many things unspoken behind them, always. The man had brutalized her. She'd barely managed to salvage her own life, make a new life for her children. What had it cost her to carry his death these three years, to spare me?

"It's one thing hearing you were getting better long distance. But to see you—with flesh on your bones. Colour." She clutched my arm as we crossed the mouth of a small cul-de-sac.

Released me. "It's like a resurrection."

"I know." I shuddered, did a slow turn. The houses steaming into the gorgeous mid-afternoon blue. The frosted grass in the shadow of evergreens. The glistening November sidewalk. I was actually here. Here. At home, my husband and children, survivors too. Beside me, my mother, weak with gladness. Burden her now, with vicarious sorrow?

No. We needed to hoard this time: in three days she'd be gone, flown back east, on the night flight. Then, I'd call Mark. (Check those addresses, the Death Registry.) With my father, all things were possible.

Almost all things.

"Come on Mom," I whispered, "We're celebrating. Let's walk." I could feel the pain under my coat, wrapped and waiting. Could hear, somewhere close at hand, the whir of pigeons passing.

CROSSING THE PIAZZA

ea culpa, mea culpa, mea maxima culpa. Rowan had quit his narrow bed and headed dazedly for the hallway. The startling phone call from Iris, marginal sleep, then the Gothic, unsettling dream. Reminded of Marie Boudreau and how grievously he'd failed her, his first impulse had been to dress and bolt to Our Lady of Sorrows for sanctuary. Cast himself down in front of the altar and lift a *Kyrie Eleison* heavenward. But at this hour, his age, with the sidewalks slick, he'd decided to make do with more reasonable refuge. He'd thrown his robe on; it billowed like a gently collapsing parachute as he took the turn in the stairs. The watery light seemed to collapse, too, as he descended, a sad streetlight orange leaking through the overhead transom, washing his face, then abandoning him to the dark vestibule.

Here, now. The rectory study, with his fine hoard of books and Jacobean furniture, felt intimately his own, as much his as any room he had known. Pride of possession niggled him sometimes; a priest should hold things loosely. Tonight, though, he passed unseeing through the comfortable sitting area, over the Aubusson carpet. Reaching across his desk, he lit the lamp, a brass Pullman. There. The business end of the room glowed. He paused. Oblique light caught the portrait of Pope John Paul II. His brow and eyes seemed boundlessly innocent and serene. Was His Holiness really so untroubled?

Surely not in the small hours. Woven into that modest white mantle was the weight of millions of souls. Millions upon millions. A man would have to be a fool to wear it lightly. Fools, holy or otherwise, were hardly ushered into the Vatican corridors of power. So what must *his* dreams be—what visions unsettled the Vicar of Christ in the night?

The portrait gave no hint. Radiated paternal, halcyon blessing. "*Et cum spiritu tuo,*" Rowan lifted his hand in benedictory salute, gripped the walnut prie-dieu in the corner, lowered himself wearily to his knees and began to pray.

"Most gracious and merciful Lord, grant peace to Your humble servant." He stopped, chastened. The words seemed fatuous in light of the telephone call and ensuing dream. In light of—Lord help him—his own role in the chronicle behind them.

The details of the dream remained remarkably vivid.

Rome, the Eternal City. Himself, in St. Peter's Square. The vast piazza oddly empty: as he hurried away from the Basilica, his footsteps beat a solo staccato on the cobblestones. No pilgrims, no pigeons, no flamboyant guards or traffic. Just the colossal space with dormant fountains. Then, an arresting voice, knifing into him across the expanse of half a lifetime, "Father! Father Rowan!"

He pirouetted slowly, theatrically, on a wave of premonition. Marie Boudreau? Materializing in dusky shadow before the Basilica, a circle of clergy in crimson, purple and black. There: dead centre, a cross; silver, irresolute, Dali-esque. Not a crucifix, not Our Lord, His arms flung wide, eternally offer-ing Himself. Instead, bound hand and foot as on a stake, Marie. Marie Boudreau.

Rowan felt a surge of old agitation; crossed himself. Lord, she was beautiful—he'd worked at forgetting how delicate she'd been under that extravagant jet hair. His mind was instant with remembered details. He headed off those thoughts at once. Adjusted his dressing gown, a silk jacquard reminiscent of the whispering soutanes of his youth.

He stared, stupefied.

She called out his name again. The atmosphere, liquid as mercury, shimmered with the sound. On either side, columns quivered like birches. His limbs felt reluctant, elastic. He shook off his stupor and began to recross the plaza, wading across the exposed square as into deepening water. The ring of cardinals, bishops and priests stood eloquently, expectantly still, watching him.

The cry was a ruse. As he approached, he saw that Marie was past caring: they must have goaded her into summoning him. The thought was unmanning. What could this magis-terium want with him, an obscure Canadian priest? He tried to shrink, to edge around them, with vague hopes of mounting the steps and buttressing himself against the stone facade of St. Peter's. But a word pealed out like a divine clarion, halt-ing him cold. The brotherhood of the cloth stirred; a dark rush of pigeons took flight from the shadows. One of the figures—crimson robed and hatted—stooped, retrieved a scroll and raised his crosier for quiet. The dying decibels of a hum, a res-onant silence.

Rowan let his head sink forward until his brow met the prayer desk. The profane accusations that followed were Marie's husband's. Spiritualized paranoia—Michael Boudreau in his apocalyptic mode—from that Cardinal's lips: *Marie a Jezebel, a painted harlot wooing men to destruction. Scenting her bed with spices, with myrrh, and with aloes and cinnamon. The Great Whore of Babylon, taking to herself strange husbands, wantonly soliciting men at the street corners.* Dear God, to have them dredged up into his dream, he must have harboured Boudreau's misappropriations of Scripture all these years.

An antiphonal litany. Indictment, refrain. Indictment, refrain. After each charge, a chorused "Woe to you!" At the finish, an odd and fleeting transmutation—the ecclesiastics taking on plumage. Feathered bodies, a glistening, quivering flange. Then a re-transfiguration, vestments, flesh.

Silence again. A ripening silence, as though someone should speak. Him? Were they waiting for him to speak to the charges? He stood as mute as the monumental witnesses overseeing the Square, saying nothing, implicating himself

At length His Eminence her accuser nodded and knelt to inscribe something in characters—Aramaic?—on the parchment. Clearly a papal nuncio now, he rose to deliver the censure. A Decree of Excommunication. Henceforth and forever, Marie-Eve Boudreau, the woman thus accused, was barred from the several means of grace administered by the Holy Catholic Church. The table of the Lord, the Blessed Sacrament: forbidden. Penance and absolution: denied. Indulgences: pronounced void. She was cut off. Anathema. Cast from the kingdom of light into the outer darkness. By irrevocable decree, through the divine office of Christ's Vicar on earth. Per omnia saecula saeculorum.

World without end, amen. Rowan shuddered. That part was no dream. Like a deluded Michael the Archangel, Boudreau had called down divine wrath on Marie. And the Vatican had delivered.

Rowan tried to efface himself, backing into deeper and then deeper shadow, wanting to cry out yet, to protest Marie's innocence. But afraid, overawed. Fear spiking his feet to the

pavement as her judge tossed the scroll at the foot of the argen-
tine cross, then faced her with his arms extended cruciform. A
jewelled rope, no, a rosary the colour of Passion Week
shrouds, wound around his right hand. He unfurled and
raised it, a royal scourge.

There Rowan had wakened. In a chill sweat, thrashing
against his sheets.

The small of his back, his hips. He quit the kneeler for
his favorite chair. Better. If he didn't exercise more regularly he'd end up one of those ancient padres who swayed
and teetered through Mass, keeping the congregation
breathless and the altar boys one step from swooping to
catch him. Well, at least his body hadn't run to flesh.
More to bone. As he massaged his jaw to release the tension, the bones were stark. The skin fine gauge sandpa-
per, steelhead grey now before shaving.

What an infernal dream. He rarely dreamt. Or if he
did, left the details in sleep. No wonder. He was too old
for such harrowing.

On top of everything else, that word worried him. The
word called out when he'd tried to skirt the circle of clergy. Something paramount, like the breaking of a seal. He
tried to evoke the shape and sound of it again. Not *adultery. Anomaly? Apogee. Ap* something. Something sacerdo-
tal. *Apologetics, apostolate, apostasy.*

Apostasy—that was it. He winced, nearly crossing himself. Another accusation. A grave one. *Apostasy* was meant
to penetrate the soul and lodge lethally. Aimed at him or
at Marie? Within the microcosm of the dream, most likely Marie on her barbaric cross. But if nightmares pan-
tomimed the dreamer's fears, the theological charge had
to be directed at himself. He glanced up nervously at His
tranquil Holiness.

Defection, unbelief—he'd never quite shaken his priestly anxieties. At his age, surely, a sign of spiritual life. Sign that the state of his soul mattered to him, that he remained a man of faith. Early years, though, doubts had so racked him in the wasteland of hours before dawn, that he'd been tempted to blunt his vision with liquor. Legions of priests did, to face their reflections in the accoutrements of sacred service, in their communicants' eyes. Liquor, or bleak late-night vigils with the wine. He had managed to resist, thank God. Not virtue or piety, though. A childhood inoculation. When the urge over-took him, he'd picture his father, puking, cowed or stu-pidly combative, and swear to become an ascetic first. Locusts and wild honey, self-flagellation, if need be, before whiskey.

It had nearly come to that, too, after Marie Boudreau's excommunication. An abyss had opened before him.

No, that wasn't fair. The abyss had been before him always, was before him yet. What happened to Marie merely forced him to confront it.

HE'D BEEN AN OVERSENSITIVE, overly devout child. Young Joe Rowan, all eyes and ears and enigma. His parents had fought, religion too often coming into it. His mother, Maureen Bernadette had been a Catholic's Catholic, a Belfast Papist, blood and bones: "Can I help it, Paddy, that I'm a godfearing woman? That my ma raised me to cherish my immortal soul?" "Godfearin'? Priestridden!" his father would bellow. "The whole lot of you. Damn priestridden women! Yer sainted virtue! What's the use in a man marryin'?" Night after night he'd slammed out of the shinglebrick row house, to come back soused. Sloppy drunk or vicious. Listening, Joe had redoubled his prayers on his reckless Da's behalf. Had worn an extra scapular against his chest, on his helpless Ma's.

Favouring his mother by instinct, he became an acolyte. He served Mass mornings for the chance to be near the Reverend Father, to watch closehand the unveiling of the gilded Tabernacle, to announce with a shake of handbells the moment of high Mystery. And after school, he fled to the sanctuary for blessed quiet. His whole childhood, he craved peace and certainties.

As Father Joseph Aloysius Rowan, he'd thought to find them. His first church though, Holy Cross, he found himself stumbling on the realities of parish life. The worst temptations weren't fleshly. Celibacy was a daily seesaw, but he had "the gift"; he'd managed through seven years of seminary to win a tenacious mastery. No, his besetting dilemmas were moral. His heart, it turned out, was more pastoral than priestly. Confronted with human need, the manifestly human needs of his people, he was ambushed by tenderness. One thing to memorize the roll call of sins, mortal and venial. Another to have them vividly enfleshed in the closeness of the closet at the rear of his church. His priestly power began to sit on him like a mitre on an altar boy. Here he was, Paddy's son, putting fear into men's wives. Maureen's son, preaching abstinence.

There was no going back. He had taken solemn vows, had been anointed with holy oil and commissioned. To celebrate, baptize and teach. With joy. To admonish, absolve and bless, with unflinching faith, for his people's sake. Never mind asking what kind of dam three Hail Marys made against passion. Never mind seeing the shadow of hard times ahead on an innocent's face. Bless him. Bless her. Because the aging needed solace against the insurrection of their bodies, and the young ached for hope. A decade after Hiroshima and Nuremburg, dazed by human holocausts on cosmic and excruciatingly intimate scales, the world had lost its faith in a benevolent universe. And that much, he had. Certainties? Put them on in the half-lit sacristy with the immaculate alb and chasuble. Breathe them in with the incense, the perpetual bouquet of candles before Our Lady. For the Kingdom's sake, learn to juggle imperatives.

ROWAN'S STOMACH RUMBLED. The clock sounded, *basso profundo,* in the front hallway. He winced. Three o'clock. He should be in bed. He liked a good eight hours. He'd be sleepwalking through seven-thirty Mass. Well, he wouldn't be alone. A couple of the regulars had to be roused by an alarmingly vigorous shake of the *Sanctus* bells when it was time to partake. He loved them for it. Only the truly faithful braved the icy pre-dawn streets or set their clocks, adding a few hours to the muggy purgatory of a mid-August day, to attend the more traditional early Mass. When he lifted the first, "I will go into the altar of God," the scattered voices which responded, "To God who gives joy to my youth," quavered with years.

That hadn't changed in four decades. At Holy Cross the same wizened faces had met him at the morning communion rail.

SO MARIE'S HAD JARRED HIM. Young and lovely both. And in trouble. The kerchief tugged forward over her cheekbones (too late) to mask a recent bruising. A man's melton coat, enormous, on her slight frame. Despair like stone dust around her mouth and eyes. Fractional hesitation before she raised her head for the Host. A physical stillness about her, beyond exhaustion. He couldn't help glancing back. Who was she? He couldn't place her, even at Sunday Masses; he'd have remembered. She was pushing herself up from her knees more slowly than the arthritic worshippers who flanked her. Wincing as she turned. Who had done this to her? He wanted, very much, to detain her. He got no chance. She'd vanished by the time he turned from the altar to bless and dismiss the congregation.

She came back a week or so later. Beaten again, he saw at once. From her posture, the way her body curled painfully in on itself, the arm bracing her ribs. This time, he saw a wedding band. A rush of anger unsteadied his hands with the elements: *Her husband, then, damn him.* But immediately, he felt the chastening weight of the chalice: *Domine non sum dignus....Unworthy, unworthy.* That cursing should spring to his lips more instinctively than prayer.

She began to attend early Mass maybe twice a week. No pattern.

He watched for a chance to speak to her—and prayed. At confession, a woman admitted listlessly that she'd cursed her husband and wished him dead. Was it she? No telling. The penitent slipped from the booth during his prayer of absolution. And the young woman continued to slip wraithlike in and out of the church. She chose pews in the shadowed alcoves, against a pillar, behind sturdier worshippers. Genuflected and left during the *"Ite missa est,"* before he could make his way back to the vestibule. Was she aware of his interest, then, and evading him? Or just preoccupied?

Once, her eyes not quite shuttered, she watched him approach along the row of communicants. When he reached her, he paused with what he hoped was obvious pastoral concern. Noting more abrasions, discoloration around her mouth and eye, exhaustion, her astonishing beauty anyway. And pregnancy, dear God, pregnancy. He stood with the bread extended. Her eyes filled—and shut him out. She took the wafer and fled, not re-entering her pew. A grossly heavy man rose from the unlit far side, by St. Joseph's niche, and followed her out. Seemed to follow her out. He hadn't come forward for Communion; Rowan hadn't noticed him during the Mass, had never seen him before. He was unkempt. Maybe just someone who'd stolen in for shelter, nothing to do with the woman. Still, Rowan knelt uneasily for a long time before Our Lady Queen of the World, reminding her, before crossing to the rectory for breakfast.

The pregnancy ran its course. But no call about a christening. No infant, ever, in her arms.

PURE COWARDICE, letting things drag on that long without acting. The shame still stung, despite all that was set in motion when he did act. He was tempted to throw open a window and stick his head out. For air, for a moment's reprieve. Too cold, though. The storm window was bound to be jammed.

The pathetic figure in his dream, shrinking from that Sanhedrin. Not this time, by the grace of God. Not when he'd been given an undeserved final chance.

The phone call earlier had been from a parishioner who volunteered at St. Joseph's Hospital. From time to time Iris would ring the rectory, anxious about a spiritually needy patient. The young chaplains were borderline incompetents, more like social workers than priest and nun, to Iris Veenstra's Old World eyes: she'd learned her catechism and caustic piety in The Hague.

This evening, she was calling about a woman who was a puzzle: one Marie Doucette, a lapsed Catholic who'd known a Father Rowan "aeons ago, in another life." Declaring herself "past redemption with papers to prove it," this Marie had ejected the chaplain. Despite a bout of Crohn's disease which should have had her saying her rosary three times a day, she'd asked Iris to put the regulation crucifix out of sight in the clothes cupboard. Unnerved, Iris figured. And she'd told her as much, too. She'd pointed out that such juvenile mutiny didn't impress anyone, least of all God The Father Almighty. He'd seen it all before. In her experience, there was always faith—or conscience—behind it. If not, why such a fuss? Now, Iris wondered, would Father chance a quick visit himself, to see what was what?

He wrapped his robe more firmly around himself and tucked the slack underneath him. His slippers weren't particularly warm; he flexed and reflexed his feet, buffed his calves and ankles with his knuckles. There, circulation.

Faith, conscience—or unabated bitterness—in his experience. *Papers to prove it.* Marie, it had to be. Marie-Eve Boudreau née Doucette.

Lord, no telling what had happened to her. Almost forty years. Crohn's disease—that could be catastrophic. Especially if they resorted to surgery; St. Joseph's wasn't the Mayo Clinic. And she was using her maiden name again, although she'd remarried years back—a second divorce? He grimaced. Would she let him through the door? And even if she did, how could he possibly minister to her?

A sobering question. He twisted around to contemplate the crucifix on the long wall behind him: no sentimental, gilded guillotine here. Appropriately, it was too large for comfort, out of scale in the intimate study. The cross was rude. Unpolished olive wood, for Gethsemane. Jesus of blood-streaked, bone-whittled ivory. The death of God was brutal as a pelvis-fracturing birth. How otherwise?

He thought about the tortured Christ, his self-relinquishing love. The Suffering Servant...*a bruised reed He will not break, and a dimly burning wick He will not extin-guish.* Redemptive love—hands cupped around a flickering wick. Pierced hands.

A tiny goad, warning pressure: something amiss, search his heart. He closed his eyes wearily, obediently. Always, in his worn, rummaged-through carpetbag of a soul, some unsuspected perversity, the stuff of human-ness. He sighed, and acknowledged it: the urge to redeem himself.

He was still cherishing hopes for a grand reconciliato-ry gesture. Something that would mitigate his sense of having failed her, of having cost Marie Boudreau her very soul. Something that would make him feel better about donning his Roman collar.

Make *him* feel better. He dipped his head ruefully. He'd been pastoring long enough to know that self-vindi-cation was a lethal motive, reducing a priest's service to sanctimonious narcissism, more wounding than neglect or hollow ritual. *Mea culpa, mea culpa,* guilty as accused.

He breathed a chastened *Agnus Dei* and traced a sign of the cross, reconsecrating brow—*his mind,* and breast—*his heart,* shoulders—*his strength,* and hands—*his service.* A yoke of ministry, imperfectly worn, in the name of the Father, Son and Holy Ghost.

So be it. Forget heroism. Content himself with cupped hands. Compassion, some unassuming act to intimate wider mercies.

FOR MONTHS AFTER HER BABY'S BIRTH—or stillbirth, he couldn't say—the striking young woman had continued to come to Holy Cross. And Rowan continued to vacillate, not quite sure of his prerogatives. Then she stayed away, completely, week after week. He speculated, worried, imagined her descent into a deeper circle of domestic hell.

He was hobbled, though: he hadn't found out so much as her name. She'd been absent for almost three months before he broke down and raised her case with his own confessor.

The Monsignor was an Irishman. An astute and seasoned old pastor. Rowan had finished his Act of Contrition, been assigned his penance and was loitering. Last chance. Another moment and the grille would be shut, leaving him alone in the darkened confessional with his dilemma.

"Monsignor? I'm sorry to keep you. But before you go—" Feeling the pulse flare at his temple, "If you have a few minutes, I need your advice."

Kindly, "I've neither the bishop nor the bursar waiting."

Rowan blurted, "What would one advise a parishioner beaten by her husband?"

"Beaten? Physically beaten?"

"Bludgeoned."

"Catholic?"

"She comes to—"

"The husband. Would he be a Catholic?"

"Possibly. I don't know." Shame. His profound ignorance, his negligence.

"Best pray he's not." Acerbic.

Because she'd have no recourse then. She'd be trapped. Rowan fingered the tender skin under his collar. The closeness of the curtained alcove.

"This wouldn't be a *young* woman, now?"

Chagrin spreading warm up his chafed neck and into his face. "Fairly, yes."

"Pretty as well?"

"I don't see—"

"Indifferent to look at, then."

He sagged back onto his heels. The old padre was ruthless. "No, Monsignor, not indifferent."

"And you've nothing else to accuse yourself of?"

Hot tongue of anger. Quelled. Self-accusation was a cornerstone of religious life. "Nothing."

"Don't be over-hasty to declare yourself pure. The heart's a slough of treachery."

Incensed, he pictured his confessor's face with its patient folds and hooded iguana's eyes. How his papery hands might be crossed meekly in his lap, over the softly tucked cassock. How he might be fingering beads, or the Scotch mints he carried like mothballs in his pockets. He must have heard and forgiven every evil a human being could think of, over the years. But there was no transgression here.

"Monsignor," Rowan whispered, "I've made a good confession."

"Glory be, then. But a word of wisdom all the same?"

Obedience. The meticulously honed discipline of submission. Fighting bitterness, he bowed his head, "Your servant." Waited for what would surely be a reminder about the sanctity of his vows. Clergy closing ranks: the woman, her pain, swallowed up, rendered inconsequential by her prettiness.

And here it came, "You'll perhaps not have realized yet, Father Rowan, that young women—I'm speaking now of women with the compassionate bent—generally want to save men from themselves. Their own inclinations and wicked influences.

"Whereas kindly men are more apt to be rescuing women from other men. Brutal devils, unworthy sods. And the like."

"Yes, but I don't see—"

"Either way, pride is the wolf at the door. Devilish

pride. Unseemly delight in one's self." The older priest must have shifted on his narrow bench, making the wood groan.

"How exactly—?"

"Women used to the other, to being treated badly, can be wondrous grateful for the least bit of kindness. Perilously grateful. Turn the head of a saint."

Galled, Rowan stepped out of bounds, questioned his superior's wisdom: "But surely, Monsignor, where a Christian priest is concerned—"

"Pride is no respecter of the cloth, son!" Fervently, "To be sure, we priests are especially *prone*. Being in the business of saving people from the unholy three—the world, the flesh and the devil—we're liable to forget where the mercy's coming from. Now, *Divine* love and mercy, that's what your young parishioner's wanting."

He rapped the ledge emphatically and continued. "And I'm not saying that pride is the beginning and end of the trouble. We've the other temptations as well. Guard yourself. I'll commend you to Saint Paul to the Romans and Galatians."

Temptation. So that was the cardinal issue here. Not compassion. He was to do nothing at all for fear of compromising himself. Like the priest crossing the road to avoid the beaten man in Jesus's parable. And the Levite, after him. Ascetic—*antiseptic*—holiness.

"Forgive me, Monsignor. I've never even spoken to this woman." His voice was tight and tremulous, "But she used to come for the Blessed Sacrament with bruises. Terrible bruises. For all I know, broken bones. And her eyes, Father, any pastor—"

"She's a regular, then?"

"Early Mass, about twice a week. She had a child recently, I think. Or lost one. Now she's stopped coming altogether. I've been worried sick. For pity's sake—I'm her priest. *Advise* me."

A prolonged sigh. "It grieves me to say it. But you'll be needing a miracle to save body and soul both."

"Then what are we doing here at all?"

Gently, "We're looking for miracles."

Rowan gripped the cross from his cincture until it hurt his hand. He didn't trust himself to speak.

"It's as likely a place as any to be looking," the older priest chided softly, "Here we are, lifting up a tablet of bread...."

"But give me something real, something significant—"

"And what, in this wide muddled world, could be more significant?" He cleared his throat, "We'll leave that be. Your parishioner, now. Even if the marriage is criminal, the odds on the bishops handing down an annulment don't bear thinking about—it would have to go right on up the ranks to His Holiness. You'd as well take it up with St. Jude. Let this be a comfort to you: I'll be joining my prayers to yours."

Jude, patron saint of hopeless cases.

"Surely if there's a life in the balance—"

"One thing *is* sure: you'll never hold history and hierarchy at bay, Father Rowan. That's the long and short of it. You'd only be martyring yourself trying. And you've a fine parish to serve. A whole lifetime ahead of you."

The truth of that was a sledgehammer. He crumpled. He was three years out of seminary. "How can we call ourselves servants of the Lord and look the other way?"

"I've not been saying you should look the other way."

"What, then?"

"Be mindful of your sacred calling. Minister within the constraints of your communion. Whatever you do. This is one woman, and she'll not be the last. She hasn't by any chance asked you to have a go at her husband, now?"

"She hasn't asked for anything at all," he whispered.

"Likely won't then, either, if he's hopeless. She'll have a fair idea where the Church stands. The women do. But if she should happen to come, see to your motives. Myself, it's pride I'd be worried about."

Pride again? He bristled.

"I know, son, I know—you're burning up with holy rage." A rustle, close up. Mint. "Still and all, I've been sitting here long enough to learn a quirk or two about human nature. It's a wonderful thing to be needed, but if self-importance creeps up on a man, it can be every bit as ruinous as the liquor. I've had my own go-rounds with it—and I've witnessed it spoil bishops and deacons alike."

Gooseflesh. Who would he be if not a priest?

Another flicker of movement beyond the screen. The shadow of a hand, poised to shut the grille. "Father Rowan?"

"Monsignor?" He leaned forward.

"You're on the way to being a fine young priest, yourself. We've a crying need for souls like yours in the Church." His voice rasped, "So try to think mercifully of us—of yourself. And remember, the rock of St. Peter's, it's substantial. A priest either stands on it. Or he's crushed by it."

A longing to be held. To lean against someone wise and loving, to feel a healing hand on his brow. To pour out all his questions, the questions behind his questions, to someone with soothing, unequivocal answers.

"I'll not forget you, son, in my Divine Offices. Nor what we've talked about here." Sliding the grate across, "Now, the Lord be with you."

"And also with you."

Alone in the confessional, Rowan made a solemn

Apostle's Creed. And another. A *Pater Noster.* When assurance had settled back over him like a dalmatic, he stepped out into the nave. The dalmatic felt brittle, ceremonial; gorgeous and stiff with filigree. He headed up the darkened aisle to say his penance.

SHE CAME TO SEE HIM, finally, on a bleak November afternoon more than a year after her disappearance. He'd finished outlining his homily and was resting. His housekeeper's uncharitable description of his caller had him up at once, praying all the way down the back stairs and along the hallway, then standing for a moment in the passage to catch his breath and calm his nerves.

He crossed himself and entered the room. She sat shivering on the edge of a wing chair, huddled in the greatcoat she'd refused to surrender to the indignant Mrs. Olivero. Her head was wrapped, too, in taupe chiffon, the scarf and skeins of escaped hair dewed. The coat, military drab with tarnished buttons, stank of mothballs and something sharp—alcohol, maybe, iodine. And melting sleet. Her shoes must have been gay once, hardly suited to the day. Her toes were bare. She looked chilled through.

"Mrs. Boudreau?" Mrs. Olivero had got the name, at least, out of her. Marie Boudreau.

She barely nodded, white around the lips. He didn't let himself scan her face yet for bruises. She looked poised to bolt.

"Father Rowan. Welcome," he introduced himself, feeling her hand tremble in his. "I've let it get chilly in here. Let me do what I can about that." To give her a minute.

The study had a fireplace, but the blaze he'd lit earlier was almost out. He took the poker and anvil to the guttering flames over-energetically. Added a log, kindling, and newspaper, noticing that his own hands were quivering, as hers had been. There. He turned around, frowning, unsatisfied. The room needed further cheer. Through the drizzle-washed window, a depressing vista. The boulevard and sky looked solidly grey and greasy. His guest seemed anxious about the window, too. Of course—afraid she'd be seen. He lit table lamps and drew the draperies. Lemon brocade, throwing lamplight and warmth back into the room; for the first time, he appreciated the effusive hue.

"That's better." He chose a chair across from her, but angled himself slightly toward the hearth. She watched him as though he were a bailiff about to beckon her. Her eyes miserable with dread.

"Marie—may I call you Marie?"

The suggestion of a nod.

"I'm glad you've come."

A slight slackening in her posture.

"You're in some trouble?" he asked carefully.

Her jaw and shoulders went rigid again.

"Why don't we talk about it."

She flinched as though he'd struck her. Swung her head away.

A clumsy start. His inexperience weighed. Being exposed like this, without the cloistering confessional, would make it harder for both of them.

Half praying and half deliberating, he let minutes lapse. His mouth was dry. Should he be taking the lead with pointed questions? He fingered the dark weave of his cassock. Wait.

The mantel clock. The quietness of the house.

Soft sputter and hiss now, of the birch being kindled. He watched the papery bark blister, curl, blacken. "Take as long as you want," he murmured needlessly.

At last, she drew a quavering breath to speak. He held his own breath and sat still. Perfectly, patiently, priestly still, projecting a grille between them.

"I left my little girl and baby with the Trappers."

He started. "The Trapp—?"

"They live around the block."

"Ah." Not Trappists, then.

"Mike—my husband—doesn't know about them. Good people. Grandma and Grandpa Trapper, Julie calls them. Julie's four."

Her eyes were deep, translucently lidded, remarkable. He lowered his own.

"Four?"

"But she's grown up for four. She looks after the baby, Markie. He's almost two."

Two children, then. With neighbours, was she saying?

"Sometimes I have to send them over in their pajamas. There's an alley, they don't go near the road. Julie picks Markie up and runs. She doesn't ask questions or argue. She just picks up her brother and runs.

"And if they're out playing and she notices something wrong when they get back, she knows enough not to come in. She'll hold Markie, hushing him, in the hedge out front. Until she's sure. We have bushes right across the front of the house, under the window, thick. With a space behind them. She can see in the front room if I leave the Venetian blinds open a bit. She can hear whatever's happening, too." She'd twisted the end of her coat belt into a tourniquet around her left wrist. "They're safe, Father, no one suspects. She tells Markie stories, whispers nursery rhymes. She takes good care of him."

Children—*infants*—hiding in the shrubbery. What must be going on inside? He shivered.

"Don't worry, if it's bitter out, or one of them needs

something, Julie knows to go to the Trappers'. Their side door's unlocked, night or day. And they never *ask.*"

Were these children baptized, even? Lord, as if that mattered at the moment.

She was rubbing her forehead with the heel of her hand as though it ached. "Here I am going on and on when you don't even know me—I haven't been to Mass for more than a year." She wriggled her feet in the flimsy sandals. Her toenails were bluish. "Father—" her voice caught, "can something be a mortal sin if it's not your fault? If you have no choice?"

"Mortal—" It took him a minute. "Missing Mass? I'm sure Our Lord—your husband isn't a Catholic, then?" Hope brightening his voice: the Monsignor's terse, *best pray he's not.*

"I didn't mean Mass. I haven't been coming because I can't get away from the house."

"Because of your children."

"No, Mike. He—ties me up."

"How so?"

"He *ties me up.*" Her eyes filled. "With his belt. Before he goes out, he ties me to one of the kitchen chairs." She watched his face. "With Julie's help, I can usually work myself loose. When he stays in, though—" she looked away.

"He drinks. Sometimes I have to sit there all night. The baby cries—you can't imagine."

"No," he said, "No, I can't." But he could remember his father's face, engorged with liquor, his mother barefoot and shivering in the chilly bedroom, shaking his older brothers awake.

He leaned forward earnestly, "So the problem is drink?"

"That's what I thought at first." She shifted her legs away from him and fidgeted with the strip of frayed gauze around her wedding ring.

"But...?"

"I don't know anymore. It has to be more than liquor. Something terrible must have happened to him before we met. The things he imagines—this craziness about corners."

"Corners."

Her flush deepened. She wouldn't look at him. "Yes. About me—" her voice disappeared for a moment. "Soliciting at every corner."

A ripple of shock. She?

"Like a streetwalker, Father. It's something he's read in the Bible."

"The *Bible?*"

"So he says. *Jezebel,* he calls me. It's crazy. I would never *dream.*

"Honestly, Father, it's all in his head. Out of the blue, he started going on about Jezebels. Wayward women. Working himself into rages. Until one day, I was perking his coffee and mentioned that I had to run to the bakery for bread. He slammed his fist on the table and told me that was it. If I ever went anywhere near a street corner again, there would be consequences."

"He must be disturbed." At a loss, "When did you say this started?"

Her eyes were veiled. "It's been gradually—. On our first anniversary. About five years."

"But how do you manage?"

"I cut through people's yards or take back alleys."

She couldn't be serious. He tried to picture it. If she lived in the older section of the parish, she'd have high wooden fences to contend with. Ruined garages and sheds—rodents. On a day like today, the alleyways would be a slough. How, in those hopeless shoes?

"I used to cheat, until he caught me at an intersection. It was slippery, freezing rain. Cars parked everywhere, all along both sides. I had a buggy full of groceries—what did he think I was going to do with *groceries–.*" She stopped and caught her breath.

"But he grabbed my arm and marched me straight home. I was terrified. You don't fool around with Mike. He cut my galoshes to ribbons and threw them out on the lawn. Threw the groceries right after them. Said he was changing the rules: I could never go out by myself again, period. I'd have to drag the kids along everywhere, and he meant everywhere. Markie wasn't toddling yet."

"This is—"

"It's even worse now. He yanked out the telephone—something about voices, airwaves—he never let me use it, anyway. But just knowing it was there.

"For the past year he hasn't let me out of the house without him. Not even with Julie and Markie. Except once or twice when he needed liquor and couldn't be bothered going out to get it. Then he told me exactly how long I had to get back and sat there watching the clock, to make sure I wasn't two minutes late."

"You weren't late."

"No."

"He spends a lot on drink?" Her cast-off coat.

"I have to hide things to make sure the kids eat. Last time the baby came down with a bad earache, I begged Mike to go to the druggist's for drops. I should have known better—but how could I take Markie out in the cold, sick and feverish? Mike finally said he'd go, but he'd take his own sweet time coming home. I gave him my last dollar. He didn't show up till the next afternoon. No medicine. All he had to show for himself was a hangover and a *comic book.* His baby's burning up with fever and he buys him a comic book!"

"The parish has a fund for—"

She shook this off. "I didn't come looking for hand-outs."

"Your children—"

"We make do."

"But surely—"

"If Mike found out, I'd never hear the end of it. He'd accuse me of shaming him. Raiding the poor box. Or worse, with his imagination. You don't know him. Things are bad enough for us now—" She looked down at her hands.

He took a deep breath. "How bad, exactly?"

Her mouth worked. Ignoring the question, she began to trace the veins on the back of her hand. Said shakily, "When I was a girl, I thought this was my initial, written under my skin—it's almost an "M". Did you ever do that?"

"Marie."

One swift, stricken glance. Her eyes glistened with tears. "I'm sorry. But if I told you the half of what—." She turned away from him, crossed her arms and leaned toward the fire. It was ablaze in earnest now, radiating heat.

He stared at her, couldn't help himself. Under the scarf, her hair was a true jet black, black as he'd ever seen. On someone with such—right now her face was awash with colour, but where she'd loosened her coat, exposing her neck—. Was she twenty three? Or his age, twenty five? No more than that.

The fire popped. She started and glanced over. Registered his gaze and turned quickly toward the wall of commentaries and classics. "All these books," she blurted. "This room. Mike would love this. He says he's writing a novel, though I've never seen a page. He used to send wonderful letters. I don't know, if he'd had a room like this when we first got married, he might have been able to start. Before he—.

"I must be a sight," she brushed fiercely at her coat, "This used to be his. But since he's gotten so big...."

She was beautiful. Achingly. And he should be pilloried for noticing. *"Marie,"* he said urgently, "Please tell me the rest."

"I can't—" She was out of the chair, "He'll *kill* me."

"Wait—"

"I'm sorry. I don't know what I thought you could do."

"Please. At least let me pray with you. I've been praying *for* you—"

She stopped, arrested, with her hand on the doorknob.

"You're safe here," he insisted in desperation, "you need help. Spiritual guidance, I don't know what else— you haven't said. But whatever you decide to tell me, before God, I won't betray a word of it. Not to your husband, not to anyone. I can't. As your confessor, not even in a court of law. So, please."

"You've prayed for me?"

"For months now. Longer than that. To Our Lady, St. Jude—ever since you first came to Mass."

She tried to say something. Shook her head. Backed over to the chair and sank down again.

Thank God. "Your coat—shall I ask Mrs. Olivero to—"

"No. No need," she whispered. She began to unbutton the overcoat with nervous fingers. Underneath, she wore a man's charcoal cardigan over a summer-weight gingham duster; graced even that. She draped the heavy coat around her legs like a car blanket. The head wrap stayed in place. *Our Lady of Sorrows.*

He touched his collar for reassurance. Like trying to light an Advent taper with the church doors thrown wide, gusts and updrafts. Why should she trust him, a priest, with no more experience of the world than most altar boys? *The office, not the man.* He straightened, moistened his lips and tried again: "You said that sometimes your little girl won't go inside."

A flicker.

"Why don't you tell me what she's afraid of?"

After several false starts, she told him. In sporadic bursts at first, then in a rush which made his head spin: weeks when things were relatively quiet, then chaos. Apocryphal denunciations and delusions—Marie a harlot, men behind every door, phantasmic voices. Rampages through the house, dumping, smashing and overturning. Forced confessions. The children, when she couldn't get them off to the neighbours, locked in the bathroom or cellar—behind the hedge—listening.

"Is that all?" he asked stupidly, when she broke off mid-sentence. *All.*

Her eyes were two minks, running away from his.

Gently, "He never hits you?" The bruises.

He'd gone too far. A fine quiver of her brow, her nostrils, her chin. A long convulsive shudder.

"I'm so sorry," he whispered.

Collapse. She crooked her arm to shield her eyes and smother the sound of her weeping.

Shaken, wanting to console her so much that he was afraid to look at her, he covered his face with his hands. He had come out in a fine painful sweat. His cassock clung—and trembled over his knees. But the Monsignor's warning; he stayed in his chair. Did not so much as touch her arm or pass his palm over her hair in blessing.

Should he call Mrs. Olivero?

He listened.

From the rear of the house, the clink of dishes and faint tang of silver polish. A phonograph record on very low. Mario Lanza.

Wait.

Without reaching for his beads, he began a silent rosary, marking his progress with his thumb on his fingertips. A trick he'd used as a boy to pray on the streetcar, in the classroom, when his brothers were around.

He finished. Stole a glance.

There. She was bunching up her sweater to pat at her face: no purse. He passed her his handkerchief wordlessly. As she reached to take it, the lamplight caught her broadside. The scarf had slipped. He gasped. The far side of her face was discoloured as old stewing meat. *Damn the man.* He leaned toward her too abruptly.

She drew away. "I'm—I'm okay now, Father. But..."

"*Yes.*" He composed himself with effort, "Yes?"

Barely audible, "The other reason I came. I did something terrible last night."

Cold sweat, his heart an instant piston.

"It wasn't my fault. We were on the landing—he'd got me down on the stairs, I kept trying to push him away, but he was at his pants—he's so heavy, he was crushing me."

At his pants.

"I got a grip on the handrail somehow and pulled myself up. Right there—on the ledge—a wooden statue of Our Lady. A consecrated statue, from Ste. Anne de Beaupré. I couldn't reach anything else, there *wasn't* anything—so I grabbed it and tried to club him." She shuddered. "He moved, it hit the wall and broke, barely touched him. When he saw, though, he screamed at me for committing sacrilege and ran out of the house. Father, I didn't mean—"

251

Relief like a warm anointing. She hadn't killed the man. But—

"You said something, Marie."

She stiffened.

Softly, looking past her to his volumes of Aquinas, Augustine, Juliana of Norwich, vicarious wisdom, "Forgive me, I have to ask. Does—has your husband forced himself on you?" The question blatant, intrusive, itself a rape.

She gasped and bent double. Buried her face in the rough melton.

Dear Jesus. He went for the poker. His temples and hands pulsed. The need to commit violence.

Pushing the screen aside, he jabbed blindly at the fire. Flares. Hissing ash. *Damn the brute.*

Well, Monsignor, what now? Beatific Surrender? Tell this woman to redeem her suffering by offering it up to God? Tell her to light a dozen candles before Our Lady? Remind her that I am a priest, I can't get involved?

Rowan felt his pulse jump just remembering. He had refused to advise self-martyrdom, immemorial consolation of Catholic women. Perish the thought! But what good was his feverish sympathy? He went to see Michael Boudreau: and Marie was bludgeoned for seducing priests. She came to see him, repeatedly: and he pleaded with her, before there were women's shelters, before restraining orders, to take her children and run—never offering her shelter himself. Physical sanctuary being beyond his jurisdiction.

Spiritual sanctuary, too, as it turned out. Naively—obtusely—he began to presume on a compassionate amnesty from Rome. As though centuries of precedent had crumbled, as though one callow priest could sway the keepers of the canon, he spoke hopefully about securing a papal decree of nullity for her. Marie was sceptical. He countered with blind conviction: *Faith is the substance of things hoped for, the evidence of things not seen.* A year after Michael fractured her skull and jaw almost fatally and was committed to the mental hospital, she finally appealed for an annulment. Still not seeing, only half-believing, she took his advice. And the rock of St. Peter's proved immovable.

Nothing mattered.

He prayed, mightily. He offered Masses. He blitzed the diocese with a ream of papers: reports of her broken nose and cracked ribs; of Boudreau's delusions; of a deliberately smashed car; of her shattered leg; her jaw and skull. White-hot and barely coherent—*was this Christian marriage?*—he went to see the bishop in person. The ecclesiastical firmament remained as brass.

Marie's faith in him wavered. She left the parish. After two years with no word from Rome, gave up waiting. She divorced and remarried in a civil ceremony, calling Rowan first to enthuse that the man had a good job with CP Rail, was fond of children, and was a practising Catholic. They were both hoping for official blessing someday, but in the meantime. *Dissuade her.* Hollow, he wished her every happiness instead.

Belatedly, Rome spoke. In a terse verdict handed down by Pope John XXIII on Vatican stationery: *To the request for a dispensation of annulment, In the negative.* The marriage between Michael Boudreau and Marie-Eve Doucette was deemed a valid and sacramental union. Indissoluble. *Per omnia saecula, saeculorum. Amen.* Her second marriage became *de facto* adultery. Her excommunication was winged.

The ruling staggered Rowan. His Monsignor had been astute: no saving body and soul both. If the Church held the keys to the Kingdom, he had cost a woman—*Marie*—her immortal soul by foolish counsel. Foolish? *Humane. Compassionate. Christian.* But if ecclesiastical binding and loosing meant nothing, if the Pope was in error....

Rowan was a priest. For him, abysmal implications either way. He lost his footing so completely that the diocese discharged him to spend a year in retreat, among the Benedictines.

It was hellish, at first. The remote community—the pervasive quiet of Abbey life—had been prescribed as a healing sedative, when what he craved was distraction, a countervailing din against the roiling of his heart. To his newly cynical eyes, the tranquillity of aging monks seemed facile; the untried piety of young ones, petty. At thirty years old, he was contending with demons in a wilderness of the spirit.

Compounding the quiet, history. As of old, the Benedictine Rule spoked the day into task and worship, task and worship. Intrusive and arbitrary, he fretted. It was 1961. 1962. But little by little, the turning of the timeless wheel of prayer: matins, Eucharist, mid-day praise, vespers, and vigils; matins to vespers to vigils; on and on around a diurnal axle of faith, began to soothe and carry him. The chanting of archaic litanies renewed him. His apostolic legacy seemed less sinister.

And the brothers more human. Behind their harmonious communion he saw excruciating personal submission—or pettiness that was distinctly impious. The bells that drew them in from the fragrant apiary and cornfields, from the sultry woodshop and press to collective worship, summoned them not from their work, but to. An intrinsic hierarchy: God, the Church, the community. Then self, least and last. Holiness might be a gift, but it made demands on the blessed, and invariably followed devotion.

He recontemplated his own devotion. He had let it

slip. Had held out an increasingly empty cup to his people. If God had ordained him to be a priest—had sealed him, Father Joseph Aloysius Rowan, with a spiritual and indelible mark at the laying on of hands—then he was a priest forever, despite Marie and all the Maries. He would minister imperfectly, he would understand incompletely.

As St. Paul had written, he was an earthenware vessel, a jar of clay. But however cracked the vessel, he had been consecrated, set apart, anointed to mediate mystery and grace. To carry "*the light of the glory of the knowledge of God in the face of Christ.*"

On that one unarguable certainty, he stood. And in time, recovered his bearings. After Vatican II, it became marginally easier.

LORD. NOW HERE HE WAS AGAIN. And Marie.

He shuddered. Swivelled around to restudy the image of John Paul II. Those unclouded eyes. Those implacable views. But who was he, Rowan, to judge?

The clock again. Tomorrow was all but upon him. He rubbed his calves and forearms with vigour. His hands and feet seemed unreasonably cold. He could do with a fire, but the grate in this study was a deception of silver birch, flame-coloured plastic and hidden Christmas bulbs. Bed for an hour?

No. He rose from the leather chair and crossed back to the prie-dieu. He had decisions to make. And perhaps unmake.

🔸 🔸 🔸

"MARIE?"

He must have come in soundlessly, he'd startled her. Without turning, she said, "Is that really you, Father? I've been watching the window, trying to calm myself. This is my favourite time of day. The way the sky deepens and everything becomes mellow as a Flemish painting." Now she turned.

A flare of anguish. The Crohn's disease; she was almost skeletal. Her face and collarbones. Her hair—she touched it self-consciously. "I've let the roots go, the rest is hennaed." He blushed. Had he been that obvious?

His own hair was silver. His cassock had given way to a black clerical suit. But as he crossed the room, she exclaimed, "You look wonderful. I was half afraid you'd become another dissolute priest, with tight, flushed skin, appraising eyes. But you've aged well. Gently. I'm glad."

Gently? He put the paper bag on the night stand and took her free hand. It felt chilly. "Marie—" He wasn't sure whether to ask about her illness. She'd always refused to discuss her injuries. "I should have stopped at the nursing station—"

She withdrew her hand, shook her head. "Later. Let's not waste our visit, now that I've so graciously let you come." She smiled wryly. Unaware of Iris Veenstra's call to the rectory, she had needed two days to reconcile herself to seeing Rowan, after the shock of hearing his voice on the phone. Two dismal days, for him. *Past redemption with papers to prove it.* "Please, sit there, for the view."

"A grand view." He took the seat, gingerly. How to overcome four decades. The wariness in her eyes.

"A *gift*. My last room faced a brick wall and pipework. Very depressing. A four-bed ward, too. This feels like the Four Seasons Sheraton by comparison." It was a semi-private, but she seemed to have it to herself. She smoothed the waffle-weave blanket. Touched where the back of her hand was bruised and obviously tender from the IV. Potassium, he guessed, for her electrolytes.

She'd run out of chatter. A lengthening silence. He waited. Prayed.

She gave in first. Sighed. "I'm afraid I've lost the habit

of the confessional, Father. And you're still better at listening than talking."

"Occupational hazard."

"So tell me about forty years in the life of a priest. Isn't that a Biblical number, forty? Something about a wilderness? Captivity? Or was it deliverance?"

"I'm not mitred or martyred yet," he said lightly. "I've had parishes here in Ontario, one on the prairies. Our Lady of Sorrows, now. Good churches, good people."

"No pilgrimages?"

"A trip to Oberammergau and the Holy Land, another to the Dominican Republic. A year at an abbey."

"Never to Rome? I'd have thought a priest—"

"Once, to see St. Peter's, the Vatican." He looked away. The dream.

"Overwhelming, isn't it? The weight of the architecture alone." She nodded, "Yes, I've been. Tagged along with my mother and sister. Disguised as one of the faithful—I bought a lace mantilla in the Square."

"I'm sorry...."

She adjusted her pillow. Took a sip of water from the glass on the night stand. "So am I."

"You must hate us." *Disguised.* Her unceremonious eviction of the chaplain.

"Hate? Maybe once."

Carefully, "Iris told me about the crucifix." He'd noticed it as soon as he came in. Afraid she meant to dissemble, keep him at a polite distance.

"Oh." She shrugged, but a catch in her voice, "You can see I've had it rehung in honour of your visit."

"So—?"

"Something Iris *doesn't* know—I sent my children to parochial schools, Father. Took them faithfully to Mass."

Hope, a prodigal flare. That was sorrow, not spite, in her voice.

"Though it wasn't easy to hide the fact that I was *persona non grata* when they rang the Communion bells. Worried Julie sick, my delinquency. But once they were both grown....I've attended three different Protestant churches, Father, but it's been a long time since I darkened the door of a—" she shook her head, looked away.

"Maybe you won't want my gift, then. But I'd like you to have it."

Her eyes went to the bag.

"No, here."

He drew the box from his jacket, a small turquoise Birks box. She took it from him hesitantly. Shook it a little, cradled it in her hands. He reached over and removed the lid. Peeled back the cotton batting. She gasped. He lifted the rosary out, kissed the cross and gave it back to her.

Still disbelieving, she fingered the amethyst beads, traced the silver medal and crucifix. "How on earth did you know?" From the tone of her voice, he had been right to bring it. Thanks be to God.

"It's a beauty. Obviously an heirloom. I remembered it from your visits to Holy Cross."

"My grandmother's—amethyst, my birthstone." She looked chagrined. "I'm—I don't think I meant to hurt you. But I was bewildered. Lost. Outraged. I had to lash out at the Church somehow."

"It was an eloquent protest." The beads had been mailed to Father Joseph Rowan, in care of the Diocesan office, with no signature, no return address. Just a typewritten three word note: *Out of Order*. They arrived a month after word of her excommunication; heartsick, he recognized them at once. In turmoil over the ruling himself, he'd put them away. Until the morning after

Iris' call. The morning after his dream.

Marie wrapped the string of beads around her fingers. Unwrapped it. "There's something–" She closed her eyes. He waited. After several moments, she continued haltingly, "Despite everything, Father, I've never stopped believing. Not in God, the cross and resurrection, the fundamentals. I catch myself hoping against hope that there's been a mistake, that in some higher court of appeal...."

Deo Gratia. He struggled to speak, "An appeal isn't impossible, since Vatican II."

"No. Higher than that," she was emphatic. "Besides, it's too late."

"You can't know that!"

"Michael Boudreau is gone. Dead. He fell out of a boxcar, drunk, in Alberta. Broke his neck. The RCMP came to tell me. You know how they traced me? Through our *marriage* records. I thought he'd been dead for years."

He bowed his head, crossed himself. Belated conscience. He had never felt much compassion for Boudreau, even though he'd obviously been a lost soul. A tormented soul. Now, to think of him dead, dying that way. He touched his collar.

"Marie?"

"Father?"

"Forgive me, I'm going to be your priest for a moment. I need to ask you something." Fear in her eyes. "Now that Mike's gone, have you found the grace to forgive him?" It would take a miracle, after all he'd done to her.

A spasm: she winced, rested her arm across her abdomen, drew her knees up. She turned her face away from him, toward the window.

Give her a minute. As long as she needs.

Most of the cloud had moved off to the east, the sky was onyx, the shivering birches looked almost bloody against it. The room had become dusky, hushed and close as a confessional. Even the hospital sounds seemed to have passed into distance. He prayed. *Kyrie Eleison, Christe Eleison, Kyrie Eleison.*

Her voice was low. "I flew out to Medicine Hat to bury him, Father, with Julie and Mark. I bought him a suit. And we picked out a marker—a tiny stone, just his name." She slipped the rosary into its box, covered it with cotton, replaced the lid. "We didn't have a service. The kids had a Mass said for him later, at Easter. But I did place a few things in the casket. A St. Christopher's medal, a pen, and a packet of blank paper. Good paper, creamy, heavy stock."

"Paper?"

"You may not remember, but Mike hoped to write a book. I'd called it a novel of air, not paper, once."

He remembered all right. And his own unkind thoughts about any book a man like Boudreau might pro-duce. *Mea culpa.* "So the paper was an offering."

"A gesture, at least. Mike had always believed that writ-ing that novel would redeem him somehow, make sense of his life. Later, he even plagued Julie about it. Wanting her to help him."

"Why Julie?"

"She writes."

He hadn't asked her anything about her children, these forty years. Later. She was sinking back on her pil-low, looked very pale. Talking about Mike, stirring the past couldn't be easy for her. She rubbed her brow with the heel of her hand, flinched. The IV needle, probably. She said wearily, "I don't know what else to tell you. We laid him decently to rest. Is that forgiveness?"

Was it? He contemplated the crucified Christ. *A bruised reed. Hands cupped around a flickering wick. His* voice was husky, "I think so; it might be.

An act of grace." And now, before his courage failed. "I brought Communion things." He indicated the paper bag. Inside it, in a small burgundy case, a ceramic cruet, salver and chalice. A linen altar cloth the size of a handkerchief. Eucharistic bread and wine. "In case you wanted to receive the Sacrament."

"Father!" Astonishment, confusion, hope, by turns.

"I don't make the offer lightly." Days—nights—of indecision, arduous prayer. Fear of failing her again, of failing his sacred calling. But as a Christian priest, his foremost call must be to imitate Christ, surely. To administer grace—healing—on His behalf. What did that mean, here? In this room? With this woman? Searching the gospels for wisdom, he had become convinced that Jesus would not withhold salvation from her, not if she still believed. Not while the wick still flickered, however fragile the flame. So he resolved to fulfil his Divine Office, to practise his priesthood, not to violate it.

Moved to tears, she told him, "No. There's no need for you to do that. The offer alone—" She shook her head. "But there is one thing—would you bless me, Father Rowan?"

"With joy." He stood. Passed his hand gently over her hair. Anointing her—*the oil of gladness for ashes*—he traced a sign of the cross on her forehead, then her cheekbone, her jaw. "In the name of the Father, and of the Son, and of the Holy Spirit...."

ACKNOWLEDGEMENTS

Some of these stories have appeared in the following magazines and anthologies: "Taxi?" in *Grain*, and "The Lesser, The Larger" in *Grain* and in *The Northcote Anthology of Fiction*. Excerpts from "Black Lancaster" and "The Lesser, The Larger" have been broadcast on CBC Radio Saskatchewan and on CKUA Radio Alberta.

The manuscript of *In the Misleading Absence of Light* (under the working title, *Myrrh and Aloes*) won the City of Regina Writing Award for 1995.

"Nights At The Lucky Moon" and "Glass Marbles" were winners of Saskatchewan Writers Guild Literary Awards for short fiction. "The Lesser, The Larger" received Honourable Mention in The National Magazine Awards for Fiction, and first prize for fiction in *Faith Today's* Christian Writing Awards; an earlier version won Honourable Mention in the Northcote Anthology Competition.

AUTHOR'S NOTES

I have been blessed by the support and encouragement of wonderful friends throughout the writing of this book. As a Saskatchewan Writers Guild member, I have enjoyed the benefits of a vibrant literary community. My writers' groups, *Notes From The Underground* and *In the Works,* offered insight and criticism, draft after draft. Edna Alford's editorial advice was unfailingly wise and meticulous. I am most grateful to all of them.

I am also indebted to the Canada Council Explorations programme, the Saskatchewan Arts Board, the City of Regina, The Sage Hill Writing Experience scholarship programme, and the Friends of the Banff Centre, who provided financial support and time to work uninterrupted.

Finally, to my family, to those who entrusted me with some of these stories, and to John, Chris, and Tim, my first and most important readers, my deepest thanks.

ABOUT THE AUTHOR

JOANNE GERBER was born in Buffalo, New York, but grew up in Toronto. Since the mid 1980's, she has lived with her family in Regina. Her short stories have been published in *Grain* magazine and *The Northcote Anthology of Short Stories*, and have won several awards. In addition to fiction, she is actively developing a reputation as a librettist, working on a chamber opera project with composer David L. McIntyre. Joanne has taught creative writing at the Canadian Bible College in Regina for a number of years. In addition to these creative pursuits, she is completing her Master of Arts Degree in Religious Studies.